COME AND GET ME

D1512333

Visit us at www.boldstrokesbooks.com

What Reviewers Say About BOLD STROKES Authors

KIM BALDWIN

"*Force of Nature* is filled with nonstop, fast paced action. Tornadoes, raging fire blazes, heroic and daring rescues...Baldwin does a fine job of describing the fast-paced scenes and inspiring the reader to keep on turning the pages." – L-word.com Literature

ROSE BEECHAM

"...her characters seem fully capable of walking away from the particulars of whodunit and engaging the reader in other aspects of their lives." – *Lambda Book Report*

GEORGIA BEERS

"Beers weaves a tale of yearning, love, lust, and conflict resolution. She has constructed a believable plot, with strong characters in a charming setting." – *JustAboutWrite*

RONICA BLACK

"*Wild Abandon* tells how these two women come to realize that 'life was too precious to be ruled by...fears, by...demons.' While these two women struggle with their issues, there is some very, very hot sex. If you enjoy complex characters and passionate sex scenes, you'll love *Wild Abandon*." – *MegaScene*

GUN BROOKE

"*Course of Action* is a romance...populated with a host of captivating and amiable characters. The glimpses into the lifestyles of the rich and beautiful people are rather like guilty pleasures...a most satisfying and entertaining reading experience." – *Midwest Book Review*

CATE CULPEPPER

"...an exceptional storyteller who has taken on a very difficult subject ...and turned it into a spellbinding novel. As an author, she understands well that fiction can teach us our own history." – *JustAboutWrite*

JANE FLETCHER

"*The Exile and the Sorcerer* is a mesmerizing read, a tour-de-force packed with adventure, ordeals, complex twists and turns, and the internal introspection of appealing characters." – *Midwest Book Review*

JD GLASS

"*Punk Like Me*...is different. It is engaging. It is life-affirming. Frankly, it is genius. This is a rare book in that it has a soul; one that is laid bare for all to see." – *JustAboutWrite*

GRACE LENNOX

"*Chance* is refreshing...Every nuance is powerful and succinct. *Chance* is not a novel about the music industry; it is about a woman discovering herself as she muddles through all the trappings of fame." – *Midwest Book Review*

LEE LYNCH

"Lynch, with a dozen novels to her credit dating back to the early days of Naiad Press, has earned her stripes as a writerly elder. She was contributing stories to the lesbian magazine *The Ladder* four decades ago. But this latest is sublimely in tune with the times." – *Q-Syndicate*

JLEE MEYER

"*Forever Found*...neatly combines hot sex scenes, humor, engaging characters, and an exciting story." – *MegaScene*

RADCLYFFE

"...well-plotted...lovely romance...I couldn't turn the pages fast enough!" – Ann Bannon, author of *The Beebo Brinker Chronicles*

SUSAN SMITH

"This disparate duo's lush rush of a romance - which incorporates reincarnation, a grounded transman and his peppy daughter, and the dark moods of a troubled witch - pays wonderful homage to Leslie Feinberg's classic gender-bending novel, *Stone Butch Blues*." – *Q-Syndicate*

ALI VALI

"Rich in character portrayal, *The Devil Inside* by Ali Vali is an unusual, unpredictable, and thought-provoking love story that will have the reader questioning the definition of right and wrong long after she finishes the book." – *JustAboutWrite*

COME AND GET ME

by

Julie Cannon

2007

COME AND GET ME

ISBN: 10-DIGIT 1-933110-73-2
13-DIGIT 978-1-933110-73-8

THIS TRADE PAPERBACK ORIGINAL IS PUBLISHED BY
BOLD STROKES BOOKS, INC.,
NEW YORK, USA

FIRST EDITION: APRIL, 2007.

CREDITS
EDITORS: JENNIFER KNIGHT AND STACIA SEAMAN
PRODUCTION DESIGN: STACIA SEAMAN
COVER DESIGN BY SHERI (GRAPHICARTIST2020@HOTMAIL.COM)

Acknowledgments

This book might not have been completed if not for Hurricane Rita. A category 3 hurricane, she hit Lake Charles, Louisiana, on September 24, 2005, in the shadow of her sister Katrina. Rita caused the worst property damage southwest Louisiana has ever seen. My partner's family lives in Lake Charles, and Rita took the homes of two of her family members, damaged another, and caused my partner's mother to be without water or power for about three weeks.

The twenty-hour drive to pick up my mother-in-law and the twenty-hour return trip to Phoenix provided me with ample opportunity to write *Come and Get Me*. Anyone who has ever driven through New Mexico and Texas knows what I'm talking about. If my mother-in-law had any idea what would come out of that trip, she might have thought differently before she asked, "Laura, will you come and get me?"

To all of the wonderful women at Bold Strokes Books: Your time, encouragement, support, and faith in me are invaluable. The simple words *thank you* seem hardly enough, yet they speak volumes. Jennifer Knight was my fabulous taskmaster editor, and I have learned more from her than anyone, even if I still get hung up on POV.

Finally, on June 14, 2006, I joined the sisterhood of women afflicted with breast cancer. During my treatment and recovery I had the privilege to meet some of the strongest, funniest, and most beautiful women in *the hood*. These women taught me a new definition of hope, faith, and love and what we as women can do together.

Dedication

To my dad: We miss you every day. We talk about you all the time and laugh because we suspect you're probably smoking a cigarette, drinking a beer, and playing pinochle with your buddies.

To my dearest friend Claire: I miss you more than you can imagine, especially on a day like today. You would love reading this book, and it is fitting it's being released exactly one year after you left us. Tell Bailey the kids say hi.

To Dude, The Devine Miss Em, and #1: You make me understand what is truly important in life.

To Laura, my partner, my life: After fifteen years I'm still all yours. Come and get me. I love you.

CHAPTER ONE

"Okay, what the hell is it now?" Elliott Foster shouted from her closet.

She was trying to get dressed, and in the past hour she had received three sales calls and one wrong number. At the sound of her doorbell she was prepared to tear into the poor soul on the other side. Fuming, she strode through the house and flung open the door.

"What in the hell are you doing here?" She'd known it was only a matter of time before *this* woman showed up on her doorstep.

"Do you greet all your lovers this rudely?"

"You're not my lover, Rebecca," Elliott growled in frustration. *I don't need this shit right now.*

Several months ago she and Rebecca Alsip had spent a long, snowy weekend in Aspen between the flannel sheets, which Elliott would hardly classify as making them "lovers." They'd hooked up for a few weeks, but when Rebecca started making demands, including the right to have Elliott exclusively, Elliott ended it. However, her short-term fling did not go quietly.

Rebecca batted her hard blue eyes and turned on her best Daddy's girl smile. "We could very easily remedy that, Elliott. You know I'm more than willing to pick up where we left off." This invitation was accented by a slow perusal of Elliott's body as she moved a step closer.

Elliott blocked the door. "I'd be more than happy to pick up where we left off. As I recall, I was telling you that anything you have to say to me, you can say to my lawyer."

She had never wanted their disagreement to go as far as to involve attorneys, but Rebecca's erratic behavior over the past few months had forced her hand. Conflicting emotions battled in her head. She didn't know if she was furious because this woman refused to accept the fact that their affair was over or because she was here, standing on her porch. She settled on the former and demanded, "What do you want, Rebecca?"

Elliott watched with a certain detached fascination as Rebecca's demeanor changed in an instant from using sex appeal as an enticement to sex as a weapon. It had been inevitable, she supposed, that sooner or later her sexual interludes would catch up with her. From the moment she met Rebecca, she'd sensed danger, but one look at the drop-dead gorgeous body in front of her had banished her caution to the wind. It wasn't a mistake she made in business. She'd spent the past three years getting to the top by being a good judge of people and of risk. The fact that she failed to heed her own instincts with Rebecca made her feel like an idiot, and even worse, an idiot who could still be tempted to touch the flame that was burning her.

Irritated, she forced her gaze away from the cleavage displayed by Rebecca's provocative blouse and reminded herself of the dozens of phone calls she'd received from the manipulative blonde. Rebecca had tried everything from coy sexual teasing to pleading to see her again and, lately, outright threats if she continued to refuse. Now a flash of triumph in Rebecca's eyes made it clear that she had caught Elliott looking.

Her confidence growing, she said with a sensuous smile, "I know what you want, baby."

"Don't kid yourself," Elliott retorted coldly. "You don't know the first thing about what I want."

"Maybe that's true. But I know what you don't want." A sneer of contempt sapped Rebecca's face of its superficial prettiness, revealing a woman who would probably pimp her grandmother. "You don't want everyone knowing you're a queer. And for three hundred thousand dollars, they won't have to."

Years of self-control in the boardroom did not fail Elliott. Her heart was racing and her mind whirling, but as calm as if Rebecca had asked for the butter, she replied, "I'm not following you."

"I'm saying three hundred thousand makes me go away." Rebecca's voice dripped sarcasm. Evidently, she believed she had Elliott by the short hairs. She had already threatened to out Elliott in an ugly, explicit manner to the board of directors of Foster McKenzie, and Elliott had already told her that since the board already knew she was gay, they would not give a damn. The demand for cash was new and completely unexpected.

Elliott took several deep, calming breaths before she spoke. She didn't like being threatened, least of all by a woman who was supposed to be just a pretty face. "That's roughly fifty thousand dollars a fuck," she said with a trace of amusement. "I don't know who you've been talking to, Rebecca, but you were definitely not worth it."

Rebecca's eyes filled with fury and her face turned a deep crimson, ready to explode. "How dare you! Just wait till I'm through with you. What will your adoring big shots think about you when I expose you as preying on and seducing innocent, defenseless straight women?" Her voice seethed with hatred. "You'll be disgraced and out on the street with nothing."

An eerie calmness settled over Elliott as she changed her perspective on this problem. The truth was that Rebecca had blatantly propositioned *her* and was far from the innocent lesbian virgin. But now, this was no longer personal; it was business, and Elliott knew how to handle business.

"Let me guess who my board will believe. Me, the owner of the company, or you, a woman who plays around behind her husband's back and is trying to extort money."

"You think you're so smart!" Rebecca responded shrilly. "Well, your business friends might be cool with you being queer behind closed doors, but just wait till your dirty secrets are all over the tabloids. You know, in your position it's really dumb to let women send you pornographic e-mails with photos in them. They can fall into the wrong hands."

It took all of Elliott's willpower not to show a reaction beyond cool contempt. Was it even possible that Rebecca could have accessed her e-mail? Elliott felt weak at the thought. Her business communications were in a separate account she never left open. But she had been using her laptop when they were in Aspen, and it was possible that she hadn't signed out of her personal e-mail. She could think of several very candid e-mails Rebecca might have found there. Two were from the closeted daughter of a family-values politician, a story the media would eat up. Elliott had recently deleted them. Not soon enough, it seemed.

Masking her concern with a tone of brazen unconcern, she said, "Don't fuck with me, Rebecca, because I'll eat you for lunch. Now get out of here or you'll need a lawyer for more than threatening me." Elliott slammed the door on a very big mistake. "Jesus, Ryan is going to bust my chops over this one," she said to no one as she walked down the hall to resume dressing.

Getting involved with Rebecca had been the biggest mistake of her life, and Ryan Smith, her attorney, had given her strict instructions not to speak to her. That was the problem—Elliott seemed to have very little control over her actions when it came to the blond bombshell, and she was definitely going to pay for it. She wondered if Rebecca was really serious about selling her story to the tabloids. If so, maybe three hundred thousand was a small price to make it all go away. The politician's daughter was a charming young woman who had been foolish. She should never have sent indiscreet e-mails, and Elliott had told her so. They had both agreed to delete all their communications, but Elliott had been careless.

It wasn't as if she'd miss the money, she thought; it would simply be another line item in her checkbook. Elliott could already hear Ryan laughing at that idea. It would just be the start; blackmailers didn't stop asking for money. But they had to do something. This was her fault and she could not allow a closeted ex to be outed in these circumstances, let alone put up with sordid publicity no one in her position needed, gay or straight.

She finished securing her cufflinks, slipped on her jacket, and stood in front of the mirror as she adjusted her collar and lapels. The woman staring back at her looked every bit as successful as she was, from the knot of her silk tie to the toes of her Bruno Magli loafers. The impeccably tailored Armani tuxedo only enhanced her lean form and made her seem taller than she really was. Her unruly dark hair had been cut recently and she continued to decline the rinse that her hairdresser, Randall, guaranteed would hide the few strands of silver beginning to pepper her temples. Elliott refused to be anything other than what she was.

At thirty-four, she was the chairman of the board and CEO of Foster McKenzie, a venture capital firm with billions of dollars invested in business and economies around the world. Until she took the helm three years ago, the most important thing in her life had been the next big adventure under the covers. She drove expensive cars, indulged in what she termed "the celebration of life," had friends all around the world, and never lacked for female companionship. It had all come crashing down when her father died and her uncle subsequently drove the company into near bankruptcy. Her younger sister, Stephanie, was neither qualified nor interested enough to run the business, so Elliott had been forced to reconsider her blithe existence and take on the responsibility that was rightfully hers.

Along with that responsibility came power and fame, both of which led to a never-ending supply of attractive women willing to share her bed. Elliott never knew if they were attracted to her or her money and, frankly, most of the time she didn't care. She always made very clear that she was not interested in monogamy or a relationship, and she cut the strings if they started to tighten. So far, no one had complained. Elliott always made sure to choose as her partners women who knew the score. *So how did I go so wrong with this one?*

The sharply dressed woman in the mirror said, "She's got some nerve trying to blackmail me into coughing up cash for our little roll in the sack. I'll be damned if I give that bitch one red cent."

Elliott combed her hair. And speaking of a bitch, this charity event was the last thing she wanted to go to tonight. Why didn't she just say no?

The tanned face scowled at her. "Yeah, right."

Without a backward glance, Elliott spun on her heel, turned off the light, and walked out the door, heading for her garage.

Just as she'd expected, traffic was at a standstill three bocks from her destination, the Lincoln Grand Hotel. This added another layer of anger to her already short fuse. The public responsibilities of her position at Foster McKenzie were onerous, and sometimes it seemed like they were more social than managerial. Tonight was one of those occasions. Elliott knew her presence mattered to the organizers, and her closest friend Victoria had insisted she attend so they could be each other's "date" for the evening, a strategy that usually served them well; Elliott would blow smoke if Victoria wanted to leave early, and her friend always did the same for her.

Cars crept forward until she was finally able to swing into the driveway of her destination. She handed her keys to the valet and entered the lobby of the historic hotel, in search of a stiff drink. Electricity was in the air and the throngs of people milling around set her teeth on edge. Small talk was a skill she excelled in, especially at these types of social affairs, but in her foul mood, benign chatter was not going to come easily. She straightened her posture as if preparing for battle and approached one of the members of her board.

CHAPTER TWO

Lauren Collier tuned out the voice of the balding man speaking from the podium. Her date for the evening was equally dull, and it took all of her willpower to pay attention to either man. As the sole female on the executive team of Bradley & Taylor, not to mention the *only* single female executive, she had been assigned the task of escorting the boss's nephew that evening. Lauren had been incensed by the assumption that she would not only give up her time for the event but be grateful for the opportunity to spend the evening with a marriageable, well-connected male. She was still pissed several hours later when the perfectly groomed, pompous Princeton MBA continued to treat her like *she* was the eye candy on his arm, instead of understanding that *he* was the guy who had to have an arranged date.

There's gotta be a law against this shit. The funny thing was, Lauren knew the law inside and out, as the chief legal counsel of a Fortune 500 company. Two years ago, she had been surprised when a headhunter contacted her as a potential candidate to fill the position soon to be vacated by the retiring counsel. She was never sure who had put the recruiter on her tail, since she was only a relatively successful midlevel attorney at a local law firm. Seven interviews and eight months later, she was in a job she loved with a high six-figure salary, an office with a view, and a secretary, and she was being ignored by the "eligible" Mr. GQ.

Her gaze swept the exquisitely decorated ballroom of the Lincoln Grand. Handsome men and beautiful women were rising in applause from tables topped with white linen tablecloths and Wedgwood china. Black tie was the dress of the evening, and by the looks of the women, and some of the men, every safe deposit box in San Diego had been emptied of its contents for this event.

The rich, famous, and powerful of her city were gathered en masse to be seen and to raise money for the Children's Education Fund of Greater San Diego County. Lauren had been to several such galas in the past year and she was convinced that these people were more interested in the tax deduction and the distinction of having their name on the benefactor list than they were with actually helping the underprivileged kids in her hometown.

The president of the Chamber of Commerce and his wife occupied the table directly in front of the podium along with the bishop of the archdiocese. Adjacent to them was the CEO of the largest bank in town, who was eyeing a platinum blonde with surgically enhanced breasts while his wife of twenty-two years glared at him over her empty glass of Chardonnay. At the mayor's table was his wife and Steven Stark, an aging movie star in town to promote his latest flick. Stark's trophy wife sat next to him wearing an expression that said that she would rather be anywhere other than here.

Lauren's gaze halted on a woman at a table on the other side of the expansive room. She was taller than everyone at her table, and even from this distance Lauren could discern a long, lean form that was evident under her formal attire as she stood and applauded the award winner. Lauren was intrigued by the fact that she was the only woman in the room in a tuxedo, and she wore it comfortably. She looked vaguely familiar, but Lauren could not quite place where she had seen her before. She would definitely have remembered if they had met.

She realized she was staring when her escort leaned over and whispered something unintelligible in her ear. She nodded vaguely and made a socially appropriate comment, thankful this farce would soon be over and she could go home and watch old reruns of *I Love Lucy*. Throughout the appeals for money, her eyes kept returning to the woman in the tux, who sat comfortably in her chair, twirling her half-empty wineglass in her hand. She looked preoccupied, Lauren thought, unhappy to be here but hiding it well.

Elliott allowed the long-winded speeches to wash over her as she mapped out her options and planned what she was going to tell her attorney this time. What was the worst thing that could happen if they just told Rebecca to go fuck herself? Elliott's sexuality was not a closely guarded secret, but she didn't want it to be a topic of daily conversation either, and Rebecca could be trouble. Elliott could handle any fallout in her personal life—her family had long ago accepted the fact that she was a lesbian—but she was more concerned with the embarrassment this could bring to her firm.

She had worked nonstop to return the company to its previous level of trust, respect, and impeccable ethical standards, the principles set by her father so many years ago. It would be a major distraction if her clients even suspected she had seduced an unwilling woman. Through some very hard lessons, she had learned that you cannot change what people think and she had stopped trying many years ago. She was well aware that the focus would quickly move from her brilliant mind and how much money she made, to their crotches, as seemed to be the case for most men when they fantasized about two women together. Various clients came to mind, conservatives she was certain she would lose if Rebecca started rumors, and there were associates who would begin to distance themselves from her firm. She was in final negotiations with the largest software developer in the country, trying to secure additional venture capital funding, and she knew without a doubt that that deal would come to a crashing halt if there was any bad "morals" publicity.

The faces of her employees flashed in front of her. These were the people who would be hurt the most in a scandal. If clients and investment managers took their business elsewhere, she would be forced to lay off people associated with those accounts. Foster McKenzie employees had already suffered under the disastrous reign of her uncle. She had been able to rehire many as the firm got back on its feet, and she now had an outstanding staff. Elliott swallowed at the thought of letting them down.

As she contemplated the tricky possibilities, the hairs on the back of her neck rose and she was distracted by the familiar sense that someone was staring at her. Elliott was used to being the subject of inquisitive eyes at company meetings, or during a speech she was delivering, or in a bar. The latter was generally the only time she paid any attention, as it was typically the prelude to an evening of delightful entertainment in the arms of a beautiful woman. But tonight a casual encounter was the last thing she was interested in. Her run-in with Rebecca was still fresh in her mind, and she didn't feel up to conducting the cross-examination that would ensure the woman cruising her shared the same ideas about sex without strings. At this moment, all Elliott wanted was the opportunity to escape after she'd paid her dues, and go home to soak in a long, hot bath.

As the speech droned on, she subtly scanned the crowd. Faces, equally bored, dotted the landscape of tables, and a head or two nodded in slumber. Finally, her eyes landed on a face carefully schooled to glazed concentration, as if the man speaking into the microphone truly commanded attention. Elliott recognized the expression. *She's as thrilled to be here as I am, and hiding it better than most. I wonder whose shit list she's on.* A split second later their eyes met.

Lauren blushed. She knew she had been caught looking. The woman in the tux held her gaze for a long, unwavering moment, and the expression on her face shifted from bored indifference and annoyance to faint interest, then she looked away. Lauren felt as though she had just been considered for something important, then cast aside as not worth the effort. *Well, piss on you too.* She returned her focus to the front of the stage and valiantly resumed her phony interest.

Twenty minutes later the speeches were over and the dancing was in full swing. A group of musicians played a mix of classical music and light jazz, which was obviously well received judging by the number of couples on the dance floor. The tables had been cleared of all evidence of the dinner enthusiastically consumed by the guests, and white tablecloths had been replaced with red.

Lauren ditched her "date" and went in search of a fresh cocktail, since she figured she would die of thirst if she waited for him to notice her empty glass. Once her mission was accomplished, she spotted an area where she knew she could hide from the crowd without being too far out of sight of the festivities if her presence was needed. Ensuring she didn't make eye contact with anyone who would want to chitchat, she headed quickly for the safe haven. As she rounded the corner, she ran almost headlong into the tall woman in the tux and froze, mumbling an apology that was ignored. The woman was so preoccupied, she barely seemed to notice.

"I know what you told me, Ryan, but I'm telling you again, I am not going to give her one goddamn cent. Yes, I know my reputation is not the only thing at stake." Elliott blinked as she virtually stepped on a guest standing in her path. Aggravated, she informed the stranger by way of greeting, "Excuse me, I'm having a private conversation here."

Lauren had to tilt her head up to look into the cold, almost black eyes of the woman who stood several inches taller than her own 5'6". It was then that she noticed the cell phone next to her ear and the telltale signs of anger on her face. Earlier that evening it had seemed a very attractive face, but right now the scathing look directed at her marred its appeal.

"Just a minute, Ryan." Elliott lifted the phone from her ear and pierced Lauren with a look that usually turned grown men into sniveling, apologetic buffoons. "Hello! Didn't you hear me? I'm on the phone having a private conversation." She emphasized the word *private* to make her point.

Lauren recovered from the initial shock of their near collision and lifted her chin in response to the challenge. "I heard you. But this isn't your private terrace, and there's no need for you to be such an ass. Perhaps if you were paying more attention to your surroundings, you might not run into strangers and find it necessary to blame them for your own clumsiness."

Lauren didn't have to raise her voice to get her point across. She was an expert in cutting people off at the knees with her tone and inflection. She gave the woman a withering look and walked away. She was still fuming from the encounter when she spotted her escort heading toward her. Quickly, she looked around and found that she did not have an appropriate escape route. Holding back a grimace, she steeled herself for whatever he wanted now.

Elliott's hands were shaking when she flipped the phone shut and returned it to her pocket. She was not upset by the scolding she had received from both her attorney and the angry woman who had just walked away, only the fact that her actions had made it necessary in the first place. *Jesus, what a cluster!* She hailed the nearest waiter for a Scotch and concentrated on her breathing. He returned more quickly than expected and she tipped him generously to ensure his continued good service for the remainder of the evening. Sipping her drink, she searched the crowd, mentally checking the list of people she needed to glad-hand before she could leave and seeking out the attractive woman who had delivered the verbal slap.

As if replaying a bad movie, Elliott recalled her rudeness and the woman's shocked dismay. Her stomach lurched. Normally, she would never have taken out her wrath on an innocent stranger, especially one so delightful to look at. Embarrassed, and knowing she had to right a wrong, she spotted the woman she'd offended and began rehearsing a polite apology.

As she walked toward her, she appreciated the elegantly understated black dress that flattered her curves but did not flaunt them, unlike the revealing dresses chosen by many of the women in the room. Her skin was nicely tanned by natural exposure to the outdoors, not the tanning salon shade that Elliott saw on most of the women she dated. *I wonder if she has any tan lines?* Surprisingly for her skin tone, she had strawberry blond hair that looked natural. It was thick and wavy and highlighted with streaks that made Elliott want to run her hands through it. She groaned inwardly. *Just make your apologies and get out of here, Foster.*

"Excuse me," she said and was struck by the most vivid blue eyes she had ever seen. They were the color of a Caribbean bay and were clear, sharp, and inquisitive. The face tilted slightly toward her own was smooth and flawless, perfectly proportioned, and suggested just a hint of makeup. She was absolutely beautiful. "May I speak with you for a moment?" When there was no immediate response, Elliott added, "Please."

Lauren felt a rush of warmth course through her body at the simple word, adding to the flush the woman's direct gaze had provoked. She'd been trying hard to carry her share of the conversation with a small group of attorneys who had gravitated together, but had been distracted when she saw the tall figure approaching. Murmuring a polite excuse, she stepped away from the group.

"I'm sorry for taking you away from your date, but I…"

Lauren interrupted before the woman could continue. "He's not my date." As soon as she'd said it, she wondered why she was explaining herself to this stranger—this extremely rude stranger.

Elliott nodded and only spent a moment wondering why she felt relief at the information. "My mistake, then. I'd like to apologize for my terrible behavior earlier. I was in the middle of something and you surprised me. I took it out on you and you had absolutely nothing to do with it. Please accept my apology." She began to squirm when the woman did not respond as she expected her to.

"And if I don't?"

"Oh, for Christ's sake." Elliott was not in the mood to be toyed with. "It's a simple apology, not a global peace treaty." Her lovely companion reacted as if she'd been slapped. *Shit, I can't even get this right tonight.* Elliott rubbed her hand cross her forehead. "Wait, please. I'm usually not such an ogre. Let me start over. I'm Elliott Foster. I was in the middle of something difficult and I took it out on you and apparently I am still not making things right. Once more, please accept my apology." She pushed all seriousness aside and laid her palm on her chest. "If you don't, I'll be crushed and have to grovel at your feet. Then I'll have to take out a full-page ad in the *Wall Street Journal* or *USA Today*, whichever you prefer. And if that doesn't work, then I'll simply have to invite you to dinner." The last statement spilled out of her mouth before Elliott knew what she was saying. She looked closely to see if she had overstepped her bounds.

Lauren frowned as she considered the listed action items. She didn't know this woman at all and was unsure of her sincerity. One thing was obvious, however: "Elliott Foster" was used to getting her way, and Lauren was sure she had begged for forgiveness on more than one occasion if she thought it would serve her to do so. She wanted to be annoyed, but for some reason, she wasn't and joined the game. "Hmm. That's a lot to consider. I'll have to think about it."

"That's fair." Elliott masked her surprise. Normally women fell into line, unable to resist her when she humbled herself. Against her better judgment, she suddenly didn't want their conversation to end. "Since that guy is not your date, may I have the opportunity to convince you over a drink on the patio?"

Lauren's heart began to beat faster at the attractive woman's expectant look. "All right. You have five minutes."

Elliott's pulse sped up immediately with the familiar cadence of desire. *The outlook for the evening has definitely changed for the better.* "I can do an awful lot in five minutes."

She didn't know why on earth she was flirting with this woman. Because of the incident with Rebecca, she'd had enough of women, at least for the next few days. But she found this one quite beautiful and it seemed perfectly reasonable to distract herself from her annoyance. Why not see where "five minutes" could lead? In her experience, it usually signaled a long, pleasurable evening.

Lauren had caught Elliott's innuendo but decided to let it drop. "I'll have a vodka gimlet," she said as they moved toward one of the many bars strategically located around the room. "I'm Lauren Collier, by the way."

"It's a pleasure to meet you, Ms. Collier." Elliott extended her hand.

Lauren felt the warm flesh meet hers, and the woman's eyes seemed to darken as they scanned her face. The heat that started in her palm quickly moved through the rest of her body and settled in the pit of her stomach. Lauren felt slightly dizzy as she listened to Elliott place the order with the bartender, requesting a Chivas for herself.

Belatedly, she realized she was still holding Elliott's hand and quickly dropped her grasp, intrigued by her physical reaction to this woman. She met people every day of all shapes, sizes, and degrees of appeal, but none ever affected her like this. Her breathing was in a race with her pulse, her hands were damp, and she wanted to get lost in the deep, liquid brown eyes that were looking only at her. If she didn't know any better, she would have thought she was coming down with something. Shaking her head to clear it, she managed to squeak out a thank-you when Elliott handed her the glass.

As they walked across the room, Lauren took the opportunity to more closely survey the woman beside her. Dark brown hair reached just below the collar of a starched white shirt topped with a contrasting royal blue bow tie. Her skin was tanned and she wore no makeup to hide the small laugh lines that surrounded her eyes. Diamond studs sparkled in her ears as they peeked out from under wavy curls. Surprising herself, Lauren found Elliott extremely attractive in a subtle but sensuous way.

She had always had a level of appreciation for beautiful woman, as she did for handsome men, but the tingling in her stomach told her something about Elliott Foster was more intriguing than usual. Lauren was by no means a prude, nor did she sleep with everyone who gave her the slightest invitation. It wasn't like her to have sexual thoughts about someone she had just met, yet here she was with unsettling flashes running through her mind. *Jesus, when was the last time I had sex?* She had to think hard on that question. Accepting the position at Bradley & Taylor had meant eighty-hour workweeks, learning about her new company and handling the multitude of litigation that piled up on her desk. Whatever free time she did have she spent refurbishing the hundred-year-old house she had recently bought. As a result, she had lost touch with all but her closest friends and had not gone out on a real date in ages.

Thankfully, she was not a woman who believed that she was incomplete without a partner or lover. She treasured her freedom and valued her privacy. She often said that she might be alone, but was never lonely. Yet all of a sudden, standing here with this woman, she was extremely aware of her solitary state. Lauren supposed it was not irrational to imagine being touched and held, although it was unusual that she had those thoughts for a woman. If she were honest, she seldom had them for anyone, in fact.

Elliott held the French doors open, waiting for Lauren to pass through. As she did, she caught a whiff of Elliott's perfume and recognized it as Charisma, the new fragrance everyone at her office was raving about. *That's appropriate.* As they stepped out onto the patio, the noise level substantially decreased and they were met with the fragrance of jasmine carried by a cool breeze.

"What brings you to this gala event, Ms. Collier?" Elliott asked as she leaned her hip on the rail that separated the gardens from the area where they were standing.

"A business obligation." Lauren didn't know why she felt it important to reiterate that she was not with Mr. Suave out of her own choosing. "And you?"

"A good friend of mine is with the PR agency that promoted this shindig. Victoria didn't have a date, so she asked me to be her escort."

Lauren was surprised by the tingling in the pit in her stomach at Elliott's use of the term *date*. It was said quite innocently but Lauren knew exactly what she was referring to.

Elliott picked up on Lauren's reaction and smiled. "Victoria's just a friend." She took a swallow of her drink. "We tried the romance thing back in college but we both agreed that we make better friends than lovers."

There, it's out in the open. Are you going to take it and run or just run? And why do I care? Elliott knew why she cared. Lauren was both beautiful and delightful, two characteristics that normally didn't go together in the women she dated. They were definitely in the beautiful category and many had charmed their way into her bed, but compared with only the few minutes she had spent with Lauren Collier, something was lacking. Elliott thought about that and decided the missing attribute was class. *And look where my usual taste in women has gotten me so far.* She scowled at the fleeting thought of Rebecca.

Lauren watched as a range of emotions played across Elliott's face, the last being cynicism. The expression reminded Lauren that she should do the politically correct thing and return to her date. *Fuck it.* For some reason she couldn't put her finger on, she'd much rather spend the rest of the evening talking with Elliott. The fact that Elliott had just admitted she was a lesbian did not dampen her interest one little bit. If anything, Lauren found it refreshing; at least one person in this room wasn't being phony.

Ignoring the call of duty, she said, "I like your name. It seems to suit you." *My God, why did I say that? I don't even know this woman. She couldn't care less whether you like her name or not.*

Elliott didn't appear to be put off by her inane comment. With a note of mock exasperation, she said, "Thank you. It was my turn to carry on the family tradition. As I've gotten older I've come to appreciate it, but there were those times, when I was growing up, that it was a pain in the ass."

Lauren smiled. "I would not have picked you for a traditionalist." Another rash assumption. She wondered what had possessed her to make such a personal comment. It wasn't her usual style.

She felt the heat of Elliott's eyes burn a trail across her body. Even encased in the black silk dress that fell in soft folds just above her knees, she felt too exposed. When Elliott's gaze lingered a little too long on the modest neckline that showed just a hint of cleavage, Lauren felt her nipples harden and knew they were visible through the sheer silk of the bodice. Her shoulders were bare except for the thin straps of the gown, and she felt very warm as Elliott's eyes moved over them. Her breath caught in her throat as she saw the reaction her looks had caused. She felt as if she had just been caressed. *Oh, yes, this woman is definitely gay.*

"So, Ms. Collier, what do you do five days a week that enables you to wear a beautiful Vera Wang gown?" Elliott asked, indicating the dress Lauren had recently purchased specifically for this event.

"I'm an attorney," she said, fighting the urge to cover her breasts or move closer to this compelling woman, she didn't know which.

"Are you in private practice or with a firm?" *You are gorgeous!*

"I'm chief counsel at Bradley & Taylor."

And smart too. Elliott realized that she liked this woman. As a matter of fact, she liked her a lot, and she was impressed. Lauren could be no older than thirty-five, yet she held the highest legal position in one of the Fortune 500 companies that made their home in Southern California. "Very nice," she said, nodding her head in appreciation.

"It's a great opportunity," Lauren replied, glad to be moving back to familiar ground. "What about you?" She threw back her recognition of the tuxedo designer that Elliott wore so well. "Something tells me a woman who wears Armani isn't entrenched in corporate America,"

Smiling, Elliott asked, "Ever heard of Foster McKenzie?" She waited expectantly for the reaction that she knew would be coming.

It took a moment before Lauren connected the name with the face. No wonder Elliott Foster looked so familiar. In the same instant she inwardly suppressed a groan. *Oh, Christ. She's filthy rich.* She recalled reading an article several months ago in the *San Diego Business Journal* that profiled Foster McKenzie as a third-generation family-owned business that had been mismanaged to the brink of bankruptcy. In the last three years the company had made a sweeping transformation into one of the largest venture capital firms in the country, all under the leadership of the woman she was sharing the patio with.

"Very impressive as well," she replied.

"Well, you know," Elliott paused, "it was a great opportunity I couldn't pass up." She barely contained her smile as she echoed Lauren's earlier remark.

She was surprised by Lauren's low-key and genuine-sounding response. It wasn't the reaction she typically received when someone realized who she was. Lauren was either very good at hiding her emotions or not overly impressed. Either way, Elliott's interest grew and she stepped closer to this intriguing woman. The diminishing space between them was filled with energy that increased as she scanned Lauren's face and settled on her mouth. Instinctively, Elliott licked her lips. "I'd ask you to dance but I don't think this crowd is ready for that yet."

There was something dangerous and exciting in the way Elliott posed the quasi-question that made Lauren want to say yes regardless of the outcome. Elliott exuded the confidence of a wild adventurer, and Lauren thought if anyone could pull off a same-sex slow dance at a society fund-raiser, it was this woman.

Elliott kicked herself for her last statement. Not an hour earlier she'd wanted nothing to do with seducing a woman, and here she was working on just that. Taking Lauren's hesitation for unease, she glanced at her watch. "As much as I've enjoyed our conversation, my five minutes are up. May I walk you back?"

Elliott moved to stand directly in front of Lauren. Her eyes darkened as they bored into her, then just as quickly the change was gone. She reached out and took Lauren's hand in hers. Her thumb gently stroked the sensitive flesh near Lauren's wrist as she said, "Again, please accept my apology and enjoy the rest of your evening."

The sound of her voice and the look in her eyes turned Lauren's knees to jelly. As they walked across the small patio, she didn't realize just how alone they had been until they stepped back into the overcrowded noisy room. She couldn't help but watch as Elliott stopped to greet people, moving through the crowd with the grace of a gazelle and the confidence of a tiger. She soon captivated a group of guests and Lauren noticed that most of the men and even some of women eyed Elliott appreciatively, a few of them more interested than others. She felt an unexpected twinge of jealousy and jumped guiltily when a voice disrupted her scrutiny.

"Hi, sweetie. I didn't expect to see you here tonight."

The space to her right was filled by Alan Stone. She had met Alan many years earlier in college and they had immediately clicked. They crashed and burned on the romantic route when they realized that sparks did not fly when they were together. They had been friends ever since and frequently accompanied each other to social events where an escort was needed.

"Hi, Alan. I didn't know I was coming until a few days ago. The boss's nephew is in town and I received a command appearance notice." Lauren's tone conveyed her continuing displeasure at the situation. She knew she should be getting back to the nephew, but her attention was still on Elliott. "What can you tell me about the woman across the room standing next to the lady in the blue gown?" She directed her gaze in the direction of Elliott and tried not to look like she was pointing.

"In the tuxedo?" With more than a little admiration, Alan said, "That delicious-looking woman is Elliott Foster."

Lauren was startled at her friend's apt description of Elliott. "Yes, she is. But she's not really your type is she, Alan?" Her friend's preference was for men in tuxedos.

"She doesn't have to be my type for me to comment on her. I appreciate all forms of physical beauty."

"Alan, you're impossible." Lauren punched him playfully in the arm. They often teased each other about the people they were attracted to. At one time several years ago, it was the same man. That had been awkward when they both discovered that the man of Alan's dreams, and Lauren's fleeting interest, was actually married to Miss Colorado.

"Hey, you'd better not treat me like that if you expect me to give up the goods on Miss Knockout," he said, rubbing his arm playfully.

"Sorry, you just bring out the best in me," Lauren threw back.

"I'd hate to see you at your worst." Alan glanced toward Elliott. "Why the interest?"

"We were talking a few minutes ago."

Before Lauren could add to her statement, Elliott's gaze shifted from the man she was with to scan the room. When she spotted Lauren, her eyes smoldered and she gave a small nod of recognition. Lauren smiled in return.

Alan turned to see what held her transfixed. "Earth to Lauren." He waved his hand in front of her face to get her attention.

Tearing her gaze away, Lauren said, "You ask too many questions. I was just a little curious about her."

"Uh, Lauren, honey, you do know that Elliott is a lesbian, don't you?"

God, I hope so. Her mind churned and her stomach tingled. She had developed her own sense of gaydar during her law school years; her roommate was a lesbian who often compared notes with Lauren on prospective hook-ups. She was not really surprised when Alan confirmed her suspicions. She knew she hadn't imagined the nature of Elliott's frank appraisal and hadn't misread her comments.

Alan was plainly concerned that she might be heading down a wrong path, so she reassured him. "Yes, Alan, I know Elliott is a lesbian." More gruffly than she intended, she said, "Now cough it up. What do you know about her?"

Alan took a breath and seemed to gather his thoughts. The fact that Lauren had so easily answered his question about Elliott's sexual orientation obviously concerned him. However, he always said it was not his place to tell her what to do, and Lauren guessed he was measuring his words now.

"She's the CEO of Foster McKenzie," he said. "She took over the reins from her uncle when he ran the company into the ground a couple of years ago. She is bright, articulate, runs a tight ship, and has a way of wooing investors and employees. Some call it power, I'd call it charisma."

"I'd definitely say that's what she's got," Lauren murmured.

"I think she's in her mid-thirties," Alan continued. "She lives in Barrington Estates. Definitely the right side of the tracks."

Lauren knew of the neighborhood that Alan was referring to. It was prime real estate along the shoreline of the Pacific, where each house had its own private beach and a minimum price tag of two million dollars.

"She gives buckets of money to her favorite charities but she keeps it pretty quiet," he said.

"Why?"

"I guess she doesn't want to make a fuss. In the last five years she's given almost a million dollars to the child crisis center."

"You'd never know it by looking at her," Lauren said. But if anyone knew about Elliott's generosity it would be Alan. He was the chairman of the awards committee for this evening's event. "She seems very unpretentious."

"She also gives to the Barrett School, you know, the one downtown for the homeless kids," Alan continued. "She pays for the school buses that drive around and pick up the kids from the various shelters and homeless camps. Do you remember the guy I dated for a while? John? He's the manager at the Blue House." He paused as if to check that Lauren recognized the name of a local clothing retailer. "She bought every kid at the school new clothes and shoes, and backpacks with all the stuff they need for school. Two hundred kids." He lowered his voice and leaned closer. "She was actually selected to receive the benefactor award tonight and she turned us down. Threw the entire selection committee into a tailspin."

Lauren was astonished. Very few people she knew would turn down a public accolade for their good works. It said something about who Elliott was, she thought: a person more interested in what she could achieve than in what people thought of her, perhaps.

"We had to regroup and pick another recipient." Alan sighed. "Jeez, she does everything for these kids and she doesn't want anyone to know! Makes me wonder if she's running from the law or something."

"What about socially?" Lauren asked none too subtly.

"Why the curiosity?"

Impatient that Alan was being cagey, she said a little too sharply, "Because I want to know, and it's none of your business why."

"Ouch!" Alan acted as if he were stung by the retort.

"I'm sorry, it's been a long day. What else do you know? If you don't mind," she added with a please-forgive-me smile.

Alan jumped in with both feet. "Now, mind you, it's all rumor and I have no firsthand knowledge or experience—"

Lauren interrupted him. "I get it, Alan."

"She's quite the social butterfly." At Lauren's look of puzzlement he clarified, "She rarely dates the same woman twice. Every time I've seen her out she's with a different woman, and they're all stunning. She's quite a catch, but it sounds like she has no plans to tie herself down."

"Really?" Lauren returned her gaze across the room in time to see Elliott shaking hands with a man and walking toward the exit. Elliott turned around and looked as though she wanted to return to where Lauren stood but changed her mind when she saw her talking with Alan. Instead, she waved a small good-bye before she moved through the door.

"It's gotta be tough wondering if a woman is interested in you or your money," Alan said with sympathy.

"Yes, I suppose it would be." Lauren was definitely not interested in Elliott's money. She had inherited a substantial amount when her grandmother died fifteen years earlier, and she'd invested wisely over the years. She was well on her way to a comfortable retirement by the time she was fifty if she so desired.

"Mmm. To listen to the girls talk, she is one smooth operator and no one goes home disappointed, if you know what I mean." Alan arched his eyebrows, reminiscent of Groucho Marx.

I don't doubt that. Lauren kept her expression even so Alan wouldn't read anything personal into her questions.

"That's the word on the street about Ms. Foster. Take it as you hear it," he said with finality.

After some general conversation, they said their good-byes, and as Alan walked away Lauren continued to mull over what she had learned. Elliott's generosity to the children of San Diego signaled that there was much more to her character than anyone would guess. At first blush, Lauren had thought she was probably too narcissistic to give a damn about others.

With a pang of regret, she glanced toward the doorway where Elliott had exited. She knew she could have extended their conversation if she'd chosen, and she now wished she had. Wondering if she would ever run into Elliott Foster again, Lauren went in search of her date. She was ready to end the evening's charade.

CHAPTER THREE

Elliott had mixed emotions about Monday mornings, and today was no different. She loved her work and was energized by the challenges she faced. Her business was investing in ideas, and the people she met were both brilliant and devious. The business proposals that Foster McKenzie assessed every day presented Elliott with the opportunity to hone her business skills on some and trust her gut instinct on others. Crafty individuals always had a scheme to get something for nothing and kept Elliott on her toes. She was responsible for billions of dollars and could not afford to be taken in by a smooth-talking con artist.

What she hated about Mondays was the traffic. There were more cars on the road than any other day of the week. Elliott separated them into three distinct categories: The first were the ones driven by people who had overslept and kept jockeying between cars to get the best position in the lane. The second group of drivers were those Elliott thought must hate their job and were in no hurry to get to where they were going. The final were those that were in either of the first two categories and were talking on their cell phones.

The blue minivan directly ahead of her was definitely in a hurry, the woman at the wheel talking feverishly on her cell phone. Elliott sank back into the leather seat of her midnight blue BMW 745i with a noisy sigh as she was cut off for the second time by this inconsiderate driver. Telling herself to keep her cool, she allowed her thoughts to replay the events of Saturday evening.

Not long after she'd arrived at the Lincoln Grand, Pamela Whitney had cornered her by the ladies' room. Pamela was the daughter of the chief of police and they had first met at a benefit a few weeks earlier. She made it very clear that she was interested in a repeat of the hours they had spent together in her condo that night. The sex had been exciting and fulfilling, but regardless of the memory, Elliott sensed that Pamela was interested in more than a casual liaison, so she backed off.

She had no regrets about going home alone. By far the most enjoyable part of the evening had been the few minutes she'd spent with Lauren Collier. Even now, thinking about her in that form-hugging black dress, Elliott had trouble concentrating on the road. She could kick herself. Why hadn't she asked Lauren out?

Rebecca. That's why.

The thought made her pulse hammer. She could actually hear her heart pounding in her ears. She had to get that bloodsucker out of her life, and soon.

Just as she was about to change lanes, the blue minivan with the distracted driver swerved and clipped the right front fender of her car. Elliott slammed on the brakes and the minivan spun around and stopped, facing her.

"Son of a bitch!" Elliott unbuckled her seat belt and jumped out of her car in a rage. She jerked open the offending driver's door and started screaming at the woman inside. "You stupid bitch! What in the fuck do you think you're doing? Get off the goddamn phone and pay attention to the road." Her anger rose two notches when the woman still had not hung up the phone. Elliott grabbed the offending object from her hand and snapped it shut. "I said, get off the fucking phone."

It was then that Elliott heard screaming coming from the backseat. She careened her head and peered inside. An infant, no older than a few weeks, was crying at the top of its lungs.

The woman grabbed Elliott's arm and started pleading. "I'm sorry. Please, I have to get my baby to the hospital. He's sick and burning up with fever and, please, please I've got to get to the hospital. I was talking to the doctor and he said to hurry. You can follow me. Please, I'll pay you anything to fix your car. I've got to go."

Elliott's stomach dropped when she looked at the face of the pleading woman. *Christ, when did I become such an ass?* Handing the phone back, she softened her tone. "It's okay. Go and take care of your baby and don't worry about this."

The woman didn't give Elliott a chance to change her mind; she sped off in the direction of the local hospital.

Elliott slumped against the hood of her car. Her hands shook and she was breathing heavily. *Elliott, you just screamed at a lady with a sick baby. You're going to hell for that one.* She was ashamed of her actions. Her patience and typical calm demeanor had definitely disappeared in the past few weeks. She found herself snapping at people for no apparent reason and had little tolerance for mistakes. And the way she had just exploded all over this poor woman was unforgivable. *I need to get it together.*

A few minutes after nine, she walked into her office, almost running into a maintenance man on his way out. She was calm outside but seething within. "Good morning," she greeted Teresa, as if all was well.

Her assistant returned the greeting, only hers didn't sound phony. "How was the party?"

"You know," Elliott replied. "Same food, same faces, same pleadings for money."

"Good God, Elliott, it's barely nine o'clock in the morning and you're in a shitty mood. You need to turn right around and go back out the door you just came in, and this time, shuck the attitude." Teresa steadied her eye contact, not afraid to confront her boss.

Elliott gave a wry smile and dropped into the guest chair across from Teresa's desk. Teresa had been her assistant for several years, and in that time they had shared their experiences with men, women, lust, heartbreak, and an occasional skirting of obsessive lovers. They could talk about anything and generally did. Elliott treated her more like a friend than an employee, and in return, Teresa kept Elliott's life in order.

Letting her briefcase slide out of her hand and fall to the floor,

Elliott leaned forward, resting her forearms on her thighs and hiding her face in her hands. She felt even smaller than she had when she'd screamed at the frantic mother earlier. *Is there anyone else I can piss on this morning?*

"Jesus, Teresa. What is going on with me? Know what I did this morning? I screamed at a lady who was on the way to the hospital with her sick baby." Elliott still could not believe she had acted so horribly.

Teresa frowned at her. "You did what?"

Elliott leaned back against the chair, feeling exhausted before the day had begun. She relayed the ugly events of her encounter with the woman an hour earlier. "She was on the phone with her pediatrician, who was telling her to get the baby to the hospital immediately, and I'm screaming in her face to hang up." If she could have rolled into a ball and disappeared at that moment, she would have.

"That's deplorable." Teresa's disgust was clearly evident. "I've never known you to do anything like that, and you've had plenty of opportunities."

Teresa was right—since taking over the reins at Foster McKenzie, Elliott had never once lost her temper or overreacted to any situation, however challenging. On the contrary, when it came to her work and particularly her actions in the office, she had the demeanor of a saint and the patience of molasses in winter. Nothing shook her or caused her to react the way she had this morning. At least, not until the steady decline in her mood over the past few weeks.

She picked up her briefcase and slowly rose from the chair. "I need a vacation. Maybe someplace warm and tropical with an unending supply of drinks with those little umbrellas in them."

"Yes, and served by bikini-clad blondes," Teresa added, knowing her too well.

Elliott thought for a moment. "No, I need to stay away from women, particularly the bikini-clad ones, for a while." She suspected from Teresa's expression that her face had given her away.

"What else is bothering you?" Teresa hesitated. "Has Rebecca contacted you again?"

Elliott had confided in Teresa after Rebecca left seventeen phone messages in the span of three days and would not let Teresa take a message other than *The bitch better call me.*

Elliott grimaced at the thought of their conversation two days ago. "She showed up at my door Saturday night and I didn't handle it very well. Now she's really pissed at me, and Ryan is pissed at me. And you're pissed at me, and I'm pissed at myself for not keeping my mouth shut." The list was even longer, in reality. But Elliott didn't want to think about her nasty-minded brother-in-law and his latest attempts to rock the boat at Foster McKenzie.

"I'm not pissed at you, Elliott," Teresa sympathized. "I'm sorry for what you're going through with her. What does she want this time?"

"Three hundred thousand dollars." Elliott dealt with amounts larger than this on an hourly basis, but there were no personal principles at stake in those transactions.

"For what?"

"For half a dozen spins in the sack." Teresa's expression made Elliott revise her explanation to be a bit less crude. "I think her exact words were something along the line of *to make me go away.*"

"You aren't considering it, are you?" Teresa asked.

One of the traits that she admired most about Elliott was her honesty and integrity. She didn't think her boss would cave in to blackmail, but at this point she wasn't sure. She sensed that Elliott had been more affected by Rebecca's threats than she was letting on. Elliott always set an example of professionalism and never allowed her personal life to interfere. She was as tough as they came in her business dealings, but always fair. Teresa admired anyone who could manage the intricacies of hosting a conference call while answering e-mails and ordering lunch and never miss a beat; however, she thought that Elliott was in a class of her own for more important reasons, namely the checks she signed on a monthly basis in the folder marked *Our Future.* These generous donations went out to several children's organizations, and Elliott never sought publicity for them. Teresa's heart ached to see a woman who was so giving and good-hearted be involved with someone as ugly as Rebecca.

"Absolutely not. I will not give that gold digger what she

wants." Elliott paused. "Oh, yeah, I'm expecting a call from Ryan later this morning to chew my ass again, so put him through."

The thick carpet muffled the sound of Teresa's footsteps five minutes later, and Elliott was startled when a cup of coffee appeared in front of her. "Thanks," she murmured, not looking up from the pile of papers she was reading.

"You're welcome. A Lauren Collier called just before you came in, by the way." Elliott's head jerked up so fast Teresa drew back. "Uh-oh, does she have something to do with Rebecca?"

"Did you say Lauren Collier?" At Teresa's nod she said, "No, she has nothing to do with Rebecca. At least not that I'm aware of. Jeez, I hope she doesn't. Did she say what she wanted?"

Elliott was surprised at her reaction to the mention of the beautiful woman from Saturday night. She normally didn't receive personal phone calls at her office, and she was certain that she had not given Lauren her number. A strange tingling trickled through her veins at the knowledge that Lauren had gone to the trouble of tracking her down.

Teresa placed the pink While You Were Out note near the top of the black blotter covering Elliott's desk. "She asked that you give her a call. She has a meeting till eleven but then she'll be free after that."

Elliott reached for the message. "What was the maintenance guy doing in here? Is it the air-conditioning again?"

Teresa paused on her way out. "I didn't call anyone. He said it was routine maintenance."

Elliott glanced around the vents. At least this guy had tidied up after himself, unlike the last one. She stared at the opposite wall, strangely unmotivated to work. She had two hours to kill before she could phone Lauren, enough time to meet with a couple of senior staff members and ensure the presentation for their client meeting tomorrow was finished. Yet she was hopelessly distracted. Annoyed with herself, she pictured her grandfather sitting right here behind this same cherrywood desk. What would he think of her now?

It didn't take much imagination for her to hear the patriarch telling her that it was about time she grew up and assumed the responsibility that was her birthright. She hadn't known the old guy very well, but he seemed to come alive when he entered this office and Elliott knew she had inherited that gene. She loved what she did; she was good at it and could hardly wait to come into work most mornings. But today all she wanted was for the hands on the Waterford clock to move. With a gloomy sigh, she turned her attention to a stack of files and forced herself to focus on business.

Across town, on the forty-second floor of the Bradley & Taylor building, Lauren was also sitting in her office, but she was not alone. She was struggling to keep her mind on what was being discussed by the three people seated around her conference table. Lauren was always focused when she was working, but her mind kept drifting back to the stunning tuxedo-clad woman she had met two nights before. Something about Elliott Foster had colonized her thoughts and she wasn't sleeping well because of it. But what troubled Lauren even more than tiredness and a loss of concentration was her uncharacteristic behavior this morning, when she'd picked up the phone and called Elliott.

Lauren never did anything without thinking it through ad nauseam, and she certainly would never waste any time on someone as fickle as Elliott. Lauren had seen her cycle through anger, rudeness, frustration, humility, and the ever-present charm and, inexplicably, she found each more enthralling than its precursor. Yesterday she'd spent hours searching the Internet for information about the intriguing woman. Fortunately for Lauren, there was an abundance of material, and a few articles even openly referred to Elliott as a lesbian. Those that did echoed what she'd pried from Alan and provided a few additional juicy tidbits.

The more she read about Elliott, the more she wanted to know until she finally dragged her bleary eyes to bed well after midnight. She was totally dumbfounded when she found herself speaking with Elliott's assistant first thing this morning. Wasn't it enough that she'd researched the CEO of Foster McKenzie as if a lawsuit could come out of it?

"I'm sorry, what did you say?" Lauren was embarrassed to

have lost track of the conversation. *Focus, Lauren.* She banished all thoughts of Elliott from her mind as the question to her was repeated for the third time.

"He should go."

"You can't be serious." Lauren didn't know whether to laugh or smack Thomas Merison over the head with a brick. He had just asked if he could fire an employee because he was *queer*, as he put it. Merison was the chief financial officer and a twenty-three-year employee of Bradley & Foster.

"Why wouldn't I be? I can't have that kind of disruption in my organization."

From their first meeting, Lauren knew this guy was a pompous ass who wouldn't know a progressive thought if it bit him in the butt. He was so far to the right he was soon going to fall off the face of the earth. *This guy and his attitude need to suffer extinction.* She smothered a smile.

Lauren knew John Briggs, the employee in question, and admitted to herself that he was a flamer, but she had never heard any complaints about him. On the contrary, he seemed to have a good working relationship with his peers and she often saw him in the cafeteria, sitting at a table full of his coworkers. She cocked her head. "And exactly what kind of disruption is happening?"

"It's so obvious," Merison said as if that was the answer to it all.

"And?"

Merison was no good at hiding his emotions. "What do you mean and? He prances around the office all nelly-like with his limp wrist and swaying hips. He's always chatting and giggling. And those clothes."

An image of Merison dressed in a Victoria's Secret teddy flashed in Lauren's mind. She took a large swallow of her coffee to erase that scary thought. "Have you received any complaints about his work?"

"No, but that doesn't mean he's not causing disruption. People are probably afraid to say anything."

"And why would that be?"

Merison looked at Lauren as if she were stupid. "They are afraid that he would start rumors and say that they were queer too."

I can't believe I'm actually having this conversation. This guy is a moron.

Merison continued with his justification. "I have to answer to the federal government. This company has an impeccable reputation and I intend to keep it that way. I run a tight ship and I don't stand for any dissension in my ranks."

So far the third member at the table, their CEO Charles Comstock, had not uttered a word during this topic of conversation. Lauren glanced at him, inviting his opinion, but he remained silent, so she said, "From what you've told me, you can't fire him, Thomas."

"What more do you need?"

Stay calm. Remember this guy is an idiot. "First of all, Thomas, the term is *gay*. Second, it's against the law to fire him solely on the basis of suspicions about who he might date in his own time. Third, this company and you personally can be sued for simply uttering the word *queer* in this context." Lauren was sure to emphasize the *you personally* in her last comment. "Fourth, no one has complained, either officially or unofficially. And finally, you have no grounds for termination."

"What do you mean no grounds?" Merison's back had stiffened, and Lauren could actually see the Windsor knot in his tie tighten.

"I mean you haven't shown me anything that he has done that would justify termination. His performance is exemplary. You've said so yourself in his last three performance reviews." Lauren indicated the file sitting in front of her. "No one has complained and he hasn't violated any company policy. He has done nothing wrong," she said with finality.

Merison turned a pleading look toward the CEO, who finally spoke. "Now, Lauren, surely there is *something* we can do here?"

She didn't miss the inflection in his question nor the expectation he had that she would support Merison's position. Lauren knew her next comment would be a defining point of her career at Bradley & Taylor.

"No, Charles, there is nothing we can do. We cannot fire him for simply being gay. I will not support a position that is unethical, not to mention morally wrong." She watched as both men tightened their eyes at her last statement as if seeing her for the first time, and she knew she had just stepped into a minefield.

"Lauren—"

"It's obvious that's not the answer you're looking for, but it's my decision nonetheless." In her opinion there was nothing more to be said about it.

The two men rose from her table. Merison spoke through tight lips. "All right, I'll accept that for now, but I can guarantee that Mr. Nelly-Fairy will be a problem. You can mark my words on that."

Before he stepped away from the table, Lauren stood and nailed him with her eyes. "Thomas, my advice to you as chief counsel is to stop using inappropriate terms and stop making derogatory comments about an employee of this company."

Lauren collapsed onto the small sofa in her office. "Holy Christ. I think I'm in deep shit now." There was no one in the room to confirm her observation.

❖

Elliott could swear that the hands on the crystal clock had not moved in the past hour. The papers on her desk had moved from one side to the other, giving the appearance of completion when in fact they had not even been read. Finally, after an hour, she gave up the pretense of getting any work done and went in search of something to eat. When she returned, Teresa handed her a pink message note. Lauren Collier had called again. She was now out of her meeting.

Elliott didn't wait to hear if there were any other messages. She hurried into her office and shut the door behind her. She had never felt this type of apprehension before making a phone call. Every day she made calls that could change the course of people's lives, but this feeling was totally foreign to her. As she dialed, her mind raced through various reasons why Lauren might have called and what she wanted but went completely blank when the line started ringing. Elliott tried to rehearse what she intended to say, but got stuck at "hello."

Lauren was opening a file that was at least two inches thick when the phone began to ring. *Jesus, why can't we lawyers just say something in fifty pages or less?* It rang several times before she remembered that her assistant, Michelle, was in the copy center making the necessary copies of the material Lauren needed for her meeting tomorrow morning.

"Lauren Collier," she answered distractedly.

"It's Elliott Foster." *Why am I so nervous?*

Lauren's heart began to race at the sound of the rich, smooth voice on the other end of the line. She let the folder drop back on her desk and removed her reading glasses. "Hi. Uh, thanks for calling me back." *That was stupid. Why wouldn't she call me back?*

"I'm sorry I missed your call earlier. I finally succumbed to an insatiable craving for a Snickers bar and went down to the snack shop in the lobby."

Lauren could hear the smile in Elliott's voice. "Personally, I'm addicted to Reese's Peanut Butter Cups," she admitted guiltily.

"Ah, you see, no matter how grown-up or how successful we are, we all have our hidden vices." Elliott laughed.

"I won't tell if you don't," Lauren said as though the secret was a matter of national security.

"Deal." Elliott didn't really know what to say next.

Lauren held back a nervous chuckle. She felt absolutely ridiculous, scared, and as excited as she had been in years. "I wanted to let you know that I accept your apology." The pause on the other end made her nervous.

Finally, the soft voice answered, and Lauren relaxed her death grip on the receiver. "Thank you. I was kind of worried. I was afraid I was gonna have to tell my sister that I made an ass out of myself and she would give me holy hell for weeks until I made amends. And trust me, that would not be a pretty sight."

"I'm glad I saved you from her wrath. Does she have many opportunities to fuss at you like that?" This insight into Elliott's life was fascinating to Lauren.

Elliott glanced over at the photo of Stephanie that sat prominently on the corner of her desk. "More than I'd like, but not as much as she used to. I've settled down quite a bit in the last few years, and she now focuses her attention on matchmaking among her friends. I don't think they're completely thrilled about it." Elliott's heart rate increased when she heard Lauren laugh. *What a wonderful sound.*

"I can only wish. I'm an only child." Lauren winced, remembering that it had been several weeks since she had called her mother.

"Yikes, and I thought I had it tough." Both women laughed.

Acting on an impulse, Lauren asked, "Will you have dinner with me Saturday night?" *Jesus, I don't believe that just came out of my mouth.* She held her breath.

Elliott didn't expect the invitation, and she suspected that Lauren hadn't planned to issue it. She was accustomed to women and even some clueless men making the first pass at her, but this time she wasn't certain that the invitation was a pass.

Not knowing what had gotten into her, Lauren was completely embarrassed and tried desperately to think of a way to get out of this. She had never been so unprepared for what came out of her mouth. "Um...I..."

Elliott quickly said, "I'd love to."

Now what in the hell do I say? Think! Think! Lauren was stunned at her reaction to this woman, and shook her head in an attempt to jog her brain into action. Her mind was completely blank as she struggled to come up with the name of any restaurant in town. Her savior came in the form of an invitation to a luncheon meeting sitting prominently in her in-box.

"Have you been to the new restaurant at the Borgotta called Madison's?" She referred to the newly remodeled upscale shopping plaza on the boardwalk.

"No, I haven't. I hear it's wonderful." Elliott sat back in her chair and put her feet on her desk.

A vivid image of Elliott sitting across from her at a small, intimate table invaded Lauren's thoughts. She saw the candlelight flickering in the dark eyes that held mystery and adventure. Long fingers held a glass of Dom Perignon that was slowly moving toward lips that Lauren could actually feel caressing her breasts.

"Lauren?"

Snapped out of her salacious thoughts, Lauren said, "Yes, I'm here, sorry. I need your address." She could not stop thinking about Elliott's lips and had to ask her to repeat the address twice. "Six thirty? That should give us enough time to get there."

"Make it six and we can have a cocktail first if you'd like." Elliott was hoping they could have a few minutes together before joining the throngs of other dinner patrons. *Maybe we won't even make it to dinner.*

"All right." Wanting to prolong the conversation, but at a loss for how, Lauren agreed, "Okay then, I'll see you at six."

"I'll be ready," Elliott said with intentional double meaning. Based on the long silence at the other end, it seemed obvious that Lauren had picked up on the innuendo.

"Right, see you then," Lauren replied weakly and hung up the phone before Elliott could tease her any further. Sitting back in her chair, she gazed into thin air, waiting for her heart to slow down. *God, what is it about that woman? I feel like I've been run over by a truck.*

CHAPTER FOUR

Elliott leaned back in her chair and rubbed her temples. After four days of back-to-back meetings she was tired and cranky, and her head hurt. She looked at the notes in front of her from this morning's meeting, noticing abstract doodles scattered throughout the pages. Frowning, she realized the scribbles reflected how often her mind had wandered to Lauren over the past few days. She had dated many women, and slept with most of them, but none had intruded on her thoughts as this one had.

She recalled Lauren in the black designer dress and was struck again by the way she'd stood out from the rest of the women at the benefit, not by sheer beauty but with her presence. Lauren radiated an energy that made everyone else in the room seem flat and uninteresting. Elliott hadn't mistaken the interest in those eyes, even from across the room, but at the time she'd been too angry about Rebecca to act on it.

She put her feet on the desk and glanced at the clock. She had thirty minutes before her next meeting, and this was as good a time as any to think about exactly what else she had glimpsed in Lauren's eyes before she dropped her gaze. Was it just curiosity? Was Lauren straight, or maybe a hobby bisexual? Elliott pondered the different scenarios while she nibbled on the salad Teresa had left on the corner of her desk. Something else nagged at the back of her mind and she couldn't quite put her finger on it. She was rarely wrong in her judgment when it came to women, or business, but the situation with Rebecca suggested a nick in her assessment ability. Very little shook her confidence, but the possibility that she was losing her judgment did just that.

She'd spoken at length to Ryan a few hours earlier, attempting to determine their strategy if Rebecca followed through on her threats. She'd ended the call disgusted and just a little bit afraid. They could handle Rebecca, but not without some ugliness. Elliott didn't like being held to ransom, and the fact that she'd brought this upon herself made the problem even more intolerable. She rubbed the kinks out of her neck and flipped the calendar, smiling when she saw the notation for dinner with Lauren the next evening. She had almost expected Lauren to call and make some plausible excuse to break the date. But instead she'd confirmed, adding to Elliott's general distraction level.

The thought of spending an evening with a beautiful woman always filled her with anticipation, but this time the familiar prickle of her senses seemed more intense. This was not just dinner with another beautiful woman; she was going to spend the evening with a woman who tantalized her as few did. If for no other reason than to find out if she was imagining the rapport she'd felt with Lauren Collier, she needed to see her again.

Needed. Elliott shifted some papers around her desk. The thought of *needing* anything made her uneasy. To need was to be vulnerable, and she could not remember the last time she'd felt that way about a woman. Her physical "needs" were something else. But now her desires had complicated her life intolerably, exposing her and an innocent third party to Rebecca's ruthless game-playing. Elliott supposed she should be thankful that her emotions had never been involved; her pride was the only thing at stake, personally. In the future she would be more cautious and that meant whatever happened on Saturday night with Lauren, she was not going to make any hasty decisions she might later regret.

Jesus, Lauren, just pick something. Lauren was in her closet examining the clothes that remained hanging neatly on the rod. She glanced at the pile of garments she'd already tried on and discarded on her bed as not being right. She was nervous and wanted to look her best. She didn't quite know how to classify this evening with Elliott. It wasn't really a date, but yet it certainly felt like one.

The butterflies jostling for space in her stomach were a clear indication that she was looking forward to this dinner engagement with more anticipation than she ever experienced with other companions. She reached for a hanger and finally admitted to herself that she found Elliott more than just attractive and she wasn't quite sure what to do with that fact. Lauren was highly educated, well traveled, and far from naïve in the ways of the world, but she was way out of her league with this one.

Frowning at the empty hangers, she couldn't remember the last time she had been this nervous. She traveled in high circles, and thanks to her upbringing she was not impressed by the accompanying pomp and circumstance, or by the people. Her father loved his job as a mailman and had taught her the importance of commitment to family, job, and country. Her mother was a teacher, and throughout her childhood Lauren had been exposed to literature and different cultures. She still retained the love of learning and acceptance of difference she had grown up with.

Money was tight in the Collier household, and Lauren had worked hard to earn enough to attend the local university, where she graduated summa cum laude and was granted entry to the Harvard School of Law. While at Harvard, Lauren encountered, almost for the first time in her life, people who believed that their bloodline or bank balance made them superior to everyone else. Out of necessity, she had learned how to adapt to her surroundings, and she took pride in the fact that she never compromised her values or integrity to do so. Harvard had prepared her well for what was to come in her working life.

These days, she was surrounded by successful men and women and also by those who would resort to anything to be a member of the club. Lauren was aware that she had foes, colleagues who resented her senior position. Typically they underestimated her strength and savvy, and if Lauren ever had to act to protect her interests, her targets never knew what hit them until it was all over. Through hard work and dedication, she had gained the reputation of being brilliant in law and extremely politically astute. Most people knew better than to make an enemy of her, even those whose advances she rebuffed.

Over the course of her career she had encountered men used to getting their way, who thought they were doing her some kind of favor by hitting on her. Like many successful women she'd spoken with on this subject, she seemed to attract men who were interested either in being dominated or in conquering her. She dated when she found time and had managed to keep two semiserious relationships going for several years. But when each man proposed marriage, she found herself surprisingly ambivalent. Four years had passed since she broke off with her last would-be husband, and she had halfheartedly dated a handful of other men over that time, but no one who meant anything. She had started to wonder if she would ever meet one who would ignite her soul.

In recent years women had sometimes expressed an interest in her as well—it was not as if she didn't know any lesbians—but she had never dated a woman seriously. Lauren took a deep breath and stopped frantically searching her closet. It was just dinner. She'd been in more intimate settings with women. What was the big deal here?

Hoping the sound of her own voice would calm her frazzled nerves, she said, "I wasn't this nervous on my first date."

Lauren smiled at the thought of Claire Bailey, the first woman whose invitation she'd accepted. Several dates later Claire was also the first woman she'd kissed, but they had not gone much further. Lauren had dated a few other women after Claire, but she hadn't hooked up with anyone. She realized that in many respects the women she dated were very much alike. Successful, confident, and sophisticated. But boring.

Elliott was different, very different. *She's the first woman that makes my skin crawl. In a good way. A very good way.* Her body confirmed the description and she shook her hands as if this would expel the tingling sensations in her fingertips. Elliott could have any woman she wanted. *Could she want me?* Lauren doubted it. She was nothing like the women Alan said Elliott typically went for.

"If I'd just shut up and admit to myself that I want more than dinner I probably wouldn't be this nervous." Her voice trailed off as the image of what she did want filled her mind. *Nervous*, hell. She was scared to death.

She finally settled on dark green silk pants and a cream sleeveless shell with a contrasting green jacket. The color worked well with her red hair and the soft tan that seemed to be a genetic aberration. Her mother had the same unusual coloring. She leaned toward the mirror attached to her dresser, inserted her earrings, and studied her face critically. *Not bad.* She had taken extra care applying her makeup, which was a challenge with her hands shaking in anticipation. The resulting effect simply highlighted her features with a clean natural look that she could barely detect. Pleased with the results, she returned the discarded clothes to her closet, smoothed the wrinkles out of the down comforter that covered the king-size bed, and fluffed the pillows.

She intended to turn away but was arrested by a mental flash of Elliott lying naked on the large bed. A shaft of white-hot heat shot from her stomach and settled between her legs. Stepping back, she knew with a sudden shock that Elliott was the first woman she had ever been able to imagine in her bed. She quickly picked up her purse and keys and left the room, her heart pounding erratically.

I guess this means I could be a lesbian. Shit, I hope I know what to do.

❖

Twelve miles away in her McComb Drive home, Elliott was seated in an overstuffed leather chair slowly sipping Chivas from a heavy crystal glass. Her body was still, but her mind raced in direct competition. She could not remember looking forward to an evening with a woman as much as she was tonight. Lauren Collier was certainly attractive and the spark of desire instantaneous, but there was something about her that heightened Elliott's anticipation. She seemed very different from the women Elliott usually dated.

Elliott never had a shortage of attractive women willing to share her bed. She believed that if two women were attracted to each other and both wanted the same thing, then there was no reason why they should not spend the night together—or in some cases the afternoon.

It was just sex, something for two consenting adults to enjoy. As a result she'd had many sexual partners, and most of her liaisons lasted days or weeks, seldom any longer. Casual affairs fulfilled her sexual needs and suited her lifestyle, especially since she had been totally consumed with managing the day-to-day rebuilding of Foster McKenzie ever since she took over the company. She didn't have any interest in establishing a relationship.

Elliott didn't fool herself thinking that her lovers were unaware of her identity when they came on to her, or when she approached them. They ran in the same circles, and if names were not specifically known, at least faces were. However, she suspected that Lauren hadn't realized who she was when they first met, and certainly didn't care who she was when she raked her over the coals for her awful behavior. Tonight's dinner invitation had surprised Elliott completely, and, for her, surprises were few and far between.

Even through the phone lines, she'd suspected that Lauren had acted impulsively, which was not a common thing for an attorney to do. Elliott had enough experience with members of the legal profession to know that they thought through everything and usually knew exactly what the answer would be to just about any question they planned to ask. She smiled at the challenge of keeping this woman off her stride.

When the bell announced her guest a few minutes later, she rose quickly and crossed the room with more haste than usual. She did not generally have a woman come to her house but rather preferred to pick them up or meet somewhere. An easier escape if she needed one, she had always told her friends, and several times it became a reality. This was another sign that Lauren was not a cookie-cutter girl.

Elliott's shoes clipped on the marble tile floor in the foyer and her hand shook when she reached for the doorknob. She tightened her grip at the sight of Lauren on her doorstep. *She's beautiful.* Elliott took in the perfect cut of the green suit and just the hint of cleavage showing at the top of the shell. Her makeup accentuated her cheekbones and highlighted her tentative blue eyes.

Lauren's throat tightened and her breathing became shallow

when she realized that she was actually standing in front of this striking woman once again. *What in the hell am I doing here?*

"Hi." Elliott's voice almost betrayed the racing of her blood as it coursed through her body.

"Hi," Lauren greeted her shyly, stunned by her reaction at seeing Elliott for a second time. She took in the familiar cut of a Hugo Boss design in the charcoal dress trousers and darker shade silk blouse Elliott had chosen to wear. *Very hot.*

"I'm sorry. Please come in." Elliott opened the door wider and stepped to the side to let Lauren enter. *Mmm, you smell delicious.* "Any trouble finding the place?"

"No, not at all." Lauren almost laughed, recalling her reactions as she'd approached Elliott's rambling house moments before. She'd parked in the center of a long circular drive and had to take several deep breaths in an attempt to rein in her nervousness and racing pulse. Then she slowly walked up the cobblestone path flanked on either side by bright, colorful flowers and an immaculately manicured lawn. The smell of salt was in the air as a soft breeze from the ocean tousled her hair. The walk would normally have been a pleasure, but the whole time she had been rehearsing how she would greet Elliott. *For crying out loud, it's only dinner. Yeah, right.*

Elliott motioned her through a spacious hallway to a living room decorated in shades of brown and tan with accent colors in the upholstery on the chairs and throw pillows on the couch. A Georgia O'Keeffe print hung above the fireplace and another on the wall to her left. The room had a warm, comfortable feeling to it.

"You have a beautiful home," Lauren said as she moved to sit in one of the high-back chairs across from the couch.

"Thank you. I'm not here often but when I am I like to be comfortable," Elliott replied almost guiltily. She wasn't home much, and at times it seemed to be almost a waste of good furnishings. "What would you like to drink?" She moved toward the wet bar on the other side of the room.

"Scotch if you have it." Lauren was typically not a heavy drinker, but she felt she needed additional fortification this evening.

"Certainly. How was your week in the world of corporate

law?" Elliott cringed at the stupid question but, surprisingly, she was unable to think of anything else to ask. Normally she had no trouble with small talk, which she generally peppered with sexual innuendo.

"Probably about the same as yours." Lauren accepted the glass with thanks. "Meetings, phone calls, tedious flights out of town, and more meetings. And let's not forget about the ever-present e-mails." She chuckled. "I think they multiply the longer they're in my in-box."

The liquor was warm in her hand but was nothing compared to the warmth spreading through her body as Elliott laughed at her apt description. She held the glass tightly and took a drink, blinking back the tears brought on by the strong beverage.

"I think the same about the pink message slips Teresa gives me. I'm not a geneticist, but I swear they reproduce like bunnies on the corner of her desk." Elliott wished she could relax.

Lauren choked on the smooth liquid sliding down her throat when the image of her and Elliott fucking like bunnies on her desk unexpectedly popped into her head.

Elliott crossed the space between them in an instant, her concern plainly visible on her face. "Are you all right?"

No, actually I'm mortified. Lauren managed to catch her breath without further embarrassing herself. "Yes, guess it just went down the wrong pipe. I'm fine, really." She blinked several more times to clear her head.

Elliott returned to her chair, never taking her eyes off her guest. "So, how long have you been at B&T?"

"B&T?" Lauren asked, tilting her head.

Elliott grinned sheepishly. "Sorry, I don't mean to insult you. Didn't you know everybody calls you B&T?"

"Everybody?"

Elliott took a sip of her drink. "Well, everybody who does business with you. Bradley & Taylor just sounds so…" She hesitated as she searched for the right adjective. "Stuffy."

"And Foster McKenzie isn't?" Lauren couldn't keep the teasing tone from her reply.

"Um. You've got a point there."

"Why not just go with Foster Mac? It has a nice catchy ring to it." This time, when Lauren swallowed her Scotch, it went down smoothly.

"I'm not so sure my clients would have much faith in a company that has a *catchy ring* to its name. People tend to get nervous when it comes to their money."

"Mmm, I suppose so."

The quiet in the room was punctuated by the ticking of the clock in the foyer. Lauren often used silence as a technique to get people to open up, and it rarely failed her. Most people became uncomfortable and babbled to fill gaps in conversation; however, the same could not be said about the woman sitting across from her. Elliott looked perfectly relaxed, which was more than Lauren could say about herself.

Elliott was far from relaxed. *What will the evening bring? Hell I don't even know what this evening is to start with.* "So, Lauren, tell me something about you."

You mean something other than I have no idea what I'm doing here? "Anything specific or just general small talk?"

Yeah, like you're a lesbian, right? Elliott smothered a grin and sat back in the chair. "Surprise me."

Her smoky-eyed regard made Lauren's pulse race. "Something tells me very few things surprise you, Elliott." She sounded more confident than she felt.

The way Lauren said her name sent a bolt of electricity through Elliott's body, making her fingers tingle with the desire to touch her. "You did."

"Really? How so?" Lauren could not believe she was carrying on this conversation with what appeared to be composure when her stomach was tied up in knots.

She's got guts, I'll give her that. Elliott took another sip of her drink and casually crossed her legs, giving herself a moment to judge where she should go from here. She decided caution was the best approach. "When you invited me to dinner."

Lauren replied without thinking. "Yes, well, it kind of surprised me too."

Elliott mimicked the question of a moment ago. "Really? How

so?" She felt as if she were on the edge of her seat waiting for the answer.

"I'm not really sure. On the one hand it seemed a perfectly common thing to do to get to know someone better..." Lauren hesitated, not quite knowing how to finish the sentence.

"But on the other," Elliott prompted, using her hands as a prop. She held her breath, afraid that her reputation had negatively preceded her. It would not be the first time a woman was uncomfortable being seen with her. Her picture occasionally appeared in the society section of the daily newspaper along with her current "gal pal," as they liked to label her dates. If she was fortunate, that was the only place the photo ran. But the local sleazy tabloids loved cashing in when they could, and sometimes that upset dates who valued their privacy.

"On the other hand, I normally don't ask someone out that quickly after meeting them. I guess it surprised me that I actually did."

"At the risk of asking another dull-witted question, why *are* we having dinner tonight?"

The chiming of the clock stopped Lauren from answering. She glanced at her watch. "Oh, my, I've lost all track of time. We need to get going."

Elliott rose from her chair, eyes twinkling. "I'd like to think that time flies when you're having fun." She locked the front door behind her and followed Lauren down the lighted path to her car. She heard the familiar chirp of the car alarm and the dome lights came on casting a warm, inviting glow inside the vehicle. "Nice car," Elliott said in appreciation of the late-model convertible Mercedes. *Well, maybe she has a wild streak in her after all.*

"Thanks. I admit it's a bit much, but it's fun."

Elliott opened the passenger door and slid inside. Buckling her seat belt, she watched Lauren walk around the front of her car. So far the evening was starting out just as she had expected. Lauren was charming, witty, and intelligent. Elliott was impressed at the way she had directly answered her questions without the coyness the other women she dated were so fond of. Her honesty was refreshing, but Elliott reminded herself that she had also thought that about Rebecca. Could she have been any more wrong?

She let her gaze rest on the smooth outline of Lauren's thighs beneath the dark green fabric of her pants. The thought of stroking a hand along the slight gap in between them made the ugly thoughts of Rebecca vanish like a bad dream. Lauren smiled at her and turned the key in the ignition. Elliott smiled in return, surprised by something. Happiness. Just exchanging a look with this woman made her feel genuinely happy.

The drive to the restaurant took about fifteen minutes, and as the valet parked her car, she instinctively placed her hand on the small of Elliott's back and escorted her inside. The maître d' led them to a table next to the window where the sun was setting over San Diego Harbor.

"This place is fabulous," Elliott said after they were seated and the wine steward had taken their order. She surveyed their surroundings, noting that every table was occupied, many by gays and lesbians. "I'm surprised you were able to get a reservation. It's obviously very popular."

"I could come back with a witty reply and say that I simply mentioned my name and a table miraculously was available, but in reality they had just received a cancellation when I called."

Elliott was beginning to enjoy Lauren's sense of humor. "I like the witty reply better than the real thing. Let's go with that."

"Okay, but don't expect my name to stop traffic." Lauren scanned the menu, and her mouth began to water at the delicious selections.

"You in that dress you were wearing Saturday night would certainly stop traffic," Elliott said.

Lauren's heart skipped a beat at the unexpected compliment. She slowly lifted her gaze from the menu and settled on the sharp eyes across from her own. *That was smooth.* "Thank you. I kind of like dressing up once in a while."

"And do you always look that beautiful?"

She doesn't waste any time. This was not the first time Lauren had been hit on by a woman, but it certainly was the first time she'd felt like reciprocating. Aiming to lighten the mood, she said, "You really don't expect me to answer that, do you? I'd be lying if I said no and narcissistic if I said yes."

"Well, I'll answer it for you, then. Yes, I'm certain you would look lovely in anything." Elliott immediately imagined what Lauren would look like in nothing at all, and her hands started to sweat.

"Now you're embarrassing me."

"Sorry, but the truth just flows from my lips."

Lauren's heart stopped as she envisioned those lips doing other things as well. She was not accustomed to having sexual fantasies, yet it did not seem the least bit odd that her mind kept straying along that unfamiliar track.

Elliott noticed Lauren's gaze drift to her lips and she read something other than a passing glance in her sparkling blue eyes. She grinned with the realization that her fresh sheets would not be wasted. This was familiar ground, ground that she had walked over many, many times, and she relaxed. "This view is fantastic."

"Yes, it is, isn't it?" Lauren replied after their drinks were delivered. "I love to watch the sun set over the water. When I was little my dad would bring me out to the beach in the evening, and we would sit together and listen for the sound when the sun touched the water."

"What did it sound like?" Elliott asked, drawn in by the look of nostalgia on Lauren's face.

"A long, slow sizzle that grew louder and louder when it hit the water and then tapered off as it disappeared in the horizon. As a grown woman, I know the sun doesn't touch the water, but as a little girl, I swear I could hear it."

"Where is your father now?" Elliott asked, hoping that Lauren would not say he was dead. That was usually a conversation killer.

"He and my mom live not far from here." Laughing, Lauren added, "You couldn't get them to leave San Diego even if they dropped a bomb. How about your family?"

Elliott was taken aback by the sincerity of the question.

Everyone she met either knew her father or knew of him, and many also remembered her mother. "Lauren, do you know who I am?" *God, that sounded pompous.* "I mean…" She didn't get a chance to finish her statement.

"Yes, Elliott, I know who you are," Lauren replied calmly after the waiter appeared and took their dinner order. "I know who you are but I don't know *you*." At Elliott's look of confusion she continued, "What I know I've either read in a newspaper or magazine or someone has told me." She hesitated for a moment. "I'd rather hear it from you."

Elliott was speechless at her remark. It had been a long time since anyone wanted to know her, really know her. Everyone thought they did simply because of her reputation or who her father or her grandfather were. They all had preconceived impressions and ideas about her, and Elliott had became accustomed to that. She hadn't realized the pattern her life had fallen into until the simple request from Lauren.

"What would you like to know?" she asked tentatively, not certain that she even wanted to go down this path. It was much easier for her to act the way that was expected of her by business associates, acquaintances, and even lovers. That, she knew how to do; this was something altogether different.

"Tell me about your family." Lauren sat back with her drink in her hand, prepared to listen.

Elliott obliged. As a matter of fact, she talked all through dinner. She told Lauren how her great-grandparents had emigrated from Europe during World War I with just the clothes on their backs and had built a successful retail business in lower Manhattan. About how their children had expanded into banking and her grandfather went out on his own, building a successful investment banking firm.

Throughout dinner Lauren detected a light in Elliott's eyes as she talked about her family. She noticed it dim slightly when she began to talk about the death of her father and how her mother's brother took over the firm.

"I was twenty-eight years old." Her tone was one of resigned dismay. "I had no interest in running Foster McKenzie."

"What were you interested in?" Lauren asked.

"Women. Lots of them." Elliott cautiously raised her eyes to the woman across from her. Lauren's expression was neither repulsed nor judgmental but rather encouraged her to continue. "I guess I was a bit self-centered back then."

"You guess?" Lauren teased.

"Okay, I was young, rich, *and* self-centered."

"And don't forget devilishly attractive," Lauren interjected humorously.

Really? Elliott was amazed at the good nature of this woman. "Well, that too." She winked at Lauren and continued half seriously, "I was never really sure if I was good-looking or my money looked good. I hate to admit it, but at the time I really didn't care."

"Do you now?" Lauren asked pointedly.

"Sometimes."

Surprised by the honesty in her answer, Lauren prompted, "Sometimes?"

Knowing that her next admission would either clinch or curse any chance she had of getting this sexy woman into bed, Elliott plunged forward anyway. "Sometimes I just need to unwind. I don't want any intense involvement and I'm not looking for commitment, so it doesn't really matter why they're with me."

Lauren held Elliott's gaze. She couldn't resist alluding to Alan's comment about her rumored sexual prowess. "I hear you unwind a lot and that you're pretty good at it."

Elliott was flabbergasted. "Well, you know how rumors are," she replied, attempting to deflect the comment.

But Lauren didn't let her off the hook. "No, how are they?"

Elliott sipped her wine. "You should only believe half of them. The other half is wishful thinking on the part of the person doing the gossiping."

"And which is the half I should believe?" Lauren continued to drill Elliott with her pointed questions. "The part about the frequency or your skills?"

Elliott smirked and decided to give Lauren exactly what she was looking for. "All right, Counselor. I'll tell you all about it. I'm one of those people who believe that sexual desire is a natural bodily function." The images that her comment brought to mind caused

Elliott to momentarily lose her train of thought. She toyed with her wineglass, using the time to gather herself. "And…well, if you have two consenting adults who think the same way, then…" She trailed off, not quite knowing how to conclude.

"You have two satisfied women."

The laughter in Lauren's eyes caused Elliott to join in. "Well yes, if you do it right." *And I'd definitely do it right with you.*

When their dinner was completed and the dessert plates cleared, Lauren asked, "So why are you running Foster McKenzie now?"

Elliott was not prepared for such a sudden shift in topic. She was always uncomfortable talking about how she'd wrested control of Foster McKenzie from her uncle. It was a long, arduous legal battle that had quickly become ugly, with her uncle slinging mud, calling her names, and pointing the blame finger in every direction but his own. She'd refused to stoop to his level and didn't acknowledge or refute any of his comments and certainly none of his innuendo. In the end, the judge had ruled in her favor and Uncle Ted was out.

"I guess this is the stage of our relationship where we start airing our dirty laundry." Elliott tried to set a humorous mood to ease her humiliation. "My uncle had more experience betting on the horses than running a venture capital firm. To him, the principles were the same. Bet on a horse to win, bet on a company or idea to win. I guess in a way they are, but the stakes are quite a bit higher. It wasn't long before he ran the company into the ground." The story sounded benign, but she still felt the pain. "One of our oldest clients tracked me down in Paris and didn't spare me details. I guess by then I'd finally grown up and realized that my father's company was my right and my responsibility. So here I am."

"And are you happy?" It was a simple question.

Elliott laughed.

"What's so funny?"

"No one has asked me that in years. I don't think anyone really cares as long as they're making money." Elliott knew her statement to be true.

"Well, are you?" Lauren still wanted her answer.

Elliott thought for a moment. *Happy* was not a word she would have associated with herself when she assumed control of Foster McKenzie. She was a spoiled little rich girl stepping into a man's world, a world filled with egos, money, and a sincere belief that women didn't have the brains for such *complicated matters*. She'd fought with clients and employees alike to prove that not only was she smart enough, she had also inherited her father's business intuition. It was a long time before she'd felt comfortable, let alone happy.

"Yes, actually, I am. I enjoy what I do and I seem to have a knack for it." Teasingly, she said, "I will admit there are times when I wish I was still running around with no responsibilities and…well, you know." She looked into Lauren's eyes to gauge her reaction. "But all in all, I'm doing all right. How about you?"

"Do I enjoy my work or would I rather run around and…well, you know?" Lauren knew exactly what Elliott was referring to and called her on it.

Elliott raised her eyebrows and cocked her head in acknowledgment. "Both."

"Yes, I enjoy what I do and I'm good at it," Lauren replied. "I haven't had a lot of opportunity in the running-around department, so I'll have to take your word on how much I'd miss it." She hoped Elliott didn't take offense to her last statement.

"And what about well, you know?" Elliott was confident the conversation was going in the direction that she wanted it to.

"What about it?" Lauren held her breath not sure she wanted to go down this path. "Are you asking me if I'm a virgin?" She was stunned at her own question and the flirtatious tone in which she asked it.

"You're a beautiful woman, Lauren." That simple statement was her answer.

"Thank you," Lauren replied softly. Her voice had a huskiness that had not been there a moment ago. She held the dark eyes across the table from her. The promise of passion she saw there made her throat grow dry. *How did this conversation turn from teasing into smoldering desire? This woman is dangerous, and I don't have a clue what I'm doing or why I'm even doing it.* Lauren reached for the check, grateful that her nervous hands had something to do.

"Thank you for dinner, Lauren, it was wonderful," Elliott said when they finally rose to leave.

"It was delicious, wasn't it?"

Elliott felt the light touch of Lauren's hand on the small of her back again as they moved toward the door. *Is her hand warmer than it was when we came in?* The car felt warmer too, once they were seated, as if both of their bodies were radiating heat. Elliott had seldom felt so aware of a woman's close proximity. She could hear Lauren's breathing and feel her eyes.

Their conversation on the ride home was minimal and Elliott's plan of attack was so perfected she didn't even think about it. When Lauren walked her to the door, Elliott asked, "Would you like a nightcap?"

Lauren knew exactly the kind of nightcap Elliott was referring to, and she also knew where an affirmative answer would take her. "I've had a wonderful time, Elliott, and you're a charming dinner companion, but at the risk of never seeing you again, may I have a rain check?"

My God, what did I just say? Lauren blinked, wanting to take it back but knowing she couldn't. Already she could see her response sinking in.

Elliott was doing a terrible job of hiding her surprise. *Did she just say no? After all of that flirting and innuendo, she said no?* "Of course." She tried to sound casual. "Another time, perhaps."

"Yes, another time." Lauren managed an awkward smile. "Thank you."

Elliott didn't push the issue but simply wished her good night.

As she drove away from Elliott's home, Lauren puzzled over her reaction to the proposition she'd anticipated all evening. *Wasn't that what I wanted? Don't I want to feel her hands and lips on my body? I want to have sex with her, right? Goddamn right I do. So why in the hell did I say no?*

CHAPTER FIVE

Lauren was tired. Tired of looking at the clock on her nightstand, tired of tossing and turning, tired of thinking about Elliott, and, considering it was five in the morning and she had not slept a wink, just plain tired. She rolled over onto her back and scanned the ceiling for answers that had not appeared in the past five hours. In the quiet darkness of the night she recalled every minute of her evening with the woman who now dominated her thoughts, specifically rehashing the fact that she had declined a night filled with pleasure. Of that there was no doubt; Lauren realized that was probably the only thing that was not in doubt where Elliott was concerned.

She'd known that Elliott would make the offer and until she'd opened her mouth and turned it down she'd been planning to accept. *So why in the hell didn't I?* That was the question keeping her awake. Lauren rarely second-guessed her decisions, preferring to analyze the situation, weigh the alternatives, settle on her choice, and move on. Her mantra was that you make the best decision you can with the facts that you have in that moment and playing shoulda, coulda, woulda gets you nothing but grief.

In the past few months she had been acting out of character, and she was starting to worry. She had worked hard over the years and used her natural ability to think logically and remain levelheaded to get to where she was today. She loved being an attorney and was proud of her accomplishments, but she was beginning to feel that her life was borderline empty. With growing clarity, she recognized that she desired the life her parents had. After forty-two years of marriage her father was still married to "the prettiest redhead in America." Dinner at the table every night was filled with chatter about the day's events and the inevitable squawking over whose turn it was to wash the dishes. Their house was the gathering place for the neighborhood and, in those days, was always filled with adolescents, teenagers, and even young adults.

Her parents had always supported her and attended as many extracurricular activities as possible. Lauren loved them equally, but she was closer to her father than her mother primarily due to his unconditional support of her, even when she wanted to participate in so-called boy sports. He had tossed the football with her, thrown thousands of pitches, hit hundreds of ground balls, and cheered her from the sidelines of the neighborhood flag football team. Without him, she doubted she would have become the confident woman she was today.

So what? So what that I have a great job, a big house, fancy car, gobs of money, and the envy of those around me? Big freakin' deal. I don't even have a fish to share it with.

Lauren had dinner engagements at least four or five times a month, but they were business obligations. She tried to remember the last time she went out socially. A persistent throbbing between her legs was a not-so-subtle reminder that it had been far too long since she'd felt the touch of another human being. She certainly couldn't remember the last time she'd had sex. *With someone other than Duracell.* It was probably seven or eight months ago, and apparently it was not particularly memorable, either. Lauren chuckled. *Jesus, I've got to get laid.*

Forcing herself to shift topics, she began wondering what her boss wanted to talk to her about on Monday. When the meeting notice had arrived in her e-mail after hours yesterday, the subject line was blank. Just a nondescript invitation that she typically declined unless she was aware of the subject. Her legal training prohibited her from going into a meeting unprepared. Unfortunately she couldn't do that when her boss called her in, so she scanned the events of the past few weeks in her mind, hoping something would pop up. There was one thing that nagged at the back of her brain, and that was her stand on firing the gay guy in accounting. She had reviewed her decision several times since and was confident she had made the right choice. But she had half expected it to boomerang, and she was determined not to let it. Apart from the ethical considerations, it would be risky for her company to fire anyone on those grounds.

Confident that she could handle any angle her boss wanted to raise about that decision, she closed her eyes and hoped for at least a few hours of sleep.

Elliott hated being on hold but she had been playing phone tag with Ryan all morning. While she listened to the inane music, her mind drifted to Lauren for at least the twelfth time that day. She had spent most of Sunday trying to determine if she had misread the signals she picked up constantly during their date. Her gaydar and experience with women seldom failed her, and she was shocked when Lauren said no. So shocked, as a matter of fact, that she had not even attempted to talk her around. She was still puzzled by the unexpected rejection.

Her friends had told her on several occasions that her reputation would one day catch up with her. Elliott's stomach churned when she remembered what she had said about her past interests. *Funny, Elliott. You practically told her you were a slut and you're surprised that she turned you down. What an idiot!* She knew that if hindsight were foresight she would have taken a different approach. She was so accustomed to dinner with a beautiful woman being a prelude to sex, she had hardly considered the possibility of a negative reaction to her openness. *And why does it matter to me what she thinks?*

When her musings were interrupted by her lawyer finally coming on the line, she complained, "Ryan you really have got to get some better hold music. If you hadn't insisted that we talk today, I wouldn't have put up with it. And so help me, if I have that song playing in my head for the rest of the day I'm going to personally stomp on you."

Their relationship of client and attorney was somewhat different than most. They had been friends for over ten years and it was natural that she would want Ryan as her lawyer. He had declined more times than she could count citing conflict of interest, but she knew he was simply afraid he would let her down. He had yet to. Elliott knew the call was serious when he didn't reply with a jab of his own.

"Ryan?"

"El, I received papers from Rebecca's attorney this morning."

Elliott remained quiet, knowing the other shoe was going to drop.

"She's suing you."

"For what?" Elliott felt surprisingly calm. She knew her best friend was holding his breath.

"Three hundred thousand dollars." He still had not exhaled.

"On what grounds?"

Ryan hesitated, and Elliott guessed he didn't want to see her hurt. Their friendship defied the common definition of a bond between a man and a woman. But Elliott seldom thought of Ryan as a man. When she looked at him she didn't see gender, she saw an honest, loyal friend and she knew he felt the same way about her. They had weathered the usual storms together, from one-night stands to failed relationships. Elliott was the first person Ryan had introduced to his soon-to-be wife Crystal, and she'd stood up as his best person at their wedding thirteen months later.

When he put on his attorney hat and plunged forward, she could tell he found the conversation difficult. "Alienation of affection, fraud, and defamation of character. Ludicrous, of course, since you have not circulated your opinions in public. I guess she didn't take kindly to being told she was a bad lay."

Elliott sighed. She was not surprised that the situation had escalated. She'd known that Rebecca was going to be trouble; it only remained to be seen how much trouble. "Go on."

She was astute enough to know that there was much more in the legal document that was now casting a shadow over her life. From their last conversation, she knew Ryan had dropped everything when the papers arrived by courier at eight that morning. He had pored over the seventeen pages, making notes in the margin as thoughts came to mind and had given his paralegal the task of scouring the Web, pulling any and all information on Rebecca Alsip. Elliott was itching to see what had been gathered, but Ryan had insisted on going through the file in detail to determine exactly what he would use to get rid of Rebecca once and for all.

"What do you want first?" he asked. "The good news or the bad news?"

For the next twenty minutes they talked about the various elements of the suit, Ryan often reiterating that although this was going to get ugly, they would win. Elliott was buoyed by his confidence but her instincts told her it would not be easy.

Her attention zeroed in on one specific phrase amid the legalese. "Say that again. She's going to call who as a witness?"

"Any and all persons with prior or current sexual contact with the defendant and any person currently with a foreseeable sexual contact."

"Let me get this straight." Elliott rubbed her eyes. "She's going to subpoena everyone I've slept with and anyone I might be thinking about sleeping with? Is that about it?" This was beginning to sound insane. She had plenty of normal human flaws, but they did not include the ones outlined in the document.

"She's gonna try." Ryan's reply indicated his commitment to not let this happen.

"Can she do that?" Elliott said a silent prayer.

"No, this is a standard ploy. Besides, if she wants to subpoena anybody you want to have sex with, we'd all die of old age before she got as far as the *M*'s."

The sound of Ryan's deep laugh lightened Elliott's mood. "I'm not sure what your intent was, but I'll take that as a compliment."

"I'm not sure that's how I meant it." Ryan's mood quickly sobered. "This issue could be a problem if we don't come to some type of agreement with her. You know who she will call first, and I don't have to tell you how Senator Jarvis will feel having his daughter's name come up. You don't want to upset this guy. He has a long reach in the financial sector."

Elliott finally snapped. "I've told you, I am not giving her anything. Not half a million dollars, not one hundred thousand dollars, not one hundred dollars, *not one goddamned red cent*! I pay you an outrageous amount of money, Ryan, and I expect you to fix this. Now." She slammed the receiver into the cradle and cursed, "Goddamn son of a bitch!"

Teresa hesitantly peeked her head around the door. She knew her boss was talking to her attorney and they were not making weekend plans. "You okay in here?" When her head wasn't immediately bitten off, she entered the spacious office and stopped in front of the cluttered desk.

Elliott dropped her head in her hands. "Jesus F. Christ. I'm falling apart." She rarely lost her temper, and when she did she never took it out on an innocent bystander. She felt as small as a flea as a result of her rant. She held her hand up, silencing any further questions from Teresa while she reached for the phone. After a very humbling apology to Ryan, she turned her attention back to her concerned friend.

Teresa inhaled sharply at the agonized look in her boss's eyes. She had never seen her so distraught, and what hurt the most was that there was nothing she could do. "Can I get you anything?"

Lauren. Elliott was shocked that her first thought was of Lauren. *I really am cracking up.* She took a moment and tried to sort out her thoughts and emotions. When nothing appeared to fall into place she sat back in her chair and sighed. "Nothing, thanks. I'm sorry if my antics worried you. Why don't you pack it in and go home." Trying to put Teresa at ease, she insisted, "I'll be fine, really. I was just venting."

But she was far from fine, and it took several hours of intense self-questioning to put everything into perspective. More troubling than the issue with Rebecca was that she still couldn't budge her mind from its determined focus on Lauren, and she was at wits' end to know why. Other than their brief conversation at the awards banquet and their dinner last Saturday night, she really didn't know Lauren at all. Certainly she was warm, witty, and intelligent, and had a great sense of humor. She challenged Elliott on every level. Without question she was the most intriguing woman she had met in a long while, perhaps ever.

It crossed her mind that she was so disenchanted over Rebecca, any reasonably decent, honest woman would seem remarkable. And Lauren was more than that. She was beautiful and independent, and she didn't seem to have any hidden agenda; Elliott was an expert in spotting those. She'd learned, growing up, that she could take very few people at face value.

Elliott wasn't sure when it had first dawned on her that most of her friendships were conditional upon her wealth and the status of her family. She and her sister Stephanie had attended the Willingham School in Pennsylvania. Willie, as her fellow classmates called their school, was one of the best private girls' boarding schools in the country, with an admissions waiting list of years. The joke was that when a woman ovulated, she put the family name on the list hoping to obtain one of the coveted slots when the soon-to-be child was old enough to attend.

Elliott had never had a problem fitting in; she was the typical rich girl with dashing good looks, lots of toys, and money to spend. She was also a hell-raiser with a bad-boy image, and all the girls were after her. But she was always aware that even if they were attracted to walk on the wild side, most still wanted something more from her, and it was seldom simply her friendship.

Her sister Stephanie, however, had inherited the trust gene, and it was the dominant factor in her life from the day she was born. Their mother had died when Elliott was six, and there was never any one special woman in her father's life to step into the mothering role. Instead it seemed as if there was a new woman hanging around each time she came home from school.

As the big sister, Elliott was protective of Stephanie. While they were at Willie, she bailed Stephanie out of many awkward and even dangerous situations. Stephanie's naïveté and belief in people's goodness not only broke her heart on a regular basis, but also her weekly allowance. Elliott did what she could to keep her sister safe and prevent others from using her, but she could not be there all the time.

Stephanie's poor judgment extended to the men she dated and had culminated in her marriage to Mark Nelson, a conniving manipulator who seemed to make a habit of dating wealthy women. Elliott had done everything she could to make Stephanie see who Mark really was; she'd even had him investigated and discovered a couple of previous fiancées who wised up before they tied the knot.

Nothing she found out made any difference. Stephanie was too far down the path of blind love to listen.

To Elliott's chagrin, her father invited Mark to join Foster McKenzie shortly after the marriage and he became a bigger asshole than he was when she first met him. When James Foster died, Mark assumed he would be in the corner office since he saw himself as the head of the family. Stephanie had no interest in business and Elliott's interests were in sun, wine, and women, not necessarily in that order. Her father's will handed the reins of the company to her uncle, and Mark had been furious; however, he soon seemed to accept that there was simply a new butt to kiss. His strategy hadn't changed much over the years, and Elliott could feel his seething resentment now that hers was the butt in question. The only reason she hadn't fired his worthless ass was because of her sister.

Mark had some allies at Foster McKenzie; opportunists always recognized others on the make. Elliott had tried to weed them out when she took over the company. Predictably, some of the people who had sided with her uncle against her suddenly acted as if they were her best friends and closest allies. She had fired them without a second thought. Loyalty mattered to her, although she knew it often came with strings attached. Experience had taught her that everybody wanted something from her and, other than a few close friends and her direct staff, Elliott didn't trust many people.

Making a conscious effort to turn her thoughts in a more pleasant direction, Elliott picked up the phone and dialed a local florist Foster McKenzie had an account with. She discussed the arrangement she wanted to send and gave Lauren's address at Bradley & Taylor. She wished she could be a fly on the wall when the umbrella containing the spring bouquet was delivered to Lauren's office with the card that said, "I'm looking forward to rain in the forecast."

Elliott shook her head. *Jeez, and we haven't even slept together.* She wanted to add *yet* to the end of that thought, but for the first time in many years she felt uncertain of herself. Confidence was one of many traits she'd inherited from her father, and on the rare occasions when it deserted her, she felt unsettled. It seldom happened in her relationships with women. She always knew what steps to take, what to say, and in what order, to get a woman into bed. There were challenges every now and then, but instinct kicked in at those times and she went home happy.

Elliott turned to her computer and her fingers hesitated over the keyboard. She remembered the first few weeks she'd sat in this chair and how scared she was. So many people were depending on her. But most importantly, she needed to prove herself. She was her father's daughter.

❖

The next day Lauren picked up her phone when it rang after lunch. "Lauren Collier."

"Hi, it's Elliott."

Lauren's heart jumped at the voice on the other end of the line. "Hi yourself." *Can't I think of something better to say?*

"I hope I'm not interrupting."

After declining the invitation to spend Saturday night with Elliott, Lauren had doubted that she would hear from her again. She was flabbergasted when the bouquet of flowers arrived a few hours earlier. She immediately suspected they were from Elliott, and the umbrella clinched it even before she read the card.

"Yes, you are interrupting, and thank God!" She took off her reading glasses and pushed her chair away from the desk.

"I take it that's a good thing?" Elliott was not sure she had heard correctly.

"That's a very good thing." Lauren turned her chair to face the window. "I'm reviewing a deposition, and it is the driest questioning I have ever read. I must have read the same page three times and I still don't know what the plaintiff's answer is. So, yes, your calling is a good thing." *That and the fact that I was hoping I'd hear from you again.*

Elliott could detect the pleasure in Lauren's voice. "I'm glad I could be of service, Counselor."

"Thank you for the beautiful flowers. Very imaginative." Lauren could still feel butterflies fluttering around in her stomach; they had arrived with the flowers.

"You're very welcome. I try not to be too predictable." Elliott was cautious when she sent flowers to a woman. She was afraid they would contradict her message of *no strings*. However, this time she was looking for a thread. "I hope it wasn't uncomfortable for you to get them at the office."

"No, not at all. It was a wonderful surprise." The delivery had caused quite a stir. Lauren had never received flowers at work, and the excitement far outweighed the inevitable speculation. Michelle knew better than to open the card, and Lauren knew her young assistant must be dying of curiosity.

"Are you free Saturday evening?" Elliott asked.

"Saturday?" Lauren quickly turned and scanned her calendar. "Yes, I am, after six." She hesitated in anticipation. Elliott was going to invite her on another date. She felt like giggling.

"I have tickets to the ballet and I was wondering if you'd like to go." *I sound like a teenager asking for a date.* Elliott stretched her legs out on the teak coffee table in front of her and tried to relax back into the Italian leather sofa in her office. Next to being in bed, preferably with someone, the couch was her favorite piece of furniture.

"I love the ballet," Lauren exclaimed. *Swan Lake* was scheduled to be performed by the nationally acclaimed San Diego Ballet, and she had been meaning to get tickets. She was an admirer of the arts, but her schedule kept her from attending as many performances as she would have liked. The fact that Elliott would attend the ballet was another nugget of information about her that Lauren found fascinating. She intended to uncover more.

"I know it's short notice, but my schedule just freed up and I thought of you." Elliott knew she was rambling, which was unlike her. "We could have dinner downtown before the curtain rises if you'd like."

Lauren hesitated. "Can we have dinner afterward? I have something that I can't get out of in time for dinner before the show."

She glanced at the photo of a teenage girl on her desk. She was in her third year as a mentor to Tonya Quinn, a teen identified by her school counselor as at risk. They had a commitment to spend the day together the second Saturday of every month. The relationship was important to Lauren, and she would never consider canceling unless it was an extreme situation. As much as she wanted to see Elliott again, social outings with sexy women did not count as "extreme."

"If Saturday is not good for you we can make it another time."

"No!" Lauren said more forcefully than she meant to. "No, really. Saturday is fine, except for the early dinner." *Am I sounding desperate?*

Elliott hadn't realized that she'd been holding her breath. "Great. How about if I pick you up at seven?"

"Actually, can I meet you there instead?" Lauren knew she wouldn't be able to get home from the aquarium and be ready in time for Elliott to pick her up. She could take fresh clothes with her in the car and change at Tonya's.

Elliott sensed the hesitation in Lauren's last comment. "Sure, no problem. I'll leave your ticket at Will Call and we can meet inside."

"Why don't we meet at the eagle statue about seven fifteen?"

Elliott knew the bronze landmark east of the entrance hall. "I'll be there." She didn't want to end their conversation and frowned when she glanced up and saw Teresa hovering in her doorway pointing to her watch. "I'm sorry, Lauren, I've got to run. Teresa's standing in my doorway, looking frantic. I'll see you on Saturday?"

"Yes. Thank you." Lauren hung up and recalled the arguments she'd had with herself nonstop over the past few days. Eventually she had concluded that she didn't want Elliott to think she was going to be another in a long line of women in her life. Lauren was not interested in her money, her fame, or her power. She did admit that at first she was in pursuit of Elliott sexually, but after their conversation over dinner she was equally interested in her as a person. To throw sex into the mix would definitely muddy the waters. *But I do love to play in the mud.*

CHAPTER SIX

"The only good thing about these events is all the skin that you get to see."

Elliott shot a scathing look at the man standing next to her. How her sister could marry slime like Mark Nelson was a question that probably would never be answered, and why she stayed married to him was an even bigger mystery.

"Ah, come on, El," Mark whined, taking a swig of beer. His eyes continued to scan the crowd of ballet patrons. "You know you like to look as much as I do."

Elliott would not describe Mark's actions as *look,* by any definition. *Leer* was a better verb. "Mark, you're a pig," she said, making no attempt to hide her disgust. "I've met your mother and I know she raised you with better manners." Mark's father had passed away several years after he and Stephanie married, and MaryLou Nelson often joined the Fosters for family gatherings.

"Yeah, she did. But she also said I was a chip off the old block too." Mark winked at her.

From all accounts, his father had been a womanizer, and Mark actually seemed to take pride in this heritage. Elliott always felt like she needed a shower after spending any time with him. He could very easily ruin her evening with his crass behavior. *God, where is Stephanie?* She searched the crowd for her sister. She started to walk away but Mark grabbed her arm.

"Oh my, look what just walked in the door."

Elliott could not help but look, and her heart stopped.

"I gotta get me some of that." Mark was almost panting.

For once Elliott agreed with her brother-in-law, but she certainly didn't say so. Her sister's husband despised her and would use anything to gain the upper hand. Mark was pissed that he had been passed over for the head of Foster McKenzie twice and had not so subtly made it clear that he didn't think she was up to the job. Lately Elliott had begun to suspect that he was up to something but she wasn't sure what, and right now she had better things to dwell on.

Lauren hadn't seen her yet, which gave Elliott the opportunity to covertly admire her. She wore a black dress held up by spaghetti straps that exposed her smooth shoulders. The bodice was held snug by pearl buttons and as she walked, the soft folds of the dress moved with her, falling to just below her knees. Her strawberry blond hair was pulled back off her face and secured at the base of her neck, and her ears sparkled with diamonds that matched the jewels around her neck. A gold watch on her left wrist completed her accessories. *I had no idea an attorney could be so beautiful.*

Elliott was rudely torn from her appreciation by an elbow in her side courtesy of Mark. "She looks good enough to eat." He licked his lips for emphasis. "What I wouldn't give to be the guy she's looking for."

The instant he finished his comment, Lauren's eyes met hers and Elliott's heart beat faster at the smile of recognition that lit her face. She could not resist saying to Mark, "What makes you think she's looking for a man?"

Mark tore his eyes from the woman walking toward them and stared at Elliott. After a moment he came to the correct conclusion and his expression changed from confusion to shock. "*You're* her date?"

"Don't look so surprised. You said it yourself. I like to look as much as you. Only in this case, I get to touch too." With a ridiculous sense of beating Mark at his own game, she walked away.

When she stopped in front of Lauren, she allowed her eyes to travel the length of her once again. The fine details she had missed from her vantage point across the room were now clearly visible. Lauren's hair shone and smelled slightly of jasmine. Her eyes were crystal clear and crinkled at the edges when she smiled. Her black dress molded to her body like a glove, with just a hint of cleavage exposed.

"You are beautiful." To Elliott's ears, the simple compliment did not adequately convey her response. But it was sincere, and she found herself marveling at the difference between her feelings now and her usual automatic flattery of dates.

Lauren had never felt as beautiful as she did the moment Elliott saw her. The expression on Elliott's face made her stomach churn and her heart must have fallen between her legs, because the throbbing there was almost unbearable. Matching her date's intense scrutiny, she let her eyes roam from the impeccably shined shoes to the razor-sharp crease in the shimmering black trousers and the dark green bow tie complementing the starched cream-colored shirt. The tanned neck beneath was suddenly asking to be kissed. Shaken, she lost all thought when her eyes traveled the remaining distance and met Elliott's.

"Thank you. You look quite smashing yourself," she replied through the lump in her throat.

The smoldering look in Elliott's eyes was almost more than Lauren could stand. As much as she wanted this woman, she had to stop this right now or risk embarrassing herself in front of all of these people. She leaned in and said softly, "You have to stop looking at me like that, Elliott."

The already dangerous look in her eyes darkened. "How am I looking at you?"

"Like you can't wait to put your hands on me." Which was exactly what Lauren wanted as well. She held her breath, waiting for the reply.

Elliott stepped closer and leaned in until her lips were a hairsbreadth away from Lauren's ear. "You're wrong, Counselor." She waited until she had Lauren's full attention. "I want to put more than just my hands on you."

Lauren shivered, not sure if it was due to Elliott's warm breath in her ear or the vision that exploded in her mind. Either way it didn't matter. She was so aroused that she was afraid she would explode at any moment. She smiled and put her hand on the center of Elliott's chest, looking into desire-filled eyes. Sliding the palm of her hand slowly down Elliott's chest, she said, "I look forward to it," then withdrew her hand and stepped back from the source of the fire.

Shock waves coursed through Elliott's body from the touch of Lauren's hand. She drew a shaky breath. "I think we should find our seats."

Lauren put on the calmest expression she could muster. "Yes, I certainly need to sit down, don't you?"

Elliott had no idea how she made it into the theater without grabbing Lauren, and once the performance began she had a difficult time trying to focus on the melodious sounds coming from the orchestra one hundred feet in front of her. Her eyes kept drifting to the tanned skin exposed when Lauren crossed her legs. After a while, she gave up trying to concentrate on the ballet and chose instead to simply enjoy the view beside her. Lauren was on her right, a long expanse of smooth thigh inches from her fingers, as if daring her to touch. Even in the subdued lighting she detected well-defined muscles that she didn't expect. *Nothing about this woman is what I expected.* She grinned and raised her eyebrows, imagining the rest of Lauren's thigh hidden by the smooth fabric. Deciding it was safer to look down Lauren's leg rather than up, she followed the trail of muscle over a knee toward a shin that disappeared out of sight.

Twenty minutes into the performance Lauren shifted positions. The angle provided Elliott with a full view of Lauren's right leg, which was equally alluring. She lavished her attention on the perfectly shaped limb, all but ignoring the crowd around her. She suspected she was blatantly staring but didn't care. The crashing of the cymbals drew her attention back to the stage. She had just about determined where in the ballet they were when she felt pressure on the outside of her right calf. Thinking it was an inadvertent bump from Lauren, she shifted her leg slightly to allow more room between them. Her heart skipped a beat when the touch followed.

Instantly tuned into the action below her knees, she kept her eyes forward and didn't move a muscle. Lauren's stocking-clad toes caressed her ankle and snaked under the leg of her pants. Her breathing quickened as Lauren's foot ran sensuously up and down her calf.

Elliott risked a glance at the limb tormenting her, and her stomach jumped at the image of Lauren's foot disappearing and reappearing from under her trousers. Her mind took an erotic turn and she imagined other parts of Lauren's body in her pants but at the opposite end. Watching the swaying of Lauren's leg was making her far too aroused and she couldn't stop herself from slowly caressing the long legs with her eyes once more. The tempo of the music kept pace as she blazed a trail up Lauren's shin, over her knee, and along her thigh until the orchestra reached a crescendo when her gaze settled on Lauren's hands folded neatly in her lap. The program in Lauren's hand was shaking, alerting Elliott that she was not the only one affected by the encounter.

She didn't know whether she felt relieved or disappointed when sudden applause and the brightening of the house lights signaled the intermission. Her legs wobbled as she stood and followed Lauren down the aisle.

As they approached the lobby, she touched Lauren's elbow. "Would you like something to drink?"

"Yes, thank you." Lauren could feel Elliott behind her even without the touch. As they moved toward the bar, she continued, "Since we're all dressed up I suppose I should order something ladylike and suitable for the occasion, but what I'd really like is a Scotch on the rocks."

Elliott couldn't help herself; she broke into a deep laugh, aware of a few patrons turning and looking around at the sound. "If I recall correctly, you were drinking pretty freely the last time you were dressed this beautifully."

God, she is smooth. She can turn anything into a compliment. "Elliott, you make me sound like a lush!" Lauren feigned outrage. "I was in no way drinking too much."

Elliott smiled at the quick retort. "I was referring to your choice of alcohol, not the quantity." She gave the bartender their order as they stepped to the front of the line. Leaning on the bar, she asked, "Are you enjoying the performance?"

Elliott's pose reminded Lauren of Humphrey Bogart in *Casablanca*. "Definitely. *Swan Lake* is one of my favorite ballets." When she accepted her drink, she intentionally let her fingers graze Elliott's and watched her eyes darken immediately. Not even attempting to hide her pleasure over the telltale reaction, she asked, "And are you enjoying yourself?"

Elliott grinned, knowing she had been caught looking at Lauren's legs. She offered her arm to Lauren and led them away from the crowd. When they reached a secluded corner of the lobby, she quickly maneuvered Lauren so her back was against the wall. "You know I am," she replied, glancing pointedly down at the legs that had enticed her throughout the first act. They were covered with the fine silky cloth of Lauren's dress now, and Elliott revealed her disappointment with a small sigh.

Feeling adventurous and emboldened, Lauren teased, "You really should pay attention to the performance as well, Elliott. It is beautiful." She had no intention of admitting that her attention had wandered constantly too.

Elliott stepped closer and her eyes grew dangerous. "Beauty is in the eye of the beholder, Lauren, and I am definitely paying attention to something that is magnificent."

Lauren laughed. "You are such a charmer. You've had way too much practice charming women out of their pants." She was curious to hear how Elliott would respond to her statement. It wasn't meant to be judgmental at all.

"Just the truth and nothing but the truth, so help me God." Elliott crossed her heart but was unsuccessful in keeping the smile off her face. "And you're not wearing pants," she added with a twinkle in her eyes.

Lauren chuckled and touched Elliott's arm. "Very observant. Now if you'll excuse me for a minute, I have to go to the ladies' room." Over her shoulder, she added, "Don't let anyone steal you away. I'll be right back."

Elliott sipped her drink and watched her exciting companion walk away. She was amazed at how much she was enjoying every minute she spent with Lauren, even aside from their flirtatious exchanges. She couldn't remember a time when she'd simply taken pleasure in the company of an intelligent woman. Foster McKenzie had season tickets to the ballet and Elliott typically allowed her employees to have the seats, but she'd had a hunch that Lauren would enjoy this production. Once more, she let herself imagine what the body that was hidden under the little black dress looked like.

"What a waste."

Elliott was startled by the familiar voice behind her but kept her composure. "That's twice tonight you've been right, Mark. Don't waste your time."

Her brother-in-law snorted. "It should be against the law for the hot ones to be queer."

Elliott's stomach clenched. She was having a wonderful evening and was in no mood for Mark's obnoxious comments. "Mark"—she looked him directly in the eye—"go fuck yourself."

"Actually Elliott, I'd rather fuck her." He used his glass to point to Lauren, who was returning.

Elliott reined in the overwhelming desire to deck the man beside her. She loved her sister and would do anything for her, but putting up with Mark's boorish behavior was always a challenge. She suspected he cheated on Stephanie and wouldn't think twice about doing exactly what he had just described. Stephanie had always refused to listen to her and remained steadfastly dedicated to him, but it was obvious that Mark only believed in the *for richer* part of his marriage vows.

Elliott quickly finished her drink and stepped out of the sludge of her brother-in-law, walking forward to meet Lauren. Her empty glass was the perfect excuse to extract them both from Mark's company.

"Would you like another drink?" she asked.

Lauren detected a strained look on Elliott's face an instant before she masked it. She suspected the man staring at her was the cause of Elliott's discomfort and soon realized why. Before she could accept the offer of a drink, he invaded her space, looking her up and down as if he thought she would be flattered by this appraisal.

"Well, hello there." His voice dripped with sleaze. "I'm Mark, Elliott's favorite brother-in-law."

Elliott cringed when she realized they would not make their escape. *What did I ever do to deserve this?* "Mark, you're my only brother-in-law," she corrected, holding her breath in trepidation of what he would say next. He did not disappoint her.

"I'm the best looking brother-in-law she has too." His eyes never left the cleavage exposed by Lauren's dress.

Lauren had plenty of experience deflecting the unwanted attentions of men like Mark. "Nice to meet you," she replied politely but did not reach for the hand that was extended to her, taking Elliott's arm instead. "I can certainly see why your wife grabbed you right up." She hesitated for a moment, then asked, "Tell me, Mark, is your wife as beautiful as her sister?"

Elliott stifled a laugh at the expression on Mark's face. Lauren had not broken stride or hesitated in the slightest as she cut the legs right out from under him. *Ouch.* Elliott had rarely seen Mark at a loss for words, and this moment was priceless.

Lauren wrapped both hands around Elliott's arm and moved closer until their bodies were in full contact. "Because if she is, you are one lucky man." Her position next to Elliott clearly indicated that they were together, and the subtle intimacy left no doubt as to that fact.

Elliott seized the opportunity to escape from her lecherous relative, quickly heading for the bar. When they were out of earshot she squeezed Lauren's hand warm on her arm. "You're ruthless."

Lauren looked as though she had no more than swatted away an annoying gnat. "Lots of practice. They're all the same." Instinctively she knew that Elliott would not be insulted at her response to her brother-in-law's actions. "Shall we go back in and enjoy the rest of the performance?"

Elliott looked down into the sparkling blue eyes of the woman beside her. "Let's," she said, and the subject was closed.

❖

Elliott had made reservations at the exclusive Barrett's restaurant, within walking distance of the theater. As they left the auditorium, Lauren saw a man hurrying toward her, waving to get her attention.

"It's my neighbor," she explained, and they stopped to wait for him.

"I hate to bother you," he said after the introductions were made and he'd shaken Elliott's hand. "But I was wondering if you could drop me home. My wife was called to the hospital halfway through the performance. You know how that goes."

"You're stranded?" Lauren could have kissed him on both cheeks. She handed him her car keys and said, "Elliott can take me home. We're about to have dinner." She turned slightly to Elliott. "If that's okay?"

There was no mistaking the look Elliott gave her. "It would be my pleasure."

Lauren gave her neighbor a bright smile and they exchanged brief farewell pleasantries, then she and Elliott resumed their stroll.

Their strides were sedate as the sounds of the city surrounded them. Streetlights overhead cast a soft glow on the sparsely populated brick and mortar sidewalk. Store windows proudly displayed trendy fashions, sparkling diamonds, and the latest bestsellers. The sounds of music floated in the air when patrons exited restaurants and bars along the street. A horn honked farther down the street and a siren wailed a few blocks over. Street vendors hawked everything from red roses to cheap perfume.

A mild breeze blew strands of reddish hair around Lauren's face, and she tucked them back into the clasp at her nape as she walked. The tall woman beside her did not speak; Lauren sensed she was enjoying their companionable silence, a fact that pleased her. She was also pleasantly surprised that Elliott appeared not to notice the admiring looks she garnered from other women. Lauren would have expected anyone with her reputation to return the occasional warm stare, but she didn't and Lauren loved how that made her feel—somehow Elliott was communicating that Lauren had her full attention, no matter what.

This continued throughout their meal. Conversation flowed easily as they dined, and Lauren was aware that Elliott's eyes kept drifting to the barest hint of cleavage at the top of her dress. Elliott finally gave up trying not to look and simply let it be known, with a warm, intimate smile, that she was enjoying the view.

When they finally stepped out of the restaurant, Lauren grasped her arm in almost the exact spot she had earlier in the evening. It felt good. Her hand remained in the crook of Elliott's arm as they strolled in the warm night air.

Elliott often had a beautiful woman on her arm, and tonight was no exception. She was comfortable with the quiet as they walked, their steps in sync. It was rare to find a woman who did not insist on cramming chatter into any gap in conversation, so Elliott made the most of it and only broke the silence when they approached the valet parking. "Are you tired or would you like to walk some more?"

"No and yes, but my feet are killing me," Lauren admitted a little sadly. She felt warm and safe and desirable on Elliott's arm and wanted it to go on forever. But the pain in her right foot was excruciating and she knew she couldn't last much longer.

On principle Lauren refused to wear shoes that did not feel good. She didn't buy into that notion that fashion overruled comfort. However, the Prada pair went so perfectly with her new dress, she chucked practicality and went for it. She had not been disappointed— she looked fabulous—but it was time to set her feet free.

Elliott took an exaggerated look at her shoes. "Ouch, I see what you mean. Those would cripple me." She handed the parking ticket to the attendant. "We'll have to continue this another time. I know a great place with sand so soft you don't even need shoes. It's like a Shiatsu massage for your feet."

The car arrived and Elliott held the door as Lauren slid into the passenger seat. Her crotch lurched and her mouth went dry at the expanse of long legs that appeared from the slit in the dress. She wasn't the only one to notice, and she winked at the open-mouthed valet as if to say, "Yep, she's mine," and gave him a larger than usual tip.

❖

Lauren's hands refused to stop shaking throughout the drive to her house, and when Elliott pulled into her driveway she knew she did not want their evening to end. "I'd like to use my rain check." She raised her eyes from the hands clenched tightly in her lap to stop at a pair of blistering black eyes. "Would you like to come in?"

"Yes," Elliott said softly.

Wordlessly Lauren unlocked the front door, fully aware of the close proximity of the woman who had set her body on fire. Once inside, she dropped her keys on the sideboard and turned to Elliott. The smoldering desire in her eyes made Lauren's knees weak. "Can I get you anything?"

"Just you." Elliott bent her head and kissed her.

Lauren's lips were softer than she had imagined, and she savored every sensation. She gently nibbled, smiling when Lauren wound her fingers tightly in her hair and pulled her closer. Wanting much more, Elliott reluctantly dragged her lips away and kissed the fine bones of Lauren's cheeks and along her jawline before returning to the enticing mouth. Lauren quickly invited her in for more. With practiced ease, she let her hands roam over Lauren's back, then she slowly reached forward to cup Lauren's breasts. She kissed her way down Lauren's neck, stopping to tease the racing pulse just above her collarbone, then continuing her journey to taste the bare shoulders that had tormented her all evening. Elliott wasn't sure who moaned but took it as encouragement.

Lauren lost all track of time as Elliott lavished her lips and skin with the kisses she'd craved all evening. She momentarily felt a draft on her chest and just as quickly a warm mouth covered her breast. She gasped at the sensation and pulled Elliott to her. Just as Elliott's mouth was about to encircle the erect nipple, the phone rang.

"Don't answer that."

"I wasn't going to."

Elliott took the full nipple in her mouth and was rewarded when Lauren grasped her shoulders for support. She had kissed many breasts, but none had tasted as sweet as the one she was exploring now.

"Lauren, are you there? Lauren, it's Charles Comstock." Lauren stiffened when she heard her boss's voice on the answering machine. "I'm afraid we need your help. Merison's daughter has been arrested. Please call me as soon as possible."

"Shit!" She stepped slowly out of Elliott's embrace. *Shit, shit, shit!* Leaning against the back of the couch, she struggled to catch her breath. "God, I am so sorry."

"It's okay." Elliott attempted to regain control over her raging hormones. For a few seconds, she watched Lauren fumble to button the front of her dress, then said, "Here, let me help you with that." She closed the gap between them that up until a few moments ago was almost nonexistent. As she worked on the buttons, her hands were as unsteady as her legs.

"I am so sorry." Sorry didn't even begin to describe Lauren's embarrassment at the interruption. "That was my CEO."

Elliott's smile was soft; she could only imagine how a call from the boss could immediately dampen amorous intentions.

Lauren made a gesture of frustration. "I'm a corporate attorney, not criminal. What does he expect me to do? They never call me at home and when they do, it has to be *now*!"

"Lauren, it's okay, really." Elliott closed the final button on Lauren's dress. She put her finger under Lauren's chin and lifted it so that their eyes met. "Better now than fifteen minutes from now, when you wouldn't have been capable of answering the phone."

The note of mischief in her voice helped Lauren relax. "You sound pretty sure of yourself."

Elliott was drawn to the gleam in the bright eyes regarding her, and against her better judgment she leaned in and kissed Lauren again. The kiss was as sweet as the one before and Lauren's response was instant, but before things could progress, Elliott pulled her lips away a fraction of an inch. "I just go where the lady leads me," she said huskily.

Lauren blushed. "I guess the path was pretty clearly marked, wasn't it?" *How can I be bantering with this woman when all I want is for her to ravish me right this minute?*

"Even though the destination may be known, the fun is definitely in the journey. And I was looking forward to identifying your landmarks along the way." *Okay, that was corny.* Elliott felt slightly foolish at her last comment.

"Is that a promise?" Lauren asked in anticipation. She had thought of nothing other than Elliott's hands on her all evening, and the call from her employer had squelched any hope of a satisfying encounter.

Their lips were millimeters apart, their breath mingling. Elliott was tempted to taste them again—her body was primed and ready to go at the slightest invitation—but Lauren had business to attend to. She quickly, almost chastely kissed the soft red lips. "Yes, it is." A long sigh escaped from her as she disengaged Lauren's arms from around her neck. "I'll go so you can get focused and deal with this crisis."

Lauren could sense Elliott's arousal, but she was taking the frustrating interruption in stride. Thankful that she was not being given a hard time, she walked Elliott to the door. "Call me in a few days?"

"Count on it." Elliott clenched her jaw so she could resist the desire to kiss her again, and walked out the door.

CHAPTER SEVEN

Summer Merison, the seventeen-year-old daughter of Bradley & Taylor's chief financial officer, had been arrested for drunk driving. She was supposed to be tucked safely in her bed at a Mt. Holy Catholic School retreat but instead was eight miles away when she smashed her Mercedes into a telephone pole. Three of her camp mates were in the car and had suffered cuts and bruises necessitating an ambulance ride to the hospital.

When the police searched her car, they added possession of cocaine to the list of charges against her and recited her Miranda rights. It was at that point that Summer mistakenly thought her beauty and money could get her out of trouble and she propositioned the arresting officer, offering sex, money, or both. She had used the two to bail herself out of jams in the past, as far as Lauren could tell, and had fully believed the cute young police officer would be a pushover. In spite of the handcuffs that were immediately slapped around her wrists, her teenage wisdom told her she just needed to raise the ante. She became belligerent and struggled with the officer as he led her to the patrol car. She was so drunk that she stumbled to the ground and gashed her knee, which only made her angrier.

By the time she arrived at the hospital, the charges against her had grown to include resisting arrest, assaulting a peace officer, and bribery. According to the medical record, Summer continued to rant while she was being examined for any additional injuries. She had refused to take a breathalyzer at the accident scene and was outraged when the nurse pulled the curtains and handed her a clear plastic cup. Because she was a minor and charged with a felony, a drug test was required by law. Her indignation was complete when she was restrained and introduced to a catheter. Only the results of her urinalysis finally silenced her. She was pregnant.

Lauren spent what should have been a night of passion dealing with this arrogant, drunk teenager and her equally pompous father. She could not convince Thomas Merison that criminal law was not her specialty. He kept insisting that she get his "little girl" out of this "situation," as he phrased it. Not only did he refuse to deal with the fact that his daughter had a serious problem, he was desperate to keep the episode quiet. Neither he nor the company wanted this all over the papers. Lauren didn't like being used and thought Summer should face the consequences of her actions. She finally agreed to speak to the district attorney about reducing the charges if Summer checked into rehab and stayed clean and sober for two years.

Lauren felt soiled when she stood beside the disheveled girl in the early morning arraignment. Under threat of financial sanctions from her family, Summer was quiet but had not lost her swagger of entitlement. She was released into the custody of her father and a court date set.

Lauren was still disgusted when Elliott called. "I still can't believe I was a party to that."

Elliott's laughter flooded from the phone into her hair, making her weak. "At least something good came out of it."

"Please tell me what, because I certainly can't see it." All she felt was embarrassment and frustration.

"An appetizer." Elliott's tone was suggestive.

"An appetizer?"

"Yes, an appetizer." Her voice grew soft and husky. "You gave me a preview of what I hope is to come. That little sampler makes me want you more now than I did then."

It took a moment for Lauren to comprehend the words. She didn't have much experience flirting over the phone while she was at work, and it was unsettling. Unsettling in a very positive way. Surprised that she was able to respond calmly to such a provocative comment, she replied, "Is that so?"

"Yes, Counselor, it is," Elliott said firmly, leaving no doubt as to her intentions.

Lauren felt the flush of desire start in her gut and spread rapidly throughout her body. Butterflies returned to her stomach and the images that raced through her mind made her legs weak. "Well, Elliott, you certainly do know how to make a girl feel wanted."

"There's absolutely no doubt in my mind." Elliott was enjoying herself immensely and wondered just how far they would take this telephone foreplay.

Lauren felt dizzy at the smooth, melodious voice on the other end of the line. She sat down in her chair, and the flashing red light on her telephone pulled her back to reality. Somehow she gathered herself together and replied. "I don't really know what to say to that other than thank you." The red light blinked at her almost loudly. "Much as I'd like to continue this line of conversation, I have to get back." *Get back, hell. I need a cold shower!*

"Okay," Elliott conceded, more than a little disappointed. But Lauren was in the middle of a meeting and Elliott respected that.

"Can I call you tonight?" Lauren asked hopefully.

A rush of heat sliced through Elliott's body and landed between her legs, betraying just how much she wanted this woman, and how soon. "I have a board meeting. I probably won't be home until quite late." *Damn.* "Are you free for lunch tomorrow?"

"No, I'm on the 8:00 a.m. flight to Chicago."

"When are you back?" Elliott studied the calendar at the top of her desk.

"Thursday afternoon."

Why does that seem like a hundred years away? "Dinner, Thursday night?" Elliott made a mental note to have Teresa cancel her meeting with the president of the local Rotary chapter. *He wants something from me, and he can just wait.*

"Dinner would be great. I'll call you when I get in."

Thursday could not come fast enough. "I'll talk to you then. Have a safe trip."

"Thanks." Lauren hesitated. "Elliott?"

"Yes." Elliott could tell by her tone that there was something else Lauren wanted to say. After several seconds of silence, she prompted, "Lauren?"

"Yes, I'm here. Sorry." Lauren cleared her throat as if she had something important to communicate, then seemed to cut herself off. "I'll see you Thursday."

Disappointed that Lauren didn't finish what she was going to say, Elliott said, "I'm looking forward to it."

"Me too."

Lauren hung up and took a deep breath. Her nice, orderly life had suddenly been turned upside down by Elliott Foster. She knew how exhausted she would be after three days in Chicago; she had back-to-back depositions that would last well into the evening hours, and even though she traveled quite a bit, she always had difficulty sleeping in hotels. However, the idea of being with Elliott banished those thoughts. She stared at the button blinking on her phone and wished she had been able to find the words to express the one small worry she had about their plans.

Most of the time, she didn't give a second thought to the difference in their relationship histories, but she thought they should be honest with each other. Elliott had been open with her, but Lauren had avoided making personal disclosures. The past just didn't seem that relevant to what she felt now. There would be an opportunity to get her minor confession off her chest, she decided, probably during their dinner. Right now, she wished she could call Elliott back, just to hear her voice again.

Feeling foolish about this teenage urge, she forced her mind back to her work and lifted the phone. "I'm back. Sorry for the interruption, gentlemen. Now, where were we?" Lauren was all business again. *Yeah, right. Two minutes ago I was almost having phone sex and now I'm talking to a bunch of fifty-year-old gray-haired white guys.*

The Boeing 757 taxied at a snail's pace toward the arrival gate. Lauren had made this flight more times than she could count but this return trip had seemed longer than most. She was in first class and the man seated next to her had snored the entire flight. After three days inside a stuffy conference room drinking stale coffee, taking depositions, and generally putting up with bullshit from the defense attorney, her nerves were fried and she was beat.

But her energy level lifted along with the top of her flip phone when she dialed Elliott's number. "Hello, Teresa? It's Lauren Collier. Is she in?"

"I'm sorry, Ms. Collier, but Ms. Foster is out of town. She asked me to forward you to her cell phone. Will you hold while I connect you?"

"Certainly." Her spirits took a nosedive as she waited for Elliott to come on the line. She had looked forward to this evening all week.

"Welcome home." Elliott's melodious voice made Lauren's pulse rate increase.

"Thanks." The background noise she heard coming through the phone sounded all too familiar. "Where are you?"

"Charles de Gaulle Airport."

"You're in Paris?"

"*Oui*," Elliott replied. "I'm standing in line at customs. Actually I'm joined by about a thousand of my closest friends, also standing in line at customs." By her count, over half the custom booths were empty, and those that were staffed appeared to be having problems with the passport screening equipment, increasing the wait time to enter the legendary capital even more.

Lauren did a quick count of the days and time zones and frowned. "Are you going in or coming out?"

"Unfortunately, going in." Elliott was not happy about having to leave the country on the day that Lauren was returning. "It was totally unexpected. A client on one of our major accounts is meeting some investors here and at the last minute he decided he needed my help, specifically my presence. So here I am. A command performance, if you will. If this guy wasn't worth a bundle to me I would have told him to go fly a kite, but I couldn't. I hope you understand."

"Of course I understand." Lauren ruefully remembered how many times she had boarded a plane a few hours after being notified she was going somewhere. Out of necessity she'd learned how to pack quickly and travel light. She tried to hide the disappointment in her voice but she was suddenly too tired to be successful. "The same thing has happened to me more than once."

"Lauren, I am just as disappointed as you are, believe me. I'd much rather be having dinner with a beautiful woman than room service."

"I've been to Paris, Elliott. There is no shortage of beautiful women you can dine with." *And that worries me.*

"But none of them are you," Elliott replied softly, realizing her statement was honest and not just fluff to keep a girl on the hook. She really did want to see Lauren again.

"Thank you, that's a nice thought." Lauren sighed over the missed opportunity. "If we can't even find time to talk to each other, how are we ever going to…" She stopped when she realized what she was about to say.

"Going to what?" Elliott prompted.

Have sex for hours. "Spend time together," she said hesitantly. Her mind swiftly filled in the gaps.

"And do you want to *spend time together,* as you call it?" Elliott gripped the phone tighter, her feet rooted to the floor.

"You know I do."

Elliott's crotch started to throb. She was often aroused in an instant at the sight of a woman, or from her touch, but very rarely from her words. Along with the pulsating sensation came a warm glow that spread throughout her body. "Lauren, I…"

The rest of her sentence was muffled and it was several moments before she came back on the line. In the interim Lauren could hear her talking to someone in French.

"Lauren, I'm sorry, I've got to go. I'm at the window and the customs agent is telling me I have to hang up or he won't stamp my passport. I'll call you just as soon as I get to my hotel. Gotta run. Bye."

And just like that she was gone.

❖

Elliott did call Lauren that night, and several other nights while she was in Paris. Since she had to be in Europe, she decided to take advantage and research prospective leads. Two weeks later she had eight new clients and had secured financing for a major development project for another one. All in all, she was pleased and it was a very productive trip.

Although her schedule was busy, she did find the opportunity to mix business with pleasure, dining with old friends and a few women who made it perfectly clear that they were willing to be her new friend, at least for a night or two. She had been to Paris on many occasions and found that French women were fabulous in bed. They had no inhibitions, were very creative, and left the next morning with a kiss on the cheek and an *au revoir.*

On her last evening in the City of Light, Elliott decided to take one up on a tempting offer, and so far she was finding Isabella an entertaining companion. The music was slow, the lights were dim, and Isabella was soft and responsive in her arms. There were times when Elliott wanted a slow, seductive evening, and other times when all she wanted was a good fuck. This evening she was definitely in the mood for the latter, and by all indications Isabella was more than willing to comply.

Ten minutes after their hot, slow dance, she was walking the short distance to Isabella's apartment near the Palais de Justice. Isabella's hand was heavy on her arm and she chatted the entire way. The sidewalk was crowded with boisterous tourists and Elliott was jostled several times, once so hard she almost lost her temper. She could not help but compare this uneasy stroll with the last time she had walked with a woman on her arm. That evening had been tranquil and she and Lauren were almost alone. Elliott had been as comfortable with the silence then as she was irritated with the noise now. *I wonder if Lauren's ever been to Paris with a lover.*

The thought drew a surprising response from her: instant dismay and something approaching resentment. She didn't want to think about Lauren in anyone else's arms. Steps loomed ahead and she forced herself to pay attention to her surroundings. Isabella opened her apartment door and barely waited for it to swing shut behind them before she pounced on Elliott, smothering her with kisses. It wasn't as if Elliott didn't expect to be kissed, but she was still thinking of Lauren so her reactions were slow. Isabella asked her something and had to repeat it before she answered.

"No, I haven't changed my mind. You just surprised me. This is exactly what I want."

Elliott let the chic French woman lead her across the room and through an open door. When her eyes adjusted to the darkness she took control. Her hands were steady as she unbuttoned Isabella's blouse, and soon the floor was littered with their clothing. The bed squeaked under their weight and Elliott frowned at the irritating noise. Isabella rolled her onto her back and kissed her again. Elliott twisted her mouth away and wondered when Isabella's kisses became sloppy rather than sensuous. She thought of the soft, feather-light kisses from Lauren and how aroused she became from them.

"Ouch!" She was startled by a bite on her neck. *Shit, that better not leave a mark. Try explaining that to Lauren.* She froze, realizing what she had just thought. She didn't owe Lauren an explanation. She didn't owe her anything.

"Are you with me, *chérie?*"

The unfamiliar voice jarred Elliott back to the dark-haired woman hovering over her. Pushing thoughts of Lauren aside, she quickly switched their positions and showed Isabella just exactly how with her she was. Legs wrapped around her and the image of lithe, muscular limbs clad in silk popped into her mind. *God damn it, Elliott, what in the fuck are you thinking? Pay attention.*

She had never been distracted while in the arms of a naked, beautiful woman, but she couldn't stop thinking about Lauren. Although she had often used sex to disengage from herself or from the pressures of work, this time she couldn't shake the feeling that she was doing something wrong. Her brain told her she wasn't, but her gut was screaming just the opposite. *Would Lauren be hurt if she knew I was doing this? Would she care?*

"Are you going to fuck *me* or the woman you're thinking about?" Isabella demanded, clearly pissed off.

Elliott could relate; she was less than thrilled herself. How dared Lauren control who she fucked? She did not need anyone's permission to sleep with a woman, especially someone she hadn't even slept with. It was none of Lauren's business what she did in her spare time, and, if their roles were reversed it wouldn't be any of her business who Lauren chose to sleep with, either.

Elliott let her actions speak for her. She had Isabella writhing under her hands and mouth and Lauren was not going to interfere with her pleasure. Unfortunately she was dead wrong about that. *Fuck, fuck, fuck!*

She pulled away from Isabella, and after mumbling a sincere apology, picked up her clothes and got dressed. She did not even bother to button her shirt before heading out the door. Her head was pounding and her stomach was tied in knots as she walked along the Seine River back to her hotel. She was angry that thoughts of Lauren kept intruding while she was with Isabella and even more furious that she could not stop it from happening, but what disturbed her most were the feelings she was having about Lauren. She felt guilty about the entire evening with Isabella and was even a bit jealous imagining Lauren with someone else.

The cool Parisian air chilled her body, but the relief only seemed skin deep. She was still churning hotly inside. The full moon lit up the deserted streets, providing ample light for her to see. It was after 2:00 a.m. and she did a quick calculation to determine the time in California. She wondered what Lauren was doing. Was she still at work? Was she having dinner alone or with someone? Stopping under a lamppost on the Quai des Orfevres, she reached for her phone.

❖

Elliott awoke on the plane to the smell of breakfast and was not surprised that she had dreamed of Lauren. For a moment she experienced a pang over her episode with Isabella but she quickly pushed the feeling aside as ridiculous. After trying unsuccessfully to reach Lauren the night before, she had walked for hours on the streets, circling her hotel until exhaustion finally drove her inside. Methodically she had showered, packed her bags, and waited for a taxi to take her to the airport.

In the first class lounge, waiting for the flight to depart, she had come to a decision. She rarely felt guilty about her sexual activity and was not about to start now. She was not committed to any one woman and, as far as she was concerned, that meant she was free to see anyone she wanted.

Elliott sighed and put her tray table down. *And it just so happens the only woman I want to see is her.*

She dozed intermittently during the rest of her long flight home, cleared customs quickly, then headed straight to her office from the airport. She would face jet lag later. Even though Teresa took care of urgent matters, she knew her desk would be piled with work, and even though it was Friday and she could spend the whole weekend catching up, she hated when work got out of control. The sooner she made some headway on the backlog, the better.

Piled was an understatement. Elliott scanned her calendar for the next few days and choked on her coffee when she saw the HRC dinner penciled in for tomorrow evening. *Holy shit, how could I have forgotten!* She was a big supporter of the Human Rights Campaign and had attended the annual dinner for the past ten years. She quickly dialed Lauren's direct line from memory, praying that she didn't already have a date for the night.

"I have no excuse for not inviting you sooner, Lauren," she said when the voice mail bleep sounded. "I'm sorry for the last-minute call, and I'd understand perfectly if you had other plans…"

"Elliott?" Lauren picked up. "It's all right. I understand and I'd love to go with you. The HRC dinner, I assume?"

"Yes, tomorrow."

Lauren paused. "It's good to have you home again."

"It's good to be here," Elliott said vehemently. She tried to find the words to express just how good it was to hear Lauren's voice and to know they were in the same city and would soon be seeing each other again.

"Pick me up at seven. And don't be late," Lauren added teasingly, perhaps to lighten the mood.

"Yes ma'am, I'll be there." Elliott had never felt so relieved to have a date in her life.

CHAPTER EIGHT

They made a striking couple on the dance floor. Lauren wore a midnight blue silk tuxedo and a white vest with no blouse. Elliott's royal blue bow tie contrasted nicely against her white dinner jacket. They danced well together and moved gracefully across the floor. Elliott was a strong lead and Lauren felt as light as a feather in her arms. When the music slowed, she drew Lauren closer, and their hips swayed sensually to the melody. Elliott had felt an initial awkwardness when she picked Lauren up, still guilty over the debacle with Isabella in Paris even though she'd convinced herself the feelings were irrational. She could barely look Lauren in the eye even when they entered the reception hall, but after dinner, she'd invited Lauren to join her on the dance floor and the feelings had passed.

Lauren wrapped her arms around Elliott's neck, pulling her closer. She felt Elliott take a quick breath in surprise, then the warm arms she was waiting for encircled her waist. "That's more like it," Lauren murmured into Elliott's shoulder. "Traditional dancing is fine, but sometimes I just want to dance close like this."

Lauren's warm breath on her neck sent shivers down Elliott's spine. "I like it too. Particularly when it's you I'm holding."

She dropped her hands a little lower on Lauren's back, lightly grazing the top of her butt, and not for the first time, Elliott noted how their bodies fit together almost perfectly. Several minutes into the song Lauren lifted eyes bright with desire and lips asking to be kissed. Not being one to require that a woman ask twice, Elliott slowly lowered her head. Lauren's kisses were as soft as she remembered, and this time the memory was sweet. Lauren nibbled on her bottom lip, and Elliott had to restrain herself from deepening the kiss even more. She wasn't sure how she remained upright and guided them around the other dancers on the floor by instinct.

Lauren's senses filled with the musky smell of the woman in her arms. Her back burned under Elliott's soft caresses. But it was the taste of Elliott's lips that had her full attention. Elliott's kiss was soft and tentative at first, then insisted she become an active participant. Lauren was more than willing to comply; she felt safe and warm. Her hands drifted into Elliott's hair and pulled her closer as she took control of the kiss. She didn't have much more than a brief chance to enjoy the taste of Elliott before they were jolted apart by the blaring voice of the DJ announcing the next song.

If she didn't want Elliott as much as she did, Lauren thought the passion she saw in her eyes would be frightening. Her legs shook and Elliott's guiding hand on her elbow was comforting as they returned to their table. Elliott resumed chatting with friends and colleagues, making every attempt to include Lauren in the topic. Yet Lauren had trouble assembling her thoughts. She made a few intelligent comments but most of the time she was content to let the discussion wash over her. There was no point trying to concentrate on politics or social issues when all she wanted was to be in private with Elliott so they could pick up where they'd left off two weeks earlier.

One by one, their tablemates drifted away until finally they were alone. The night was cool but Lauren felt quite warm. She removed her jacket and slid it over the back of her chair, then stood, reaching for Elliott's hand. "Let's dance."

But Elliott didn't move.

Sweet Jesus! The back of Lauren's vest was completely devoid of fabric, exposing her smooth, tanned back and shoulders. She couldn't catch her breath, and the only thing she heard was the blood roaring through her ears. Muscles danced under the exposed flesh, and a small tattoo on Lauren's right shoulder blade dared Elliott to step closer to make out exactly what it was. She couldn't move, she couldn't think, and she couldn't do anything but stare with her with her mouth gaping open.

"Elliott?" The expression on Elliott's face and the longing in her eyes made Lauren feel more desired than she ever had in her life. Feeling like the most powerful, feminine woman in the room, she gave Elliott a shy smile and tugged on her hand. "Come on. I want your arms around me again."

Elliott was unable to do anything other than follow Lauren out onto the dance floor. It took several moments before she regained her composure. As they danced she noticed the reaction of other guests to Lauren's provocative attire. Some seemed shocked, while others looked completely envious.

"You seem to have created quite a stir." Elliott could not remember the last time she had felt such a visceral reaction to a woman.

"What do you mean?"

She really has no idea of her beauty. "Your vest," Elliott replied. "Every pair of eyes in the room is on you."

Lauren didn't bother to pretend she didn't know what Elliott was talking about. "The only eyes I'm interested in having on me are yours."

Elliott stumbled a little and knew, from the twitch of Lauren's mouth, that her reaction was a dead giveaway. Soft hands slid behind her neck and began stroking the baby fine hairs at her nape.

"Have I created a stir in you, Elliott?"

"Yes." *Yes to anything you want.*

"Good." Lauren moved closer.

Elliott's mind reeled with the feel of bare skin and the smell of warm flesh. Tight muscles jumped beneath her fingers and sent pulses of heat directly to the sensitive spot between her legs. The familiar pounding of arousal coursed through her body, and her silk boxers did little to stop the juices threatening to slide down her leg. She could not remember ever being so turned on by a woman still fully clothed. If she were not careful, there was the distinct possibility that she would embarrass herself on the dance floor. She had been in the arms of many women, but none made her feel like this. She wanted to make love to Lauren; of that she was certain. But there was something else as well, and she struggled with exactly what that was. Inhaling the fragrance of Lauren's hair, she gave up trying to decode her responses and simply closed her eyes and lost herself in the woman she was holding.

The music ended way too soon and Lauren led them slowly back to their table. Elliott was not quite as shell-shocked as she had been when she first saw Lauren's naked back, but she still couldn't take her eyes off the skin she'd so recently caressed. She pulled out Lauren's chair and lightly stroked her bare shoulders after they were both seated. Elliott lifted her water glass and the ice clinked erratically against the sides due to her shaking hands. *I need more than a glass of cold water to quench this thirst.* Her dance partner was flushed and breathless and gazing back at her.

Elliott stood. "Let's go outside for some fresh air." *Maybe it'll cool me off enough not to ravish her right on this table.*

She reached for Lauren's hand, and when their eyes locked her breathing became shallow. She lowered her head to kiss Lauren again, but a couple leaving the dance floor bumped into her, offering a halfhearted apology. The interruption was enough to break the spell, and Elliott did her best to appear effortlessly in control as they moved out the door. As soon as they stepped into the evening chill, Lauren lifted her hair to catch the cool breeze and Elliott saw a light film of sweat on the back of her neck. She wanted to run her tongue over the damp skin and catch the liquid, but before she could satisfy the urge, a high-pitched cry of recognition intruded.

"Lauren, I thought it was you."

Lauren turned with barely concealed dismay. "Marcie…" The unmasked desire in Elliott's gaze almost made her fall in a heap. Gathering strength from God knows where, she smiled at her business acquaintance. "It's good to see you again." *Bullshit.*

"Lauren, what have you been doing? You have *got* to come with me to meet Samuel Parker." In her usual manner, Marcie didn't give Lauren the opportunity to answer any of the questions she rattled off in her Southern drawl. "You look fabulous in that outfit. Where ever did you get it?" She reached for Lauren's hand, and almost as an afterthought said to Elliott, "I'm Marcie Webster, by the way. You'll excuse us for a minute, won't you? We won't be long."

Lauren flashed Elliott a pleading look that said, *What am I supposed to do?* She had always found Marcie abrasive, and the impression was not dispelled when Marcie pulled her into the ballroom and demanded in a loud stage whisper, "Have you given any more thought to the opportunity we talked about a few months ago?"

Rattled, Lauren glanced around. She hoped no one she knew was standing within earshot. "I'm sorry, Marcie, I'm not sure if..."

"Oh, don't give me that false modesty," Marcie chided. "The community needs an attorney with your skill and connections, and you'd be great at it. Private practice is definitely the right move for you."

Wonderful. Just tell the whole world. She and Marcie had been adversaries on a case almost two years ago and Lauren had been surprised when Marcie approached her at a legal seminar in Los Angeles. She'd spent the entire evening talking to her about a prominent attorney who was ready to retire and was looking for someone to take over her practice. The woman represented women and children in their county and was highly respected in the legal community. Lauren had considered the possibility, but she wasn't anywhere near making a decision to change. She loved working at Bradley & Taylor.

"I haven't really given it much thought, Marcie," she said.

"Well, I told her you'd give her a call."

Lauren sighed. She hadn't agreed to anything, but Marcie was a steamroller once she got an idea in her head. "Okay, I'll think about it."

After a few more minutes of polite conversation she excused herself and returned to the patio where Elliott was waiting with a fresh drink in her hand. "Sorry about that. She caught me off guard."

"She was quite a hurricane, wasn't she?" Elliott handed her a fresh drink, and Lauren was relieved to see amusement in her eyes, not the irritation she'd expected. "Who is she? An ex, perhaps?" Elliott finished the question with raised eyebrows.

"No!" Lauren responded vigorously. She didn't want Elliott to think that she would be attracted to someone as tactless as Marcie. "No, not at all. She represented an employee who sued Bradley & Taylor for wrongful termination." Lauren lifted her chin proudly. "She lost."

"Good girl." Elliott allowed her eyes to drift to Lauren's lips, and her heart skipped a beat when Lauren ran her tongue over them. She lowered her head to kiss Lauren again. "I'd like to—"

For the second time that evening, they were interrupted. This time it was a law school classmate, and after introductions and several minutes of catch-up, the woman left.

"You were saying?" Lauren prompted, ready to kill the next person who dared intrude on them. She read the sexual tension in Elliott's body language and it thrilled her to know she was the cause.

Elliott took her arm and led her into the vegetation surrounding the patio, where they were hidden from view. "You're very popular tonight, Counselor."

"I didn't set out to be popular." Lauren stopped just a few inches in front of Elliott.

"What did you set out to do?"

"Seduce you."

"It's working."

Elliott's eyes darkened more than Lauren thought possible, and the air surrounding them cracked with electricity. Their ragged breathing formed a faint mist between them. She let out a growling moan of pleasure as Elliott's lips found hers in a kiss that rapidly became hot and demanding. Lauren molded her body into Elliott's and stood on her toes to get closer to the tantalizing mouth. She had been kissed many times but never like this. She was being devoured but was also expected to be an active participant. Her heart beat so hard in her chest she expected to see bruises in the morning. Her mind was completely blank, but her body was full of the millions of nerve endings that came alive in Elliott's arms.

After several minutes, Elliott broke away, fighting her natural urge to take Lauren right then and there. It would not be the first time in her life that lust overruled caution, resulting in ruined clothing, hers or the other woman's and sometimes both. But she wanted it to be different with Lauren; she didn't want a quick fuck, she wanted all night.

"That was nice," Lauren said weakly. *Nice, hell, that was breathtaking!*

"Yes, it was."

"Can we do it again?" Lauren was not sure she would survive another kiss like that but would die a happy woman if not. She wanted to be kissed again and again by this woman and float away in desire like she had never known. And she wanted it now.

"Definitely." Elliott kissed Lauren's nose, her eyes, her jaw, and quickly returned to her lips. Simultaneously she shifted and inserted her thigh between Lauren's. Her hands were equally busy, and Lauren gasped as Elliott cupped her breast. Elliott received the message loud and clear and began a journey of kisses to the top button of the daring vest.

Lauren pressed her throbbing clitoris against Elliott's leg and released a long sigh signaling her pleasure. *God, that feels good.* Placing a hand on Elliott's shoulder, she pushed slightly. "I think we should take this somewhere a little more private."

Elliott raised her eyes. "Are attorneys always so levelheaded?"

"Actually, yes. They teach you that in law school, you know."

Elliott laughed and reluctantly lowered her hand from the breast that fit so perfectly in her palm. "They must. My attorney is equally levelheaded."

"I hope you don't kiss her like you just kissed me."

"He's not my type."

"What is your type?"

Elliott hesitated a moment. "A woman who is confident, bold, warm, charming, witty, intelligent with smoldering sensuality, and eyes the color of the summer sky."

"Anyone like that around here?" Lauren teased. She was not

sure if she was fishing for a compliment or if she simply enjoyed hearing about Elliott's attraction to her. Either way, it made her heady.

"Yes. Particularly the smoldering sensuality part." Elliott's body was playing the familiar song of desire, but there were several new verses emerging, and she didn't know the words to them. There was tenderness for the woman in her arms, a tenderness that belied explanation. She wanted Lauren to be happy. She wanted her to have everything she needed. She wanted to keep her safe. After what felt like an eternity, she asked, "Are you ready?" There was definitely a double meaning in her question.

"Yes."

Lauren was shocked at how a simple three-letter word would forever change her life. She had struggled on and off with her growing attraction to women, not knowing if she was ready to make a commitment to lesbianism. She had ruled out bisexuality. She was not interested in men, even when she tried very hard to be committed to one, and most importantly didn't think it was safe. Crossing the line into another lifestyle, especially a controversial one, was not something she took lightly. The decision might impact her career, her friends might desert her, and her family might disown her. Deep down she felt sure her family would respect her decision, but she could not be so sure of what might happen in the other areas of her life. The only thing she was completely certain about was that she wanted to make love with Elliott Foster.

They made their way to Elliott's car and somehow drove to Lauren's home with their libidos in check. As they pulled up outside, Lauren took a calming breath. "Would you like a nightcap?" *Jesus, what a stupid question.*

Elliott turned in her seat to face her directly. The twinkle in her eyes defused some tension. "I'd be more interested in breakfast."

"How do you like your eggs?"

They abandoned the car and just made it inside the spacious foyer before they fell into each other's arms. Elliott didn't waste any time. She pulled Lauren close and kissed her directly on the mouth, her excitement rising again. She couldn't drive fast enough, getting here, anticipating what was to come. Now here she was, holding the woman she desired, knowing how much she was desired in return. Thrilled by that certainty, Elliott slipped her hands under the lapels of Lauren's suit jacket, her palms lightly brushing already hard nipples. Lauren removed the jacket and tossed it on the chair beside her, enabling Elliott to explore the expanse of skin that had tormented her all evening. This time when she kissed her way down Lauren's neck to the top of the vest there was no reason to stop.

She trailed kisses back and forth from Lauren's lips to the flesh she exposed with each button she unfastened on the silk vest. When all the buttons were undone, she nibbled her way back to Lauren's mouth and captured it in a kiss. She moved her hands inside the vest and gently cupped the warm, full breasts that swelled in her hands. *God, she feels good.* Lauren's rapid breathing was echoed in the rise and fall of her breasts in her hands. Spurred on by her silent encouragement, Elliott used her lips and tongue to trace the path mapped by her hands.

"Oh, God," Lauren moaned as Elliott's mouth closed over her nipple.

She stumbled a few steps backward, using the wall for stability. She wasn't sure if she was clinging to Elliott out of necessity or desire. Either way it really didn't matter. This was the first time she'd experienced desire this intense, and it didn't frighten her. Her body was on fire and Elliott's lips and tongue were stoking the flame even higher. The sensations were almost overwhelming, and she shivered thinking about what was to come. This was as close as she had ever been with a woman, and she needed the reassurance of Elliott's kiss.

As if Elliott sensed her need, she placed a final soft kiss on an eager nipple, then shifted her attention to Lauren's mouth. Somehow Lauren found the strength to remove Elliott's jacket. She dropped it to the floor and was trying to unbutton Elliott's shirt when both quivering hands were gently grasped.

Elliott looked into eyes brimming with uncertainty. "Your hands are shaking," she commented gently.

"I'm nervous," Lauren confessed.

Blue eyes bored into her soul. "I'm nervous too."

For some reason Elliott found that statement to be surprisingly true. She couldn't remember the last time she had felt this way in the arms of a woman. She knew passion, desire, anticipation, and occasionally boredom, but never nervousness. It was as though this was her first time again, and she didn't want to disappoint her lover. She bent to kiss Lauren again.

"But you've done this before."

Elliott's mouth stopped a fraction of an inch from lips that were open and inviting and held the promise of so much more. "What did you say?"

Lauren was taken aback, not immediately realizing what she had said. Once she did, she hesitated, knowing that this was a defining moment. Her mind raced, but in her aroused state, she couldn't think clearly. Eyes lowered, she whispered, "I said you've obviously done this before."

"Does that mean you haven't?" Elliott wasn't certain she wanted to hear the answer. She could feel the heat draining from her body.

"Not exactly." Lauren sensed Elliott's withdrawal and tried not to panic.

"Exactly what is *not exactly*?" Elliott held her breath. *Please don't tell me this.*

"Exactly...no." Lauren spoke so quietly that she wasn't even sure if she had spoken at all. With crashing disappointment, she knew that she had and it was too late to take the words back.

Elliott dropped Lauren's hands and carefully pulled the vest closed, leaving it unbuttoned. She clenched her hands into tight fists. She knew that if she reached for the buttons, her hands would end up back inside, on the hot inviting flesh, and her lips would certainly follow.

"I need to go," she said curtly, looking for her jacket.

Lauren's body reacted to the sudden chill in the air and the coolness where Elliott's hands had once been. She reached out and touched Elliott's arm. "Elliott, wait."

"Were you going to tell me?" Elliott's frustration came out in anger. Lauren's touch on her arm sent searing heat through her body and in a fraction of a second, she visualized those hands all over her. She picked up her jacket, using it as an excuse to step away from the contact.

"I did tell you," Lauren pleaded. Even to her own ears, her reply sounded evasive. Whatever hope she had of making love with this woman was rapidly evaporating.

"But were you *going* to tell me?" Elliott felt blindsided by the entire conversation.

"I don't know," Lauren answered honestly. She had thought about whether she needed to tell Elliott since the moment she realized she wanted to sleep with her, but in her typical fashion, she had methodically listed the pros and cons like she was preparing an argument before the Supreme Court. Unfortunately, she was unable to come to a definitive conclusion. She'd simply hoped that it would never come to this, or that somehow the perfect night together would miraculously materialize, precluding any need for awkward disclosures.

"You don't know?" Elliott was shaken by her answer. "Don't you think I should have known about this?" She paced around the room running her hands through her hair. Her surprise had turned from anger to confusion and back to anger.

"Would that have changed anything?" Lauren asked, already knowing the answer.

Elliott stopped pacing. "What kind of question is that? Of course it would have." She put her hands on her hips defiantly. "I think it's pretty obvious that it changed everything."

Lauren didn't know what to say, so she said nothing.

"I'm not a lab rat for you to experiment with, Lauren," Elliott said curtly. She didn't know if she was more upset that Lauren had never been with a woman or that she could have so misjudged her companion's experience.

Lauren cringed. "That's not what I'm doing." She was desperate to get her point across. *And just what is my point? That I wanted you to be my first? She'd really like to hear that now.*

"That's exactly what you're doing, Lauren. You are thirty-four years old and you've just now decided you want to be a lesbian? I'm sorry, but you'll have to find somebody else."

"Elliott, let me explain." Lauren didn't know what she would have said even if Elliott had given her the chance.

"No, I'll explain for you." She came across the room and stood face-to-face with Lauren. This time her eyes were filled with fury, not passion. "It's very simple, Lauren. I'm a lesbian," Elliott's finger touched her own chest then moved to Lauren's, "and you're not. I will admit you did an excellent job of hiding it. I didn't have a clue. Not a fucking clue."

"Elliott…"

"I'm sorry, Lauren, but I don't sleep with straight women. Good night." Elliott stalked away, refusing to listen to another word.

The door closed soundly behind her, leaving Lauren frozen with shock and rejection.

CHAPTER NINE

W hat has your butt out of balance?"
Elliott looked up from the papers she'd been signing
and across her desk to Teresa. "Excuse me?"

"I said, what has your butt out of balance? You've been a
royal bitch for two weeks, and I for one am tired of it." Elliott's
startled protest did not deter her from speaking her mind. "You have
everyone walking on eggshells around here, and whatever it is, you
had better fix it, find it, or get over it, because you are making us
miserable."

Elliott was accustomed to Teresa's directness; they had been
friends long enough that she could get away with it. But she had
never scolded Elliott like this before. "Sorry. I guess I have been a
little on edge."

"A little?" Teresa raised her eyebrows.

"Okay, more than a little," Elliott admitted, ashamed of her
behavior. "I'm just preoccupied." That was an understatement.
She'd been obsessing over Lauren ever since that night, dissecting
every minute they'd spent together, seeking any clue that Lauren
was not gay. *I still can't believe I misjudged her.*

Teresa scooted her chair closer. "Elliott, I've seen you juggle
more balls than humanly possible and you've never been like this.
Not even a little. Is everything all right?"

*You mean other than the fact that I have had one of the biggest
disappointments in my life, I feel like a fool, and I can't stop thinking*

about the most beautiful woman I've ever met? "I'm fine. There's something I have to work out, that's all."

"Anything I can do to help?"

Elliott wished there were. She relied on Teresa to take care of just about everything for her, both professional and personal, but this was one problem she had to work out herself. "Just do what you just did, Teresa." She smiled for the first time in days. "Keep me in line, tell me when I'm out of line, and smack me if I don't get back into line."

Teresa didn't seem convinced. "You need a break. I'm serious."

Elliott shrugged off her concern. "Don't worry. This will pass."

She left the office later than usual and, on automatic pilot, drove home and was soon sitting on the couch with two fingers of Scotch in a glass. As she sipped, she pushed Play on her answering machine.

The only message was from Ryan, insisting on seeing her. Elliott groaned. She really wasn't in the mood. The very last thing she wanted to do right now was spend another hour trying to figure out how to stop Rebecca from pillaging her life; she didn't need any outside help with that. Maybe Teresa was right. Maybe she really did need a break. It wasn't like her to vacillate in a situation that could affect her company. She had to get some perspective, and soon.

Elliott poured herself another Scotch and stared around the room. Comfortable, perfectly decorated, her private retreat was an oasis of solitude she treasured. She had never felt lonely here before, yet suddenly she did, and all she could think about was getting away. Shocked and angry, she set her drink aside. How could this be happening to her? She felt displaced—from the life she'd built, from the person she was, from everything that felt familiar and comfortable. And she had no idea how to get back to normalcy, or whether she even wanted to. *I'm a mess. What am I going to do?*

❖

Lauren listened to the sound of rain for the fourth morning in a row. Crisp, cool air whooshed through a large vent into her hotel room, raising goose bumps across her skin. She glanced at the large red numbers across the face of her travel clock and groaned. Only ten minutes had passed since the last time she'd checked. Frustrated over another sleepless night, she threw the covers back and flipped on CNN. For a few minutes, she sat shivering in her silk boxer shorts and tank top as she watched the usual depressing news coverage, then she padded to the bathroom to prepare for another tedious day.

The trip had come up suddenly when Bradley & Taylor was notified by the Securities and Exchange Board in India that they were being investigated as part of an internal investigation of the Bangalore Stock Exchange. The charges were bogus, but Lauren was still required to appear in person. She'd had all of two days to get her office in order, pack, and be on a plane headed to the other side of the world.

She brushed her teeth and was about to turn on the shower when she froze at the sound of a familiar voice. Slowly she inched around the bathroom door and her heart leapt into her throat. Elliott's face filled the television screen as she responded to questions from a business reporter. Lauren studied her, noting the circles under her eyes that the television makeup couldn't quite conceal. A dark red jacket accentuated her coloring, and diamond studs twinkled when she talked. She looked thinner, and Lauren detected an edge that she had not seen before.

The corner of the bed dipped as Lauren positioned herself there, transfixed. Her stomach lurched when Elliott laughed at something. The charisma that had attracted her at their first meeting was evident even over the airwaves. *Whatever made me think someone like that would be interested in me? Look at her.* Lauren stared at the screen, caught up in the melodious voice. Elliott was rich and famous and brilliant. She was on worldwide television, for crying out loud. *Oh, and let's not forget about gorgeous.* She could have any woman she wanted.

Lauren turned off the television and laughed as she marched back to the bathroom. *Shit, no wonder she hasn't called.* She scrubbed her body hard but couldn't erase the cloak of self-doubt that followed her into the shower. During the twenty-three-hour flight a few days earlier, she had rehashed the ultimatum she'd left on Elliott's answering machine the day of her departure. She had never begged for a lover's attention, and she certainly wasn't going to start now. Her message had been clear and to the point. She had explained how she felt and why she was attracted to Elliott, and she'd left the next move to her.

Like all virgins, and she laughingly considered herself a virgin, Lauren wanted her first time to be with someone special. From the moment Elliott practically ran her over she knew she had never met a woman like her, and perhaps she never would again. Since their abrupt parting, she had come up with many different reasons why Elliott had not called her. They ranged from the totally absurd to the vividly morbid, but she kept coming back to something that nagged at her.

Did Elliott think so little of her intelligence that she believed Lauren would blindly stumble into a woman's arms on some kind of whim? Had she not even considered the effect this could have on Lauren's career? Elliott had been gay her entire life and was simply accepted for who she was. Lauren, on the other hand, was risking everything. She had no intention of living in the closet; she wanted to share her life openly with the one she loved, when that time came. She had everything to lose. Did Elliott think she would make such a choice lightly?

Toweling herself dry, she examined her reflection in the mirror. What she saw was not appealing. Along with her pride, her self-respect was bruised. She was reliving her teenage dating years and risking the confidence she'd spent her entire adult life cultivating over something as unimportant as whether or not a woman would return her call.

Elliott was startled by a car horn blasting somewhere in the distance. The crick in her neck told her she had dozed off briefly. Blinking several times, she gazed out at her surroundings.

The old neighborhood still looked the same. The trees were

taller, the shrubbery fuller, and other than different cars parked along the street, Claude Boulevard was just as Elliott remembered it. She'd spent the early years of her childhood in the house with the winding driveway, and no matter how many places she'd lived since then, she still thought of this as home. She rolled down the window and turned off the car. The silence was peppered with the sounds of a dog barking and birds welcoming the early morning. The only movement on the street for the past hour was an empty school bus driving by.

Elliott settled deeper into the comfortable leather seats and sipped tepid coffee from a plastic cup she'd filled at the mini-mart a few blocks away. From her vantage point across the street she could see curtains closed over the window where her mother used to stand, waiting for her to return home from school. She remembered the last time she ever saw her there.

Elliott was six years old and had hurried home with her first report card clenched in her fist, filled with letters and numbers that she had not yet learned, but she felt sure they were going to tell her mother how smart she was. She still remembered how she felt when she rounded the corner that day and saw her mother waiting: she was proud of herself and eager to share her news. She felt safe, certain her mother would always be there. She was also waiting anxiously for the arrival of a baby brother or sister; her mother was eight months pregnant. Elliott hadn't known then about the pregnancy complications.

When her sister Stephanie came home a few days later, Elliott was the one standing in the window watching as the car halted in the drive and her father stepped out carrying a pink bundle. He was a solid man, standing well over six feet, but he looked small and broken walking up the front steps. Her mother was not coming home, and Elliott would never feel completely safe again.

She leaned her head back, suddenly very tired. She hadn't slept at all the previous night and had only managed broken sleep in the period that preceded it. She'd spent some time out of town on what was supposed to be a short vacation that would clear her head. It hadn't, and that was the reason she was sitting alone in her car on the street she grew up on. She never fully understood why coming here gave her a sense of belonging and peace, but it did. She would often sit in this same spot on different days, in different cars, refreshing the memory of her mother and recalling the happiness she'd known until that loss.

At the sound of an approaching car, Elliott checked the rearview mirror and caught a glimpse of herself. The dark circles under her eyes didn't surprise her, but the hollowness did. She had never noticed the flat emptiness in her gaze and she pulled the mirror closer. Gone were the intensity and drive that she saw in the bathroom mirror every morning, and in their place was nothing. *Is this what my life has become?*

Shaken, she brushed off her appearance as mere tiredness. On most nights, her dreams were filled with images of Lauren, and she couldn't escape her during the day, either. Elliott was usually extremely focused at work, but images of Lauren standing in front of her, alive with laughter and burning with passion, drifted in and out of her brain. She wondered what it would take to drive the beautiful woman from her mind. Maybe she needed to put her head down and escape into her work even more. Maybe she needed to have sex with someone else—or several someone elses. Either was a typical modus operandi when she was troubled about something, but both had failed her this time.

Another possibility hovered: maybe she should just face her feelings head-on and accept that avoiding them hadn't worked so far. Perhaps the only way she was going to get Lauren Collier out from under her skin was to go ahead and sleep with her. *So why does that scare the hell out of me?*

The insistent echo of her heels clicking could be heard throughout the lobby as she approached the front desk. Glancing at her watch, Lauren informed the desk clerk that the cab she had scheduled had still not arrived. She fumed at the insolence of the man behind the counter, so she asked to speak with the hotel manager, who, after another ten minutes, was only able to generate an apology and not a cab. Frustrated with the lack of amenities, including reliable cab service, she decided that if she was to get to the meeting with any time remaining she would have to walk.

Five minutes into her decision, she regretted it. The rain had stopped and in its place was air so muggy that steam rose from the puddles she was forced to sidestep. The streets teemed with people, all in a hurry to get somewhere. A large woman dressed in a traditional Indian sari almost knocked Lauren's briefcase out of her hand in her haste to get across the street. Sweat dripped down the side of Lauren's face, and she cursed as her shoe emerged from a pile of mud she could not dodge. "Great. Just fucking great."

Lauren usually traveled well, but this trip had drained her, physically and emotionally, and her temper was getting shorter as the sun climbed higher in the hot Indian sky. Seeing Elliott on television that morning must have unnerved her more than she thought. A limousine crawled to a stop a block in front of her, and an exquisite-looking woman emerged from the air-conditioned interior looking as fresh as Lauren wished she was. The woman was so much like Elliott, she stopped suddenly, causing the man behind her to practically run her down. She mumbled a halfhearted apology as the woman disappeared into a building.

Squinting against the sweat that burned her eyes, she finally spotted the building she was looking for a few blocks ahead and heaved a sigh of relief and picked up her pace. *If she were going to call, she would have done so by now. It's history. Let it go.*

The cool air in the lobby sent a chill through her body as she approached a bank of elevators. Beads of sweat continued to trickle slowly down between her breasts and lower back. The clock behind her chimed, indicating the half hour, and she pushed the Up button impatiently. She hated being late for a meeting, and she particularly hated losing the edge she needed if it was with an adversary.

Lauren composed herself as she exited the elevator, then took another moment to control her breathing as she stood outside the conference room.

God, what a brutal trip. Thomas Merison had accompanied her to India, and she detected not-so-subtle hostility and resentment from him. On several occasions she'd caught him looking at her peculiarly, almost as if he were trying to figure out if she played for the boys' team or the girls'. No doubt her stance on John Briggs, the gay employee Merison wanted to sack, had aroused his suspicions. But Merison had a strong sense of self-preservation, and he was also depending on her to be discreet about his daughter, so he wasn't making any overt comments. Instead, during their meetings with regulators in Bangalore, he questioned the correctness of her position on specific legalities, and often his comments were made in a room filled with parties on both sides. He was clearly attempting to undermine her authority, and after dinner on the first day she called him on it.

Lauren was incensed at his condescending denial and insinuation that she would rather settle than fight the trumped-up charges. She stared at him without speaking until he started to squirm, then told him in no uncertain terms never to question her credibility again. Merison was on his best behavior for the rest of the meetings, but she was forced to be on her guard much more than usual.

The door squeaked when she opened it, and all heads turned to look at her. She surveyed the occupants seated around the table and was not the least bit surprised that every one of them was wearing a dark suit, white shirt, and a perfect Windsor knot in his silk tie. *Jesus, not only do these attorneys think alike but they dress alike too.* This was not the first time she'd been the sole woman in a room, and she knew it was going to be another long day.

Elliott tossed her car keys on the counter and peeled off her clothes as she walked through her house. She needed a hot shower and a stiff drink. Opting to combine the two, she stopped at the bar to pour Chivas into a thick tumbler. She was naked by the time her feet hit the cool tile on the bathroom floor.

The scalding water pelted her neck and back, and she stood motionless for several minutes, willing it to wash away her melancholy. Then she reached for the soap and lathered her entire body before rinsing. The familiar scent of the liquid was reassuring. Shampoo dripped into her eyes and the burning reaffirmed that she was still alive. Mechanically she turned off the water and wrapped herself in a towel.

The blinking light of the answering machine reflected in the mirror above the bar. She refilled her glass, padded over to the desk, and pushed Play. A familiar voice captured her complete attention.

"Elliott, it's Lauren. Are you there?" A few seconds of silence. "I'm sorry if I misled you, that was not my intent. I was going to tell you, it was just never the right time." Elliott gripped her glass with both hands and stared down into the golden liquid as Lauren continued. "Elliott, I am not a naïve, bored housewife looking for kicks." She sounded angry now. "I'm an educated woman with a law degree from Harvard and a PhD from Princeton. I've given this a lot of thought, and trust me, I don't do anything without thinking it through. Just because I've never made love with a woman doesn't mean that I'm not a lesbian. Jesus Christ, Elliott. Everyone has to have a first time."

Yeah, but it's not going to be me. Been there, done that, and learned a valuable lesson.

"I like you, Elliott, and I am very attracted to you. Obviously, I'm attracted to you." Lauren chuckled as if she realized the absurdity of her statement. "Most importantly, I respect you, what you think and what you believe in. You challenge me, and quite frankly, very few people do. I want to spend more time with you. I could very easily say more. I'm an attorney…I could plead my case for a very long time, but I won't beg for this." There was a long pause and Elliott thought she had hung up. The finality of Lauren's voice surprised her. "The ball's in your court now, Elliott. I won't approach you again. If you want me, you'll have to come and get me."

CHAPTER TEN

The annual fund-raiser for Children's Hospital was one of Elliott's favorite events, and she often bid on several of the items in the silent auction, then gave them back to the hospital for the kids to enjoy. She had spent most of the evening catching up with old friends and business acquaintances and was finally alone sipping her drink when Lauren walked into the room.

Her head began to spin and her stomach dropped. Immediately the taste and feel and softness of Lauren's body came flooding back. If it were possible, she was even more beautiful than Elliott remembered, and she wasn't the only one who noticed. As Lauren strode confidently over to a group of people, the eyes of one specific woman casually roamed her body and lingered on her breasts. Even from this distance Elliott recognized the hunger; this woman was on the prowl. Her stomach knotted and she felt oddly flushed.

Elliott was stunned by the feelings tracking through her body. It was a combination she could not recall ever experiencing. She was hot with desire, but hotter with what? Jealousy? *Am I jealous that someone else is interested in Lauren?* She wasn't even sure what jealousy felt like. She did know that the thought of someone else touching Lauren made her crazy. What was worse, she didn't have the first clue what to do about it.

She should have responded to Lauren's phone call. She'd saved the message, and when she had finally been able to listen to the words and tone without anger, the logic of Lauren's argument began to make sense. Hadn't they all been virgins at one time? Wasn't it actually a compliment that Lauren had wanted to share herself with Elliott instead of some other woman? There could be no shortage of offers. Perhaps she had already satisfied her desires, or curiosity, with someone else.

Pushing the thought from her mind, Elliott followed every small movement of Lauren's hands, imagining them moving over her body and answering her desire. She focused on Lauren's mouth and yearned once again for the teasing brush of those lips against her own. Weeks had passed and there had been no contact between them. Elliott wondered if it was too late; she had a feeling charm didn't cut much ice when you blew it with a certain type of woman. Lauren had left the ball in her court and apparently wasn't kidding. Elliott had half expected to get a follow-up call. She had imagined Lauren trying to persuade her into another date. Instead she had walked away. If nothing else, that said something about her agenda; for once Elliott's wealth was not the drawing card.

After several minutes of benign conversation, Lauren knew she was being watched. Not wanting to appear rude, she casually moved her gaze from the woman she was speaking with and immediately connected with a familiar pair of warm brown eyes. *Elliott!* She had suspected she might see her at the benefit, given Elliott's commitment to children's charities, and she had prepared for this moment. A rush of turmoil swirled in her stomach anyway.

Elliott looked composed, holding a drink and leaning against a decorated pillar. With something approaching despair, Lauren realized just how much she still wanted her. *God give me the strength to keep it together.* She was determined to not approach Elliott; whatever pride she had was damn well going to stay intact. She nodded a polite but distant acknowledgment, and Elliott's eyes darkened even though her expression did not change. Lauren held her gaze for a few aching moments, then returned her attention to the people around her. One of the women in the party had been trying to catch her attention ever since she'd arrived. She was mature and in good shape. Lauren gave her a warm smile.

She didn't see Elliott again until much later that evening, when a blonde who looked like a stripper cut through the room and stopped about a foot away from the enigmatic CEO. As Elliott turned, the woman said something Lauren could not hear, then slapped Elliott's face hard. Amidst a chorus of gasps and a cloudburst of flashes as the few social page reporters swarmed, the blonde spun on her heel and walked away.

For a couple of seconds, Elliott stood where she was, apparently stunned, then her eyes flashed at Lauren and her one pale cheek turned as red as the other. She shifted her gaze immediately and it seemed as if every muscle in her body contracted; her face was drawn and her stance stiff. Then she was herself again. Ignoring the buzz of speculation, she stalked off after her busty assailant.

Lauren wasn't the only one staring open-mouthed.

Alan, her ever-dependable escort, remarked, "Well, it had to happen sometime."

"Who is she?" Lauren asked. If *that* was Elliott's "type," no wonder she hadn't called.

"I have no idea." Alan offered a philosophical shrug. "But if Elliott Foster ever thought she had a private life, it's history now."

"Elliott, what a lovely surprise." Rebecca's voice dripped with sarcasm.

"Don't play games with me." Elliott dropped her car keys into her pocket. "May I come in?" She couldn't bring herself to say Rebecca's name.

"You're always welcome in my house, and in my bed." Rebecca swept a lust-filled glance over her and stepped back to allow her by.

The practiced discipline of her emotions prevented Elliott from shuddering. She knew her way around Rebecca's house, so she headed to the living room.

"Scotch?" Rebecca asked with saccharine sweetness.

Elliott declined. "Let's get to the point. What in the hell was *that* all about?"

"You send the FBI here and you need to ask?" Rebecca's nearly bare breasts rose and fell sharply.

The FBI? Elliott schooled her features. Had Ryan taken some

drastic measure without consulting her? Cautiously, she said, "I'm sure they explained the situation."

"Oh, yeah. They explained it, all right. I'm being set up. They've got the telephone recordings and tapes from your house. You think you're smart, don't you?"

Smart? Elliott felt incredibly obtuse, but she couldn't let Rebecca see that none of this made any sense to her. "What are you going to do?" she asked blandly.

"Duh! I'm supposed to drop my lawsuit, hand over my evidence, and have no further contact with you or they're going to arrest me. They've got me for blackmail, and then there's that bullshit about national security. Puh-leeze."

National security? Elliott couldn't even imagine what Ryan must have said to the authorities. She pointed out the obvious. "You *are* blackmailing me."

"I could go to prison."

"Those jumpsuits are hideous." Elliott was baffled, but she could definitely see a funny side to this bizarre conversation.

Rebecca's outrage gave way to a pouting whine. "Come on, Elliott. I know you don't want me locked up or they'd have arrested me already. Things could still work out between us. I'm willing."

Elliott ignored the seduction attempt; however, she was intrigued. Why hadn't the FBI arrested Rebecca? The answer presented itself before she could draw a breath. Rebecca's behavior must have rocked the boat somehow, but if they made an arrest, their operation—whatever it was—would be out in the open. They would have to justify how they came by the evidence of blackmail. *They're investigating me and they don't want me to know.* She almost laughed. They had imagined Rebecca would keep her mouth shut. *Wrong.*

"Rebecca, it's time to quit," Elliott said. "We're done. I suggest you cut your losses and walk away while you can."

"I don't get it." Rebecca sounded genuinely bewildered. "A few hundred thousand is nothing to you. Why didn't you just pay?"

"It was a matter of principle."

"You spend millions of dollars on kids who are worthless, but you can't even give me a gift for our time together?"

I slept with this woman. Disgusted, Elliott said, "If you were sick with some terrible illness, I would help you. But you're not... unless an overdeveloped sense of entitlement is a sickness."

Rebecca produced some crocodile tears. "You took advantage of me."

"How so?"

"You seduced me. You got me in bed before I had a chance to say no. When it was over and I realized what you really are, I was in shock." Rebecca sat stiffly in her chair.

"And exactly what am I?"

"A predator," Rebecca spat.

Elliott laughed, and from the angry expression on Rebecca's face, that was maybe not the most prudent thing to do. "And at what point when you were naked and on top of me did I become a predator? Before or after you shoved your fingers so far up my cunt the back of my throat tickled? Was it when you joined me in the shower and begged me to make you come? Or how about when you fucked me in the ladies' room at the Ritz? Tell me, Rebecca, which one of those times was it? Because those were the only times we were together, and I seem to recall you were a *very* willing participant. As a matter of fact, every time I tried to leave, you fucked me again." By the time she was finished, her anger had the best of her and she was almost shouting.

"That's not the way it happened."

"That's *exactly* the way it happened. You know it and I know it. You were bored with your life and wanted a walk on the wild side. We went for that walk, Rebecca, and you were leading the way." For a second time she watched Rebecca transform.

"Does your new girlfriend fuck you like that?"

Elliott was unable to hide her shock at Rebecca's question. She had no idea what Rebecca knew, or thought she knew, about Lauren. The knot in her stomach tightened.

"That's right, your new squeeze. The pretty redhead. She's

a lawyer, right? I wonder what she'd say if we had a little chat? Maybe I'll sack my attorney and hire her."

Whatever control Elliott had snapped at the mention of Lauren in the context of this disgusting conversation. "Don't you dare bring her into this."

"Or what? Hmm? You're gonna do what? Tell my husband? Big deal, he doesn't care. Tell my mama? Who do you think I learned it from? Hey, I know, maybe you'll get your FBI friends to make me disappear. Poof." Rebecca used her hands to accentuate the disappearing act.

Elliott leapt out of the chair and in an instant was in Rebecca's face. "Listen to me, you conniving little bitch. I told you I'd eat you for lunch, and if you say one word to her…one word…any word, I guarantee you I will."

Lauren stared up at her bedroom ceiling, unable to sleep after the strange turn of events at the benefit. Obviously an angry ex wanted to embarrass Elliott publicly, and she'd succeeded. The media would be all over this story until the next scandal came along. Lauren was thankful she hadn't gotten involved with Elliott; her face would be everywhere too, and how would she explain that to Thomas Merison and Charles Comstock?

She thought about calling Elliott with a few words of support. Whatever happened, or did not happen, between them, this was going to be a tough time for her and the decent thing to do would be to reach out. For several minutes, she rested her hand uncertainly on the telephone next to her bed. Her alarm clock said one a.m. Friends did not phone each other in the middle of the night. That was something only lovers would do.

This was not an emergency, and if she were completely honest with herself, she had an ulterior motive. Certainly she wanted to make sure Elliott was okay, but she also wanted to feel Elliott's lips on hers, and the touch of her hands. She needed to hear Elliott say that there was no point in hoping. She rolled onto her side and felt very alone in her bed, but despite her yearnings she reaffirmed her position: she was not going to approach Elliott again. *If she wants me, then she's going to have to come get me.*

❖

"Ryan, who do we know at the FBI?"

"It's one in the morning," Ryan mumbled.

"I know what time it is, Ryan." Elliott could make out noises in the background. He was saying something to his wife, then it sounded like he carried the phone to the kitchen and opened the fridge. "For God's sake, wake up. The FBI. They talked to Rebecca."

"What? Why would the FBI talk to her?"

"I was hoping you could tell me. You didn't call them in, did you?"

Ryan yawned. "No, but this is extremely interesting. What exactly did she say?"

"Something about a national security issue. They told her they have recordings of her blackmail threats and she could go to jail. She thinks I orchestrated the whole thing so I could beat her at her own game."

"Rebecca is all about getting what she wants," Ryan noted. "Are you sure this is not just another game?"

"Why would she lie about this stuff?" It would be nice, at this point, to believe that Rebecca had figured out another way to manipulate her, but Elliott knew what she'd seen. "She was frightened, Ryan. She's dropping the lawsuit and she slapped my face in front of everyone."

"Well, we probably should have involved them," Ryan said. "I guess you're not the only person Rebecca's tried to scam. They must have been watching her."

"No," Elliott said grimly. "They'd have arrested her if she was their target, but they just told her to back off."

"The plot thickens." Sounding lost in thought, he asked, "Are you saying it's you they're interested in?"

"Well, if she's telling the truth, they've been listening to my phone calls."

"And if your phone has been wiretapped, your house is

probably bugged too," Ryan concluded. "So, we should take this discussion somewhere else."

Elliott felt ill. Was this her life? How could things have spun so far out of control, so fast? "I don't believe this."

Ryan launched into rapid speculation. "You know, this may not be about you specifically. You could be caught up in a wider probe. Let's not assume anything in that regard. We need to get to the bottom of this."

A *probe*? She was hearing things.

"By the way, I saw the fund-raiser incident on the late news." Ryan sounded unflustered. "I've already started—"

"It was on television?" She should have guessed someone would have a cell phone recording.

"I'm afraid so. As I said, I've already started damage control. Your brother-in-law called me right after it ran. You'll need to keep an eye on him."

"Oh, Mark's going to *love* this." He would use it against her if he could, no question about that. Elliott hoped he wouldn't track Rebecca down; she'd have to find some way to tie his hands before he did.

"I told him she's a stalker," Ryan said. "But we really shouldn't have this discussion now. We need to meet as soon as you get into work. I'll swing by. No, better yet, let's meet at the diner on Sandstone Drive. At least we know that's not bugged."

"Okay," Elliott agreed with grim resolution. She spoke her next thought out loud. "I let this go on too long." She'd allowed herself to get distracted, and she'd been stubborn. Her refusal to pay Rebecca off had been a matter of principle, but sometimes principles were a luxury.

Ryan read her mind, as he did more frequently than she liked. "It's a good thing you didn't pay her."

"Somehow, I'm not getting that."

Elliott's dry humor drew a small chuckle from her old friend. "Think about it. Guilty people are usually the first to pay up, and you're innocent, so why would you?"

His cautious tone and careful wording made her suddenly intensely aware of her situation. Right now, FBI agents were listening in. Whatever she and Ryan said could be misconstrued or used again her.

"None of this makes any sense," she said. "Why the fuck would the FBI be interested in me?"

"That's something we'll have to find out. How's eight a.m.?"

"I'll be there."

"Meantime," he warned, "don't talk to anyone."

As Elliott agreed, the line went dead and she was certain she could hear weird clicking noises. Disturbed, she dropped the receiver in its cradle and began a methodical search of her study. She wasn't sure how big a hidden listening device was, but if they'd been planted around her home she needed to find them. It would take all night, and even then she might miss one.

Elliott stopped looking under cushions and sank down on her sofa. This was a nightmare. Her life had been flowing along perfectly, and now, out of the blue, it had turned to shit. Really scary shit. Blackmail by a greedy ex was one thing, but the FBI? National security? It was so far-fetched, she felt like she'd just been zapped into another reality. Her mind lurched to Lauren. She had called her from this house, using her tapped phone line. Unwittingly she may have involved Lauren in something.

Elliott felt sick to her stomach. She had to tell her. Ryan wanted her to keep her mouth shut until they could meet and agree on how to manage the situation, but she owed Lauren more than that. Lauren had a big career to think about, and she could not risk being caught up in something like this, whatever "this" actually was. No matter what Lauren must think of her after tonight, Elliott would have to risk falling even lower in her opinion by telling her everything she knew.

She rose and located her car keys, trying to remember where she'd put her cell phone. What would Lauren make of a bizarre phone call from her at this time of night? She would sound like a crazy woman, talking about the FBI and wiretapping. *I have to see her, face-to-face, and this can't wait.*

Chapter Eleven

"You're where?" Lauren elbowed herself up and groped for the switch on her lamp, switching her phone from one ear to the other.

"Parked in your driveway," her late-night caller said.

Pushing hair off her face, Lauren swung her legs over the side of her bed and padded across the room to peer out the window. Sure enough, Elliott was standing propped against her car, gazing up at the house. "I see you."

"I see you too." Elliott waved.

"What are you doing here? It's two thirty a.m."

"Is it okay if I come in out of the cold?" There was a hint of irony in the question.

"Is that a double entendre?" Lauren queried.

"Would you like it to be?" Elliott asked softly.

Lauren's heart traded its already rapid beating for a more erratic pattern. "I'll meet you at the door."

She tossed the phone onto her bed, pulled on a robe, and hurried from her room. Elliott was at her home in the middle of the night and was talking to her as if there was something between them, or perhaps that was simply her wishful thinking. Sometimes Lauren had the impression Elliott flirted with women automatically. Now that she thought about it with some perspective, it almost seemed like a pleasant way to avoiding more meaningful conversation.

As she descended the stairs and approached the front door, she checked that her robe covered her thin silk teddy, then reached for the handle.

"Thank you."

Elliott looked as untidy as Lauren had ever seen her, in jeans and a crushed shirt, with her hair uncombed. She was still the sexiest woman alive. "Please. Come in."

"I'm sorry about this," Elliott said as they walked to the living room. "I need to talk to you."

"I'm listening." Lauren sat down in an armchair, inviting Elliott to do the same. She didn't say anything more. If Elliott wanted to talk, she was going to have to carry the conversation.

The silence seemed deafening, and Elliott finally registered that Lauren was waiting for her to state why she was here. *She's not going to make this easy for me.* She sat in the corner of the large sofa, the nearest she could get to Lauren. It hadn't escaped her that Lauren had chosen to sit alone.

"It's hard to know where to start," she said.

"I'm sorry, I didn't offer you anything." Lauren glanced toward the bar. "Would you like a drink…or I can make hot chocolate or coffee."

"No, but thanks. I don't want to drag this out." As soon as she'd spoken, she realized her remark had hurt Lauren. The soft blue eyes looked away and Lauren's shoulders tightened just enough to disturb the folds of her robe. Elliott could not ignore the outline of her body beneath the heavy satin. She was so beautiful, it was torture not to reach out and touch her. Suddenly desperate not to be misunderstood, she said, "What I mean is, it's late and I know you should be sleeping. I wouldn't be here if it wasn't important."

"Yes." Lauren nervously waited to see where Elliott was going with this.

"What happened at the fund-raiser…there's something I need to explain."

"You don't need to explain anything to me," Lauren said.

Until very recently, Elliott would have agreed. She'd just spent the past couple of weeks trying to convince herself that she wasn't in any way accountable to the woman opposite her. Yet here she was, about to explain herself and ask for understanding.

"The woman who slapped me is Rebecca Alsip. I had a brief affair with her a while ago." Lauren's expression did not alter, but Elliott could sense the emotion in her and wondered what it was. Embarrassment? Distaste? Jealousy? *I can hope.* "For the past couple of months, she's been trying to extort money from me."

This time a discernable emotion stirred the smooth perfection of Lauren's face. Her eyes widened and her mouth parted in shock. "Blackmail?"

"Yes. When I wouldn't pay, she threatened me with a lawsuit. I can show you the paperwork." Elliott wasn't sure why she made that offer. The last thing she wanted was for Lauren to read a list of sordid lies intended to assassinate her character.

"You don't have to do that," Lauren said with a perplexed frown, as if there was something strange about the offer. "I believe what you are saying."

"To cut a long story short, she came to the fund-raiser because she was angry. The FBI had just told her to back off."

"You called the FBI?" Lauren was relieved. Too often people being blackmailed were afraid to inform the authorities because they were in a vulnerable position. A blackmailer usually had some dirt and counted on their victim's desire to keep it hidden. If the FBI was involved, that meant the threat would be dealt with, and it certainly explained why Rebecca had been angry enough to create a public spectacle. She'd embarrassed Elliott out of spite.

Elliott was so distracted by the warmth flooding Lauren's gaze that she forgot to speak for a few seconds. She allowed her eyes to linger on Lauren's lips, and memory swept order from her mind.

Hoarsely, reluctantly, she said, "No, I didn't call them, although I probably should have." She met Lauren's puzzled stare. "I don't really know how to say this, but I think I'm being investigated. They told Rebecca that they recorded her blackmail threats. They said it was about national security."

Lauren could feel the blood leaving her face. What on earth

was Elliott involved in that she'd attracted the attention of the feds? "Do you have any idea what this could be about?"

"I promise you, I have absolutely no idea. This came out of the blue. I haven't done anything wrong. Why would they be investigating me? It doesn't make any sense. It's making me crazy." Elliott grasped Lauren's hand like a lifeline.

"I don't know. And it's really interesting that they risked contacting Rebecca. If she told you, that could ruin their case. Their cover would be blown. She must have been a problem for them, somehow. I'm sure they don't want media sniffing around you and your company, and she was planning to create publicity if she wasn't paid off. Perhaps that was the issue for them."

Elliott was still baffled, but Lauren's theory made more sense than anything else she'd considered, including the possibility that Senator Jarvis had somehow learned of the situation. Obviously the FBI would not want nosey reporters hanging around. "What am I going to do?"

"Find out anything you can about what they're doing, and start looking for a problem close to home...people behaving strangely around you, unusual happenings at work...something must have attracted their attention."

"But they can't tap my phone without a warrant, can they?" Not that she would know. Wiretapping was not like searching her house.

"Legally, no, but that doesn't mean it doesn't go on. The FBI has been known to use *national security* to justify just about everything they do these days."

"Shit."

Lauren stared down at the hand holding her own. The contact made her flesh tingle with awareness, reminding her that there was so much more she wanted. She imagined standing up and drawing Elliott with her, leaning into that unforgettable body, letting her robe drop to the floor. Elliott must have mistaken her distraction for expectant silence; she started talking again in a rush.

"I thought about what you said." Elliott plunged into the other subject crowding her mind. "In your phone message. You made some good points." It was still difficult for her to admit that to herself, let alone to Lauren.

"Well, I am an attorney, you know." Lauren's heart began to beat evenly again.

Elliott laughed, and some of the tension left her body. "Yes, and somehow I don't think I would have a chance to win an argument with you."

Warmth spread through Lauren's limbs as Elliott laughed. She realized just how much she missed it. "Sure you do. I don't think a woman as successful as you lacks the skill to be persuasive and win an argument or two."

"Yeah, well, I've been lucky once or twice."

"Once or twice? You're far too modest, Elliott."

The sound of Lauren speaking her name sent shivers up and down her spine. *I've been a fool.* With rare impulsiveness, she said, "I've missed you."

"I was here," Lauren replied, making her point gently but firmly. Elliott could have called her anytime, but had chosen not to.

Her subtle reproof hit home, and Elliott tried to lighten the conversation. "I spent some time in Paris."

"And I was in Bangalore."

"Maine?"

"Not Bangor, Bangalore."

"India? How long were you there?" Elliott cringed at the stupid question but was relieved that they were talking about the mundane for a moment. She needed some time to plan the conversation she knew they had to have.

"Almost two weeks," Lauren said. "I have a whole new appreciation for our taxis and air-conditioning." She stifled a yawn.

Not wanting to outstay her welcome, Elliott said, "Look, I'll let you go. I just wanted to give you a heads-up about the FBI because they probably have you on tape as well. I have to assume my phone is tapped and my house is bugged."

She didn't want to release Lauren's hand but she felt a small tug and relaxed her fingers, surrendering that one tingling point of connection between them.

Lauren was disappointed that the conversation was coming to an end, but she would not do anything to prolong it. If Elliott had anything else to say to her, she knew how to form a sentence. They stared at one another, and Lauren had the distinct impression Elliott was waiting for a signal from her.

Lauren adopted a tone of friendly concern. "Thank you for telling me about this. It was the honorable thing to do."

"Actually, it was more than that," Elliott admitted tentatively. "I wanted to see you."

"All right." It was difficult for Lauren not to add anything more.

She's making me go there. Elliott had to admire her companion's strength of will. She'd laid down her ultimatum and she wasn't budging. The ball remained in Elliott's court. Hesitantly, she said, "I'm sorry."

Lauren studied her intently but said nothing.

"For backing away. I can't explain exactly why I did, but I'm not enjoying myself one little bit." Elliott sighed. "Lauren, I have a lot of experience in casual affairs, but I'm a beginner as far as anything else is concerned, which, if you think about it, makes us both inexperienced in our own ways."

She held her breath and was rewarded with a smile that transformed Lauren's face from placid distance to something so inviting and real that Elliott could only smile exactly the same way in return.

"I'm glad you said that," Lauren responded simply.

"So am I."

"What are we going to do about this investigation?"

"We?"

"You can't imagine I'll just stand by and wait for something unfortunate to happen to you," Lauren said. "Obviously there's been some kind of mistake, and we need to get to the bottom of it."

Elliott checked her wristwatch. "Well, I'm meeting with my attorney later this morning."

"Any objection if I sit in?"

Since when had a woman ever stood by her, other than a family member or Teresa? It was the last thing she'd expected, coming here. "No, none at all." A foolish smile tugged at Elliott's lips.

"Good." Lauren rose to her feet and the front of her robe parted just enough to deliver an image Elliott knew she would not be able to get out of her mind all day. "Where's the meeting?"

Elliott stood and took a business card from her wallet. Lauren supplied her with a pen from the rolltop desk in one corner of the room, and she jotted down Ryan's details on the reverse. As they walked to the front door, she said, "I appreciate this, Lauren."

"I'd do the same for anyone I care about."

There it was, a clear opening. Elliott sidestepped it, not quite ready to jump in the deep end. "That means a lot," she said warmly. "Get some sleep."

"You too." Lauren made no move to invite the kiss she sensed floating between them. She let Elliott walk away and waited for her to look back.

And Elliott did.

❖

The late-morning sun was warm on her face as Lauren sat on her deck enjoying her second cup of coffee while she waited for Elliott to pick her up. She'd been surprised by the invitation to the baseball game that weekend. Elliott had called her after their Monday meeting with Ryan, thanking her again and asking if she wanted to join her. In the days since, Elliott had sent her a fruit basket and phoned her a couple of times to update her on their progress with the cloud hanging over her. So far, they hadn't found out much, and Ryan was urging Elliott to arrange to speak to a special agent he knew. Elliott had said she would think about it.

Lauren's eyes were drawn to one of several people jogging along the shoreline. She waved in acknowledgment as a slight woman in an orange running suit passed in front of her. Anne lived next door, and over the past five years they'd become friends. It was clear to Lauren early on that Anne was a lesbian, and occasionally they'd discussed the fact.

Lauren recalled the first party Anne invited her to. She had been slightly nervous as one of the few straight women in a group that was primarily lesbians, but Anne had assured her that she would not be hit on and would probably meet some interesting women. Lauren had enjoyed herself thoroughly, and during the evening she'd been intrigued by the way the guests interacted with each other and with their partners. Several couples were obviously deeply in love, some on the second or third decade of their relationship, and a few women were clearly singles on the make.

What struck her the most was the bond she felt with these women. This connection strengthened as she spent more time with Anne and her friends, and it slowly dawned on her that she was missing a lot in her relationships with men. She had dated throughout college and law school and into her professional years. She had come close to marrying one man in particular but broke off the engagement at the last minute. Somehow, deep inside she knew that she did not want to spend the rest of her life with him.

Over the past few years, she'd talked with Anne about her growing suspicion that she was a lesbian, and Anne had been wonderful in guiding Lauren through her thoughts and feelings without leading her down any specific path. Over pots of coffee, glasses of wine, and miles of walking the California shoreline, Lauren had vocalized and debated with Anne what she was thinking and feeling, and ultimately she came to her own conclusion.

Throughout this process she had dated women sometimes and had come close to sleeping with one of them, but she had not felt comfortable enough to make love with her. She had attributed her hesitation in losing her virginity this time around to her level of maturity, compared to twenty years ago when she was fumbling around with Steve Casper in his backyard. She knew that the first time she made love to a woman would be the defining moment in her life, and she wasn't going to jump into it without being absolutely sure. Lauren was not naïve enough to believe that she would have to be in love with the woman, but she knew that she would know when it was right.

"Lauren?" Elliott was standing at the corner of the deck, looking at her curiously.

And it is definitely right with you, Elliott Foster. "Hi."

"I thought you might be out here. I rang the bell several times and you didn't answer." Unbeknownst to Lauren, Elliott had taken the opportunity to silently observe her before she announced her arrival. Watching Lauren took her breath away. She was absolutely beautiful sitting relaxed with the ocean breeze ruffling her hair.

Lauren sat up straighter in her chair. "Sorry, you caught me daydreaming."

"If this were my place, that's all I'd be able to get done. I can see why you love it out here."

"I could sit here all day. As a matter of fact, some days I do," Lauren said with a wistful smile. "But not today. Today I have a baseball game to go to, and I *love* baseball!"

The afternoon was beautiful, she thought yet again an hour later when they were finally in the stadium. "These seats are fabulous," she said, looking at the field. They were on the second level, directly behind home plate.

"Thanks. We get a lot of foul balls, so we need to pay attention to the game." *And you are too cute in that baseball cap and your Ray-Bans.*

Elliott had been surprised to learn that Lauren was an avid baseball fan. Elliott enjoyed the experience of going to a game, eating a hot dog and drinking a beer or two as she cheered for her home team, but Lauren kept a running dialogue of the players and their stats throughout. Several times during the game Lauren reached over and touched Elliott's arm when she couldn't control her enthusiasm at a particularly exciting play. Each time this happened, Elliott could feel the heat travel from her arm and land in her crotch. *Good God, it's hot today.*

It was one of the most enjoyable games Elliott had attended in quite a while, ending on a positive note as the Padres beat the Astros in extra innings. Elliott suggested they have an early dinner at the Dugout, a crowded, noisy bar and grill not far from the stadium, and they rehashed the game over pizza and beer, sticking to their agreement not to talk about work or "the situation," which was how they referred to Elliott's FBI dilemma. The sun was just beginning to set by the time they pulled into Lauren's driveway much later.

"I had a great time, Elliott. Thanks for inviting me." *God, I love saying her name.*

"Had I known that you'd be my own personal play-by-play commentator, I'd have invited you earlier in the season," Elliott teased as she walked Lauren to her door.

Lauren cringed. "Was I too chatty? My friends are always telling me to shut up when we watch a game." She cast a cautious glance at Elliott and was met with laughing eyes.

"Absolutely not. As a matter of fact, when you went to the restroom the man sitting beside me asked if you were a scout, you know so much about each player."

"Oh jeez..." Lauren was slightly embarrassed as she opened her front door.

"He even asked me if you were coming to the series next week with the Diamondbacks. I think he really enjoyed you." *As did I.*

"Well, sometimes I kinda get caught up in it all." Lauren swept away a piece of dirt from her threshold with her foot.

"Kinda?" Elliott tilted her head mischievously.

Lauren knew that Elliott was teasing her and she relaxed. She didn't want the day to end and yearned to invite Elliott in. But when Elliott did not make any move to suggest she would welcome the invitation, Lauren simply said, "Thanks again, Elliott," and retreated indoors.

Left standing alone on the porch, Elliott contemplated knocking, but she was strangely reluctant to change the mood of their day together by making it about the night.

She had just been on a date, she realized, an ordinary date that was not about getting the woman she was with into bed as quickly as possible. Even more astounding was the fact that she had enjoyed it for what it was and she couldn't wait to be with Lauren again, regardless of the circumstances.

CHAPTER TWELVE

A card arrived two days later from the director of the children's shelter thanking Elliott for tickets to the same game she and Lauren had attended. It was signed, in different levels of penmanship and ink colors, by the twenty kids who had gone to the game. Smiling, Elliott opened the plain wooden box on her desk that was almost overflowing with similar notes. Before she slipped the card inside, she studied one particular signature.

The print was so small she could hardly make out the name. She knew nothing about handwriting analysis or the children but she had the impression the author was a small, frightened girl. She pictured a blank stare exactly like the one of the little girl who sometimes haunted her dreams.

Elliott hadn't dreamed about her regularly in years, but she knew the dream by heart. She was fifteen and was sitting in the backseat of the car assigned to pick her up at the airport for Christmas. She was to meet her father and sister and spend a week skiing in the Rockies, but she knew from previous Christmases that she would most likely be spending the holiday without her father.

It was bitterly cold outside, but she was more than comfortable in the well-heated limousine. The windows were tinted almost black but provided her a view of the world outside. The scene was one she would never forget. The limo had stopped at a red light, and she saw a mother huddled in a doorway with a child in her lap. Both were wrapped in a ragged blanket, trying to keep warm. The little girl was no more than four years old, and she lifted her head and seemed to look directly at Elliott. The haunted look in her eyes spoke of despair and hopelessness instead of excitement at the upcoming holiday. The light changed to green then, and the limo pulled away.

Elliott had never forgotten the look in that little girl's eyes, and she'd spent most of her break searching for mother and child, wanting nothing more than to put a smile on that little girl's face. The child had practically nothing, but she had her mother. Elliott, on the other hand, had all the trappings that money could buy but she'd lost her mother long ago, and what she really wanted was her father. She remembered going to a party where the icebreaker was to tell the worst thing you had ever done. She lied. How could she tell a room full of strangers that the worst thing she ever did was let the chauffeur drive away from that little girl and her mother?

She tried every day to make up for that by giving hundreds of thousands of dollars to help bring a sliver of hope to an unhappy child. A tear slid down her cheek and she wiped it away, cursing the emotions that were still so close to the surface after all these years. After returning the box to its usual place, she swung her chair around at the sound of her door opening and came face-to-face with the one person she did not want to deal with first thing this week. She wasn't surprised to see him in her office, however. "Why do I think you're not here to give me good news?"

"Elliott…"

She hated it when Ryan used that tone with her. It made her feel like a petulant child.

"They want to talk to you." Ryan didn't need to say the *they* was the FBI. He had made some calls and was finally passed on to the special agent in charge. He was given very little information other than they wanted to talk with her.

The mere thought set her teeth on edge. Why should she, an innocent member of the public, have to account for herself to a federal agency that had completely ignored her right to privacy? They should be in here, explaining themselves to her.

"You have to take care of this. If you don't do it your way, it will happen their way, and trust me on this, Elliott, you don't want that."

She slammed her fist on the desk. "You know as well as I do that rich people pay all the time to make this kind of shit go away. Can't you just file a motion or something? Make them bring charges or get out of my life."

His patience was wearing thin. "It's not that simple. We need to know why they targeted you. If you cooperate now, at least we can see where their questions are going."

"It can't be anything personal." She lived her life as she wanted to, not the way others expected her to, but she wasn't doing anything illegal and the longer she was at the helm of Foster McKenzie, the less of a personal life she had anyway. "I know I'm not exactly establishment, but they must have better things to do than hassle me because of..." She trailed off. "We still don't have a clue what it's about."

"We can't be certain it's you they're investigating," Ryan reminded her. "It's just one possibility. Anyway, when was the last time you looked in the mirror? You are establishment, whether you like it or not. You're just damn lucky you've sailed through life the way you have before now." When she didn't reply he pulled out all the stops. "I'm surprised, Elliott. It's not like you to run away from a challenge."

He was right. She had never backed down from a fight in her life. She could live with tittering media speculation on the face-slap—her publicist was making sure their spin also made it into print: the wealthy CEO stalked by a gold digger who was making up stories about their association.

Thankfully a couple of tabloid reporters had done their homework on Rebecca and found she'd once worked as an exotic dancer for six months. This, coupled with a husband thirty years older than her who had announced his plans for divorce, made the newspapers careful. So far it was Elliott's story they believed. One of them had even run a flattering profile of her as a philanthropist, commenting in the article that she, like many wealthy people, was the target of opportunists. The damage control was working well. What they didn't need was a headline that read FBI INVESTIGATES CEO.

"Okay," she said. "I'll cooperate."

❖

Lauren opened the door to Elliott wearing faded jeans that accentuated her long legs, a blue chambray shirt, and boots. *Oh my God, she looks hot. Keep your cool, Lauren.*

"Hi, I'm sorry I didn't call. Are you up for dinner?" Elliott asked hopefully.

She'd sat in her car at the end of Lauren's street for thirty minutes before ringing the bell. She knew she should have called first, but the meeting with the FBI that morning had been unsettling and she had an overwhelming need to see Lauren. She'd answered questions for hours, and at Ryan's urging took the Fifth Amendment on several. When it was over, she and Ryan had nothing concrete, but the direction of the questioning gave them some clues. The FBI wanted access to all Foster McKenzie's client information. They refused to single out individual clients or identify any particular industry they wanted to explore. However, among the questions they'd asked, Elliott had detected a slant toward foreign companies. They'd also asked her a lot of questions about her overseas travel, including the predictable ones about contacts in the Middle East.

Elliott had told them she would think about their request for access to confidential files. She needed to buy herself some time to investigate the current client list and any deals on the table.

"Dinner? I'd love it," Lauren said. Work had been so busy over the last few days that she had been skipping meals. She now felt deprived; Elliott's surprise invitation couldn't have happened at a better time. "Come in." She opened the door wide and glanced at the clock. She needed to check in with her office before she went out for the evening. "Want to pour yourself a drink while I get changed?"

"Thanks, I will."

Elliott stepped into the foyer and Lauren had a brief, unsettling flash of the intense kiss they had shared right here just weeks ago. Her knees began to shake and her eyes were drawn to the lips that had burned her skin with such passion. Somehow she managed to close the front door.

"There's beer in the refrigerator. Why don't you go out onto the deck?"

As she moved toward the stairs, Elliott said, "Dress casual."

"Even better." Elliott heard the delight in Lauren's voice, and her blood beat a little faster.

After the initial thrill of seeing Elliott again, Lauren had calmed down but her pulse still raced. She wasn't sure what this evening was all about but was anxious to find out.

Elliott watched color stain Lauren's cheeks. She could almost taste her skin and hear her low moans of excitement. Her fingers ached to touch the soft skin, but she didn't give in to the desire. "Would you like me to fix you something as well?"

"Sure. A beer sounds good. I'll see you out there."

Elliott found the kitchen and poured their drinks, enjoying the contented, domestic feel of sharing this simple after-work ritual with another person. Lauren's deck faced the ocean, and Elliott was immediately hit with a cool salty breeze when she carried their glasses outdoors. She could just barely see the waves cresting on the shore in the dying sunlight. Inhaling the clean air, she started to relax. She still wasn't sure why she was here, but she was glad Lauren had accepted her invitation. She leaned against the deck railing and got lost in the quiet sounds of the ocean.

At some point she sensed she was being watched, but she didn't hear Lauren come outside until she was standing beside her, dressed casually in comfortable khakis and a blue short-sleeve shirt that brought out the flecks in her eyes. *Oh, shit. I need to be careful here.*

"This is my hideaway from the world." Lauren gazed toward the horizon. "I step out here and immediately start to decompress. When I think I'm getting too big for my britches I look at the water and it brings everything back into focus. It makes me realize I'm just a puny little speck in the overall scheme of things." When Elliott chuckled, she inquired, "What?"

"Your comment just surprised me."

"Why?"

"Well…" Elliott hustled to find the right words. "It's probably stereotypical and I apologize up front if you're offended, but most attorneys I know are pretty arrogant and would never consider themselves just a puny little speck in the overall scheme of things."

Lauren sipped her beer as she contemplated Elliott's observation. "You're right, that is a stereotype that unfortunately is more true than not. But I don't define myself as an attorney." Lauren hoped she didn't sound as defensive as she felt. She knew that the seedier side of her profession created the lawyer jokes but she was not one of them and would never become one.

"How *do* you define yourself?" Elliott was fascinated by what her answer would be.

Lauren thought for a moment. "Well, I'd say that I'm a woman first." She was proud that she was a woman and had always strived to be poised and articulate.

Yes, you are definitely a woman. "What comes second?"

"I'm a daughter and then a friend."

"And where would you place being an attorney?" Elliott thought that this conversation was an interesting way to learn more about the chic woman standing so casually beside her.

"Being an attorney is somewhere further down the list. It's a job, it's what I do, not who I am." Lauren had never really verbalized this but suddenly it was very clear. "And what about Elliott Foster? How do you define who you are?"

Elliott immediately became uncomfortable when the questioning turned her way. Actually, she didn't really know how to answer it anymore. "Best definition right now? I'm starving. Shall we go?"

Lauren didn't miss the not-so-subtle way that Elliott deflected the question. "I'm ready."

"Would you like to take a stroll along the water?" Elliott asked as they pulled into Lauren's drive several hours later. She'd had an enjoyable evening and was not ready for it to end.

"I'd love it. I need to walk off this dinner."

She had eaten way too much, including a decadent piece of cheesecake, and she was feeling more than a little stuffed. A little exercise was just what she needed, and she loved the peacefulness of the shoreline. She walked silently beside Elliott, remembering a similar walk they'd shared the night of the ballet. The stillness of the night was broken only by the waves softly rolling onto the sand at high tide.

Breaking the silence, Lauren commented softly, "After spending two weeks with the 6.2 billion people in India, I think I appreciate this place even more. And thank you. This evening was wonderful." What she really wanted to say was that it was wonderful to spend the evening with Elliott and it wouldn't have mattered what they had done.

"I'm glad you had a good time. I did too." Elliott had thought several times just how enjoyable the evening was. She found Lauren to be charming, witty, and very well versed in politics, social events, and the arts. As the lights of Lauren's patio came into view, she realized that outside of a bedroom, she had never been in the presence of a beautiful woman for so long without feeling like she had to exchange a single word.

The experience was new for her and slightly uncomfortable, but before she could dwell on it, Lauren angled her head and asked, "How did your interview go?"

"I wish I could say enlightening, but I can't."

Lauren wanted to ask more questions; she'd known about the meeting with the FBI. But Elliott was clearly unsettled, so she changed the subject. "Elliott, I'd like to ask you a favor, but I don't want you to feel obligated." That was an ominous way to begin a conversation, but she wanted to say it right up front.

The slight brooding in Elliott's expression lifted, as if she were relieved to focus on something else. "Okay, no obligation felt. What is it?"

"I'm a mentor to a teenage girl, and one of the things I'm doing is exposing her to successful women to give her an idea of what she can accomplish in life if she stays in school and keeps out of trouble."

"Really?" *Will this woman always surprise me?* "How long have you been doing this?"

"About three years now. Tonya is one of eight children and lives in the public housing on Third and Lancaster."

Elliott knew the location. The children in that school district often were the recipients of her anonymous donations.

"She has a lot of potential, and in the last six months or so she's finally started to realize it." Lauren smiled, remembering the first time Tonya began to see this in herself.

"How old is she?" Elliott took note of the way Lauren's eyes lit up as she talked about the girl.

"Fifteen, going on thirty-three." Lauren joined Elliott's laughing.

"How can I help?"

Lauren took a deep breath. Despite what was going on between them, or not going on, Elliott would be an excellent role model for Tonya. "I'd like for her to meet you. You don't have to prepare anything."

"I'd be happy to," Elliott said without hesitation.

"If you could spare an hour to talk to her, answer her questions."

"Absolutely."

Elliott's response seemed to fall on deaf ears; Lauren kept her sales pitch going. "Just talk to her about the challenges you face as a woman who owns a business and how important it is to stay focused on your goals. You know, that sort of thing." Lauren had barely taken a breath.

Calmly, Elliott said, "Lauren, I said I'd be happy to."

"You would?" Lauren had not expected her to agree, yet at the same time she was not really surprised at all.

"Of course. I love kids and I'd be more than willing to help someone not make the same mistakes I did." Elliott looked at her calendar. "When?"

"Is Saturday too soon?" Lauren hoped Elliott was free that day. She met with Tonya every two weeks, and Tonya needed support and encouragement quickly now that she was on the right track.

"No, Saturday is fine."

They agreed on ten thirty and Lauren said, "That's perfect. Would it be too much of an imposition if we came to your office?" She was sure it would impress Tonya, and she was not above using everything at her disposal to help her, including the trappings of a fine office.

"No problem. It's after hours, so no one will be around. Do I need to do anything special?"

"No. Just be yourself. I think Tonya will be suitably impressed." *As am I.*

"I think I can do that. I'll try not to be too flamboyant and outrageous." Elliott breathed a sigh of relief when Lauren laughed.

"Thanks, Elliott, I appreciate it."

"My pleasure." Elliott's voice was soft and husky.

Lauren liked the sound of that and the sound of Elliott's voice saying it. She wanted to get lost in the feeling that voice sent cascading through her.

Elliott wondered how much it had cost her to ask for this favor. She was intrigued by the character that emerged the more she got to know Lauren. She had to admit that the opportunity to see her again was definitely pleasing. After spending time with Lauren, she had come to realize that she was missing companionship. Pure and simple companionship, without the pressure of business or sex, and with no intent other than spending time with someone special.

As they neared Lauren's house she said, "I'll walk you to the door."

"You don't have to do that."

"My father raised me better than that. He'd come back to haunt me if I let a beautiful woman walk to the door unaccompanied." Elliott placed her hand on the small of Lauren's back as they climbed the few stairs to the front door.

Lauren's mind raced as she unlocked the deadbolt. *Was this a date? What do we do now? Is she going to kiss me?* After several moments it was apparent that Elliott didn't know the answers either. "Thanks again for a lovely evening, Elliott. Good night."

Elliott was surprised and relieved when Lauren closed the door. Her mind and body had been in direct conflict over what she wanted to do, standing with Lauren on her porch. She battled over whether or not to simply say good night or kiss her senseless. Lauren had given no indication of her preference, and Elliott sensed she would not be rejected if she moved toward her. But before one could overrule the other, Lauren had taken the decision out of her hands by saying good night. With sharp realization Elliott recalled Lauren's words: *I won't approach you again.* As she strolled back to her car, she understood that Lauren meant exactly what she'd said.

❖

"Mark, I've told you before, I don't want you in my office if I'm not here." Her brother-in-law had his ass in her chair and his feet on her desk. She wanted to slap the smug look off his face but refrained. She was just about to her limit with him, Stephanie be damned.

"Good afternoon to you too, Elliott." He didn't move.

Elliott walked around her desk and batted his feet off the polished cherrywood. The momentum made him stand up, and he strutted to the chair across from her. She often thought he walked like a stuffed peacock. "What do you want?"

"No small talk, El? No how are you, Mark, or how are Stephanie and the kids? Tsk, tsk. I know you have better office etiquette than that."

She hated it when he called her El and hated it even more when he reminded her he was married to her sister. She pasted a look of boredom on her face and didn't answer him.

"I came by to let you know I had the preliminary marketing materials drawn up on the Gallien deal."

The Gallien deal was a multi-million-dollar investment proposal that Mark had pitched unsuccessfully to her several weeks earlier. As she'd listened to his proposition, she detected more than the usual amount of greed in his eyes. Apparently Mark hadn't heard what he didn't want to hear.

"I told you that Foster is not going to recommend Gallien to anyone."

"Elliott, this could mean millions to our clients and to us. We could write our ticket with this one."

You mean millions to you. "We already have our ticket. It's built on things like honesty and integrity. I'm not going to endorse a deal that doesn't meet our standards."

"I don't understand." Mark was trying to keep the edge out of his voice but she knew him better than that. "You read the prospectus, you saw the numbers. It's cash in the bank."

She didn't have time for his bullshit and was not interested in pacifying him. "Mark, the answer is no."

His expression turned ugly. "Elliott, you're making a mistake. Gallien is going big, and the board is going to want answers as to why we didn't get involved."

She refused to take the bait. She would not have Mark's insinuations of going to the board determine what she did. This was a bad deal and she knew it. "Is there anything else, Mark? I've got things to do."

His answer was to slam the door behind him. A split second later it opened again and Teresa entered. "Rebecca's here."

CHAPTER THIRTEEN

"Christ." Elliott's stomach seized. This was not going to be pretty.

"Do you want me to get Ryan on the phone?" Teresa offered.

"No, he's in Cancun with his family. Go ahead and show her in. If no one comes out after ten minutes, call 911. Okay?"

Teresa gave her a grim smile. "It's your funeral."

Elliott steeled herself. She had just started to kid herself that Rebecca was out of her life for good, scared off by the FBI and exposed by the media. But the blond bombshell walked in like she owned the place and sat in one of the wingback chairs in front of her desk. She was wearing an expensive suit, and the skirt bared most of her thigh when she crossed her legs. It never crossed Elliott's mind to sneak a peek.

"Rebecca," she said by way of greeting. It was too soon to guess at her mood, so she remained on high alert.

"I'll get right to the point," Rebecca said. "I was thinking about our last chat."

Chat was not the word Elliott would have used. "What about it?"

"We ended things badly. I don't think you understand my position, Elliott." Her voice was soft and sweet.

"Refresh my memory."

"I hate to talk about money. It is just so uncouth." Rebecca fancied herself as upper crust when in fact she had simply traded on her looks to leave the trailer park behind. "But thanks to you, my husband is divorcing me, and that's a problem."

"Shit happens." Elliott relaxed back in her chair and smiled.

An eerie sense of calm settled over her. She could handle Rebecca. Every last trace of desire had vanished. She allowed her eyes to drift over the body that had once distracted her so completely. Something had changed about Rebecca's appearance. Maybe she'd lost weight or had "work." Her eyes seemed flintier and her nose more porous. Her mouth looked puffy instead of pouty. Elliott didn't even find her attractive, let alone irresistible. Knowing she finally had the clear-sightedness to deal with her appropriately, she listened to the latest demand.

"So I'm owed some sort of compensation. I'm now suffering because of you. If it wasn't for who you are, I wouldn't have television reporters pestering me."

Elliott shrugged. "You would not have hit on me if it wasn't for who I am, either. Or attempted to blackmail me."

"I've dropped the lawsuit and I'm not talking to reporters, just like the FBI said. And they took away my computer, so I can't do anything with those e-mails. What more do you want?"

"I want you to walk away," Elliott said. "Just get out of my life."

Rebecca's eyes glittered and she smoothed her tight top down over her ample breasts. "Then we can do each other a favor. I'm willing to leave San Diego if I have enough money to get settled somewhere."

"Sounds like more blackmail to me," Elliott noted.

"Call it whatever you like. I call it buying peace and quiet."

Elliott leaned her elbows on the desk and steepled her fingers under her chin. "My life will be peaceful if I pay you to be quiet. Is that how it is?"

"I knew you would see it my way." Smug satisfaction plastered Rebecca's face.

"No, I don't." Elliott picked up the phone. "Teresa, please show Ms. Alsip out."

"No?" Rebecca's voice became as hard as the glare in her eyes. "I don't think you want to do that."

"Why, because you'll call me names to my board?" Elliott laughed. "Be my guest. I told you, they know I'm a lesbian, and anyone who forgot has seen it in the newspaper by now. My clients also know, and as far as they're concerned, as long as I continue to make them rich, they don't care."

"They will when I put a video of us on the Internet." Rebecca announced her trump card with tangible glee.

Elliott had no idea if Rebecca had kept her most embarrassing evidence until last or if she was simply inventing a new lever now that the FBI had prevented her from going public with the damaging e-mails. It no longer mattered. She reached calmly under a stack of papers and pulled out the small recording machine she habitually used to record her thoughts about various projects. Teresa later converted her ramblings into coherent notes.

"You don't have an edge, Rebecca. You have a cliff, and I have what it takes to push you over. I'm calling your bluff. I'm going to give this tape to the FBI and you'll be out of my life for good. You know, Rebecca, I don't think they're going to be happy to know you acted against their instructions in a matter of national security. But relax, I'm sure you'll make new friends in prison. You might even learn how to fuck better."

Rebecca blinked uncertainly. "You wouldn't do that to me."

From the doorway, Teresa spoke up. "Ms. Alsip, may I call a taxi for you?"

"Elliott?" Rebecca finally seemed to understand she had no bargaining chips. Her chest heaving, she stood. "What am I supposed to do? I can't *work*."

Teresa snorted.

"There is one thing I will do for you, Rebecca," Elliott said in a benevolent tone. "You're asking me for money because we had sex, correct?"

Rebecca nodded uneasily. "If you put it that way."

"Hookers are entitled to be paid for their services. I will admit, I wasn't aware that our arrangement was supposed to be professional, but I know my responsibilities." Elliott opened the side drawer of her desk and pulled out a stack of bills, then rose and walked around her desk to stand in front of Rebecca. She tossed the bills in her lap. "This is what you're worth. Now get out."

Rebecca didn't say another word. She put the cash in her Gucci purse and walked out.

❖

"She seems to be a great kid," Elliott observed as she and Lauren waited outside the dressing room for Tonya to finish trying on jeans. Their discussion earlier that morning had turned into lunch and a shopping spree.

Lauren smiled. "Yes she is. She's come a long way."

"I'm sure you're the reason. She obviously looks up to you."

Lauren acknowledged the compliment. "Thanks. It's a big responsibility, but Tonya's done all the work. I'm just enjoying myself helping her get there. We haven't missed a scheduled day the entire time we've been together. It's important to both of us."

"You continually surprise me," Elliott said, thinking out loud.

"I'll take that as a compliment…I guess," Lauren teased.

Further conversation was thwarted when Tonya emerged from the dressing room, determined to find a shirt to match the jeans in her hand. "And Lauren needs a swimsuit," she announced eagerly.

"I can help with that," Elliott offered. "I have swimsuit expertise." She looked long and hard at those areas on Lauren's body that would be covered by a suit. The tinier the better.

"I'm sure you do." Lauren waited until Tonya was distracted by a display of swimwear, then elbowed Elliott sharply. "Stop it. You're making me—" She almost said "wet" but inserted, "nervous."

Elliott's bold stare and raised eyebrows only made matters worse, and Lauren took refuge in the racks of skimpy costumes. Under relentless pressure from her companions, she finally agreed to try on a suit that Tonya picked out. It took several minutes of cajoling and outright begging by Tonya to get her to come out and model the suit. *I can't go out there dressed in this! Actually, I can't go out there undressed like this!* Lauren took one last look in the mirror and spoke so only she could hear. *On second thought, maybe I should.*

Elliott was sitting next to Tonya, both of them giggling, when Lauren stepped out. The giggling ceased and her wide-eyed audience stared in silence.

Elliott's breath stopped in her throat. *Holy Mother of God.* Her blood pounded and her ears roared as she surveyed the expanse of skin left uncovered by the bikini. She was thankful to be sitting down, because she began to feel light-headed as her eyes locked on the bronzed body that was so close she could touch it. She gripped the bottom of the seat to keep from reaching out and caressing the beautiful form. As Lauren performed a slow turn, Elliott felt a gush of arousal dampen her panties.

Bingo! Lauren was in no doubt of what she saw in Elliott's eyes, and she was proud to know that she could make her react this way. She knew Elliott had desired her once, and there was always a level of flirtation between them, but until this moment she had been uncertain of her true feelings. The undisguised desire in her eyes was as loud and clear as if she'd shouted it from a mountaintop. Lauren's body grew hot in the places where Elliott's eyes traveled and she knew her nipples had grown hard when Elliott's eyes widened at that spot.

Fortunately, or unfortunately, Tonya stepped in front of Lauren to show her another suit before either of them could act, and Lauren wasn't sure if she was relieved or disappointed. She stepped back into the dressing room on shaking legs. She had never felt as bare as she had when she saw the look of burning longing in Elliott's eyes. She took her time dressing, reluctant yet anxious to come face-to-face with the woman who had ravished her with her eyes. Her cheeks were flushed when she returned to her companions and when her eyes met Elliott's she felt as naked as she had a moment ago, even though she was now fully clothed.

Elliott was subdued for the rest of the shopping trip and kept her distance from Lauren to ease the temptation to reach out and touch her. If she acted on her urges, she knew she wouldn't be able to stop and that frightened her. As they wandered from store to store,

Elliott distracted herself by talking with Tonya and taking charge of the increasing number of shopping sacks.

"How about I take you two beautiful women out to dinner?" She directed the question to Lauren when everyone had agreed their feet were killing them and it was time to stop.

Tonya excitedly accepted, and after a dinner of hamburgers and ice cream they took her home, then Lauren drove Elliott back to her office parking lot to pick up her car.

"I had a great time today," Elliott said as Lauren parked. "I can't remember when I've had so much fun, especially shopping. I generally hate shopping." She rolled her eyes expressively.

"You hate shopping? Elliott, that's almost un-American!" Elliott laughed and Lauren continued. "If you hate shopping, why did you want to come along?"

Elliott hesitated a few moments as she thought about her answer. She decided that honesty was the best policy. "Because it sounded like fun." Okay, a half-truth was still honest.

"Well, I know Tonya enjoyed having you along. Thanks for agreeing to meet with her."

"It was my pleasure."

Elliott's voice seemed tense, and Lauren turned to face her. She'd noticed that Elliott had withdrawn from her after the swimsuit display and she tried not to speculate on the reasons. In a way, it was a relief. Lauren knew she would not be able to drive away alone if she caught another glimpse of that naked desire. She knew she should be pleased that the comfortable Elliott had returned, but she felt let down and slightly bitter.

Trying not to show it, she said, "I had a good time too."

There was a moment of awkwardness in the interior of the car before Elliott got out and closed the door behind her. She leaned in through the open window. "One more thing." Her eyes grew dark and sultry. "You looked really hot in that suit." She said good-bye to a bright red Lauren.

❖

I can't do this! I can't do this! Lauren's face flashed in front of her eyes, and Elliott rolled off the naked brunette lying beneath her. "I can't do this, I'm sorry." She quickly gathered her clothes and was out the door before the woman got out of bed.

She didn't stop moving until she'd parked her car in an empty lot eighteen blocks away. Her heart pounded as she turned off the ignition and sat in silence, leaning her head back on the headrest. *Oh my God, what did I almost do?* She opened her eyes and looked through her windshield into the black night. The panic that engulfed her when she was about to make love to the woman had subsided. Her breathing was returning to normal and her head was starting to clear. As it did, she struggled to sort through her thoughts. *What in the hell is going on with me?*

But she knew exactly what the problem was. She had allowed Lauren to drive off. They should have spent the night together. All it would have taken was for her to to tell Lauren the truth, that she wanted her and cared about her. It didn't seem that complicated, yet she had chosen the safe and familiar path, an evening in a bar with strangers.

After several drinks she was sitting close to a brunette who had a body she wanted to get lost in, and for at least ten minutes Elliott had felt like her old self. The woman was more than willing and had her hands all over Elliott the minute they were inside her apartment. Unfortunately, from that point on, everything went to hell.

Elliott started her car and got back on the road. She wasn't in the mood to go home to her empty bed, so she headed for the nearest source of comfort and support. Twenty minutes later she was sitting on a red leather couch with a large mug of coffee, and Victoria's soothing pronouncements.

"So, let me get this straight—no pun intended. You've met this wonderful woman, a woman like you've never encountered before, who challenges you, is interested in you, and just so happens to be beautiful. So...tonight you went out and drank too much and slept with someone else? Did I get it all right?"

Ouch. "I didn't sleep with her," Elliott clarified.

"Elliott, you were naked in bed on top of her. Let's not quibble over semantics."

"I felt like I was cheating on her." Elliott was shocked to hear herself saying this. "I've never felt this way about anyone. I want to know everything about her, what she does, what she thinks, what she likes for breakfast, and where she likes to go on vacation. Does she cry at sad movies, what's her favorite ice cream…" She trailed off and rubbed the back of her neck. "I want to be a better person for her."

"That doesn't sound like you." Victoria frowned. "You haven't had an accident or something, have you? Maybe a head injury…"

"You think I'm crazy?"

"No, I think something has knocked some sense into you at last. I was just wondering how it happened."

"I might have known I'd get no sympathy from you." Elliott paused, lost in thought for a moment, trying to analyze the problem. "I don't know what to do, Vic. I mean, my God, we've gone out a few times, and apart from the very beginning, we've barely kissed. If I don't have a woman in bed by the second date, I move on."

"So why are you still around?" Victoria's question was simple.

"Because I like her. I mean *really* like her. I don't think I've ever *liked* a woman before."

"Elliott, you've only ever been interested in getting into a woman's pants, not her head. Who is this goddess, anyway?"

"It's Lauren Collier."

"The woman you met at the Mayor's Award?"

"Yes."

"I'm not hearing why there's a problem," Victoria said.

Elliott drew a deep breath. "She's straight."

"What? You're kidding!"

"I wish I were."

"Holy shit. I never would have guessed that. Start from the beginning," Victoria commanded, "and don't leave anything out."

Elliott did start at the beginning and concluded her story with Lauren's phone ultimatum. "She's made it very clear that the next move is mine. Hell, every move has had to be mine. She doesn't even call me." She ran her fingers through her hair. "She's different from any woman I've ever met, Vic. She's warm and witty and extremely intelligent. She challenges me and makes me think about things I've never even thought of before. She's not interested in my money. She's honest, has a respectable job, and is a mentor to a teenager. She's not self-centered and I don't think she has a clue as to how beautiful she is. She is the first real woman I've met in I don't know how long."

"It sounds like you've been getting to know Lauren for who she is, not what she is. Stop and think about it, Elliott. Don't make this wrong just because it's different. It could be quite wonderful."

"I know."

"Then what's the problem? So far she doesn't sound very straight to me, so it can't be that."

Elliott looked at her like that was the fifty-thousand-dollar question. "I really don't know what's going on." She rose from the couch and walked over to the window. "I want to take that step, but every time I come close, I can't go through with it."

"What are you afraid of?" Victoria asked.

Elliott sighed with frustration. Struggling with a business problem was never this difficult. "I'm not sure. I suppose I don't feel I have the right to begin something…to make promises. You know me. I don't do commitment. If I started something with her that's what she would expect, and I wouldn't want to let her down…"

"So you don't trust yourself in any situation except a one-night stand?"

"That's harsh." Elliott had a thought. "Maybe I'm afraid of another Rebecca."

Victoria studied her quizzically. "Elliott, Rebecca wasn't a relationship, she was a fling. Are you saying Lauren is a similar kind of woman?"

"No. God, no!" The illogic of that thinking struck her forcibly. She fell back on her standard position. "Vic, I guess I'm just being realistic about who I am. There are far too many interesting women in the world for me to settle down with just one." However, she immediately thought of Lauren. *Could there be anyone more interesting than Lauren?*

"Come on, Elliott. Are you that shallow?"

"Excuse me?"

"You're what now, thirty-six, thirty-seven? Christ, that's almost forty. The babes dry up when you dry up."

"Jesus, you make me sound like I'm on the verge of becoming a dried-up old prune." She didn't take offense; she'd always relied on Victoria to be real with her. *Maybe not this real.*

Victoria wasn't finished. "Elliott, what do you see in the mirror every morning?"

"What are you driving at?" She knew Victoria cared about her, and there was sense in what she was saying, but she was fed up with defending herself.

"Who are you, Elliott? I don't mean Elliott the CEO or Elliott the rich girl who donates millions to charity or even the one who gets all the girls. I'm talking about Elliott the woman. Who is she?" Elliott didn't answer. "I'll tell you who she is. She's someone who is afraid. Afraid to get too close to anyone, especially a woman, for fear that she may start to have feelings for her and have to trust her. She hides behind her job and uses her money to make people happy when she should be using her wit, intelligence, and personality. But no, that's too personal, and she'd never get personal."

"What in the fuck is going on here?" Elliott demanded, at her limit now. "I'm the same person I was yesterday and the day before and the day before that. Now all of a sudden I'm shallow and a slut? And let's not forget about being a coward." She paused and forced herself to speak more calmly. "Well, let me tell you something. I've been on national TV, stood up in front of thousands of people and talked for hours without any notes, brokered millions of dollars of deals and invested billions of dollars of other people's money. Trust me, Victoria, I am not afraid."

"But have you ever said 'I love you' to a woman?" Victoria spoke quietly and calmly.

Elliott's stomach dropped to the floor. Victoria had described her better than she could herself, and it took the words of her oldest friend to see it when she herself could not. A soft, warm hand covered hers.

"El, you know I love you more than anyone on the face of the earth. Yes, you are the same person you were yesterday and the day before and the day before that. And that's what's so sad. You can't let yourself go so you can grow as a human being, as a woman. You need to change that, Elliott, or you're gonna be alone the rest of your life.

"You've met someone special. She's not just another plaything you can use and throw away, and you know it. Please, El, do yourself a favor. Don't blow this."

CHAPTER FOURTEEN

Elliott's hand shook as she rang the bell. She and Victoria had talked well into the night and she'd finally collapsed in her friend's guest room. After a breakfast of muffins and coffee Elliott had driven home, taken a hot bath, and fallen asleep under the cool covers. She woke refreshed and certain of her next move. *Okay, almost certain.*

Lauren was not expecting anyone as she looked through the security peephole in her front door. *Elliott?* She opened the door.

"Hi." *Why can't I ever think of something else to say?* Elliott shifted her weight from foot to foot. "I know I didn't call. I hope I'm not disturbing you."

"No, not at all. Please come in." Lauren opened the door wider to allow Elliott to enter.

Elliott passed across the threshold. "Thanks." She stopped in the middle of the room and turned to face Lauren. "I…" She did not get a chance to finish.

"Ms. Foster!" Tonya was standing in the doorway to the kitchen, her wavy chestnut hair loosely drawn into a ponytail.

"Tonya, hi. It's good to see you again." Elliott felt foolish for not calling first. She turned back toward Lauren. "I'm sorry, I didn't know you had company. I don't want to interrupt your time together."

Lauren put her hand out and stopped Elliott from moving back to the door. "You're not disturbing anything. As a matter of fact, we were just talking about you. Tonya was hoping she could talk to you again. Would you stay and have dinner with us?"

"Dinner?" Elliott was trying her best to shift her focus from her original mission to this new chain of events.

"Yeah, you know. The meal you eat in the evening, typically followed by a decadent dessert." Tonya chuckled at Lauren's light teasing. "Please. You're not interrupting anything. We'd love to have you." Lauren drew Elliott toward the other room. "We were just getting started in the kitchen."

After a few steps Elliott recovered and felt like her old self; as a matter of fact, she felt a little giddy. "You can cook too?"

"I have many hidden talents."

Elliott's eyes scanned Lauren's body from head to toe, stopping for a long time at her breasts. "I can't wait to find out," she said huskily.

Lauren stared at her intently.

"You heard me right," Elliott said, with a dangerous gleam in her eyes. "Let's go, I'm starved."

Dinner was delicious. The conversation was dominated by Tonya and Elliott, and Lauren was thrilled that they were getting along so well. It would be a difficult situation if Elliott did not respect her involvement with Tonya or if Tonya didn't like Elliott. Thankfully, it appeared she had no need to worry.

After dinner, Lauren and Elliott cleaned up the kitchen while Tonya finished some homework. They adjourned to the deck with a bottle of wine after Tonya settled in for the night. Facing the ocean, their hands on the rail, they were quiet for a moment. The glow of the full moon created a softness to Lauren's face that took Elliott's breath away.

"Lauren?" Elliott slowly bent her head to kiss the lips that had been tantalizing her for weeks. She stopped a fraction of an inch from touching them.

"Yes." Lauren's blood raced and her stomach did a flip. Elliott's lips were a scant hairsbreadth away from hers. All she needed to do was close the gap, but she waited for Elliott to make that choice.

"Come here." Elliott drew Lauren into her arms and lowered her head the remaining distance to take her lips. The kiss felt different this time, and by the way Lauren responded, she noticed as well.

After several moments, Lauren drew back to look into Elliott's eyes. It was all she could do to drag her eyes from the mouth that had just rocked her world. "What are you doing?"

"Kissing you. Some people even go so far as to call it foreplay."

"Are you sure?"

"Absolutely," Elliott answered firmly. They kissed for several minutes until Elliott reluctantly drew back. She leaned so that their foreheads were touching as they both struggled for breath. "However, as much as I'd like to continue this, you have a houseguest. I'd better go while I still can."

Lauren's heart soared at the knowledge that Elliott wouldn't be able to leave her if they continued. Her arousal was so intense that her panties were already wet in anticipation, and she clung to Elliott for support. Taking a deep breath to steady herself, she remarked, "Timing sucks."

Elliott smiled and kissed her again. This time she intentionally kept it brief because if she kissed her too long, she knew there would be no stopping until she kissed every square inch of the body that haunted her thoughts. "Anything good is worth waiting for."

"You're implying that you would be good." Lauren had missed their sexual banter and was enjoying it now.

"I promise to be on my best behavior." Elliott held Lauren with her hands on her waist.

Lauren gazed hungrily at her lips. "It's not your best behavior I'm interested in." They moved into a deeper, longer kiss. Lauren felt Elliott's hands move across her back in a sensual dance.

She trailed hot, wet kisses across Lauren's face, stopping to nibble on a delectable earlobe. Lauren gasped her pleasure and tightened her grip in Elliott's hair as her breasts were claimed and Elliott kissed her exposed neck. Through muffled sounds Lauren called her name and her passion ignited. Lauren shuddered at the touch and would have fallen if she were not leaning on the deck rail. She could barely breathe due to the overwhelming sensations she was experiencing in Elliott's arms. She arched her back so that her breasts filled Elliott's hands more fully and moaned her pleasure. Removing her hands from Elliott's hair, she reached behind herself to pull her T-shirt over her head. *I need to feel your lips on me.*

Elliott gloried in the feel of this woman's breasts in her hands, and her fingers closed around two pert nipples. *Oh God, she feels wonderful!* She didn't know what brought her back to reality, but she slid her hands from under the shirt to cover Lauren's, stopping her movement. At the same time she ceased kissing the soft, smooth skin and raised her head.

The look of hunger in Elliott's eyes shot right between Lauren's legs. Her clitoris throbbed and begged to be touched, and her breath stopped in her throat. She wondered if Elliott had again changed her mind.

Elliott read the look in her eyes and softly kissed her. "No, I'm not backing out. On the contrary, I want you so badly I can hardly think straight. But you have company, and when I make love to you I want you all to myself."

Lauren didn't know that she could become more aroused than she was at that moment, but Elliott's words took her to a place she had never been before. She was incapable of speech. Elliott gently took her hand and walked with her through the house to the front door. As she opened it, she turned and placed a quick kiss on Lauren's cheek. This time when she said good night and closed the door, Lauren knew she'd be back.

The familiar scent filled Elliott's nose as Lauren passed her. "You look great." *Actually, you look fabulous.*

Lauren was wearing navy pants and a white long-sleeve oxford shirt with a button-down collar. Her brown loafers matched her belt and there was a clip at the base of her neck holding her hair away from her face.

"Thanks." She suddenly felt her nerves settle and she was amazingly calm. She had been a wreck ever since Elliott called and invited her to her house for dinner.

Elliott was so wound up she could barely eat, let alone enjoy the taste of the cuisine catered by one of the finest restaurants in the city. When Lauren smiled at her, she dropped her fork and mumbled an embarrassed apology. Her uncertainty about where the evening would lead overruled her confidence. Dinner was often a prelude to sex, and on some occasions was an irritating barrier to her ultimate goal. Tonight, however, was different. She wasn't sure she wanted the meal to end, yet she couldn't wait.

The more nervous Elliott was, the calmer Lauren became. It was almost comical to watch Elliott struggle through the evening when she had always been so polished and sophisticated.

At the conclusion of the meal Lauren offered to help clear the table.

"No, that's not necessary. Ruth will come in tomorrow and clean things up."

"Ruth?"

"My housekeeper," Elliott clarified. "Actually, she's more of a family fixture than a maid. She's worked for my family for probably twenty-five years. I can't eat carrots without remembering Ruth threatening that if I didn't eat them I'd have to wear glasses."

They took a bottle of wine out onto the deck and pulled two patio chairs together, then sank into the plush cushions. The air was cool and the night was clear. Thousands of stars twinkled like tiny diamonds overhead. Neighboring houses were far enough away to be specks of light to her left and right. Elliott handed Lauren a glass of merlot and set the bottle down on the table between them. The warm wine relaxed her, and she leaned her head back to gaze at the sky. Beside her, Elliott fidgeted and Lauren wondered if she had changed her mind about the direction of their relationship. She had barely looked at her all evening and had not made any move to touch her. The evening certainly had not picked up where they last left off.

"Elliott, is there something bothering you?"

Elliott was silent briefly, perched on the brink of what felt like free fall, then she inhaled deeply and made the dive. "If I don't touch you soon, I'm going to explode."

Lauren put her glass on the table. Her heart was beating double time and her breathing was shallow, but she was amazingly calm. "Then do."

Elliott reached out and touched Lauren's face softly. Her fingers traced the lips that were inviting her, and the expression in Lauren's eyes took her breath away. She released the clip that held Lauren's hair. Strands fell through her fingers like bands of soft gold. Elliott pulled her forward and kissed her tenderly. The kiss continued in its sweetness despite Elliott's body commanding her to ravish the woman in her arms. She wanted to savor this moment, and she found that she couldn't get enough of the soft lips responding to hers. Lauren's arms encircled her neck and she simultaneously pushed Elliott back against the railing. The aggressive move ignited her passion beyond the bounds of restraint.

Without a word, she took Lauren's hand and led her down the hall to the bedroom. She stopped just inside the room and kissed her again. Lauren's lips were eager and nibbled a response. Before she totally lost control, Elliott pulled away and turned on the light next to the bed. A soft glow bathed the room. "Is this okay?"

Lauren swallowed the lump in her throat. "Yes."

"Are you scared?"

God, I can hardly breathe. "Yes and no. But I'm with you, and I want you."

Elliott's eyes hungrily searched Lauren's face as she gently cupped her chin. "You are so beautiful."

As their lips met, Lauren wrapped her arms around Elliott's neck and their tongues began the dance of desire. She was unsure which one of them moaned, because she was totally focused on the consuming kiss. She needed to feel Elliott's lips on her body and reluctantly pulled away, signaling her desire.

Elliott's lips moved over the fine skin. She kissed her way to the opening of Lauren's shirt, moving her hands slowly from caressing her back to cupping her breasts. Lauren moaned at the contact, and Elliott continued her kisses and slowly began to unbutton the shirt. As she opened each button, she kissed the exposed skin on the taut stomach, feeling the muscles quiver under her lips. She kissed her way back up to Lauren's neck and nibbled on a shoulder now bared as the shirt fell to the floor. Lauren's breasts were still hidden by her bra, and Elliott traced her tongue along the silky perimeter, returning to kiss Lauren's lips as she opened the front clasp of her bra. Lauren swayed into Elliott as her breasts were freed and spilled into Elliott's hands.

Lauren was almost overcome with pleasure and her knees turned weak as Elliott took a nipple into her mouth. *God, the last time you were in this position you said something that threw cold water on this passion. Don't say a word.* She quickly pulled Elliott's shirt out of her pants. When she reached under the material, Elliott jumped, and the response to her touch made Lauren's heart soar. She explored the hard, smooth flesh with both hands and Elliott moved away from her slightly, an instant before the snap on her pants opened.

Lauren encouraged her the only way she knew how, with her body and her hands, and soon her zipper was sliding down. Elliott's fingers moved inside her pants and lightly pressed between her legs. Through the roar of her own pleasure in her ears Lauren worked her hands slowly over Elliott's stomach to her breasts until Elliott moaned and increased the pressure of her fingers on Lauren's crotch.

Lauren dragged her mouth away from the lips that continued to devour her. "Elliott?"

Elliott's passion raged on at the breathless sound of her name. "Hmm…" She nuzzled Lauren's neck.

"I don't think I can stand up anymore."

Elliott smiled against her neck. "Then maybe we'd better lie down."

Their eyes locked as Elliott reached behind them and pulled back the covers on the king-size bed. She lowered Lauren to the crisp sheets and Lauren drew her down, ensuring their contact remained complete. Elliott quickly turned to the breasts that were begging for her attention, and what started out as butterfly kisses rapidly grew more profound as her lips and tongue could not get enough.

The sensation was so exquisite that Lauren grabbed the sheet with both hands. Her breath caught in her throat as Elliott kissed her way down to the top of her pants. Elliott lifted her mouth only long enough to slide them down over Lauren's hips and toss them to the floor. This time, she returned to trace a pattern from the top of Lauren's legs to the bottom of her feet, gently tickling her toes. Her hands joined the trip back and settled on the wet triangle between Lauren's thighs, the last barrier to her pleasure. She slowly removed the silk boxers and leaned back on her heels to regard Lauren with awe.

"You are so beautiful," she said and leaned over her to kiss her, this time keeping their bodies from touching.

You're torturing me! Lauren could stand no more and unclenched her hands and pulled Elliott's shirt over her head. Elliott didn't have on a bra, and Lauren quickly felt skin touch skin. *Holy Jesus.* She explored the flesh under her fingers while Elliott resumed her kisses. Her hands encountered stiff material and she was able to choke out, "Take off your clothes. I want to feel all of you."

Elliott froze, completely overcome with desire. Slowly she stood up and removed her pants, her eyes never leaving Lauren's. When she was completely naked, she hesitated silently, indicating to Lauren that it was her choice to go on.

There was no turning back now, and not even considering it, Lauren reached for Elliott, drawing her down so that Elliott's body completely covered hers.

Elliott sighed with pleasure. *Slowly, go slowly.* She wanted to prolong the sensations for as long as she could and make this as wonderful for Lauren as it was for her. Lauren's fingers were in her hair.

"You feel so good," Lauren said with wonder.

Elliott smiled and gently caressed Lauren's cheeks with the backs of her fingers. "This is only the beginning." She kissed her again. *Will I ever get enough of this mouth?* Moving lower, she took a breast into her mouth and gently bit the nipple. Beneath her, Lauren arched her back and moaned loudly. Elliott continued to feast on the breast as she slid her hands to Lauren's stomach and hips, caressing ever so closer to the warmth that awaited her. She paused at the inside of her thighs and came agonizingly close to her clitoris, waiting to be invited. Lauren raised her hips in anticipation, and Elliott stilled her hand just a fraction from Lauren's clitoris and looked into her eyes.

The fire Lauren saw mirrored her own and left no doubt as to her partner's desire. She moved her hand from Elliott's back and ran it slowly down her arm, feeling Elliott's muscles respond. She placed her hand over Elliott's and moved it to her clitoris. *Oh God, please touch me.* At the first brush of contact, she closed her eyes and moaned with pleasure.

Oh sweet Jesus! It took Elliott's breath away to feel the warm, moist center of the woman beneath her. She slowly explored with her fingers while gently kissing Lauren, their tongues expressing their mutual desire. Lauren began to move rhythmically beneath her and her hips began to thrust. Elliott responded in tempo to Lauren's increasing wave of desire. *Slowly, slowly. I want this to last forever.*

The touch of Elliott's hand on her was more than Lauren could bear, and she buried her face in Elliott's neck, her body arching off the bed, as she climaxed into Elliott's hand. Lights flashed behind her eyes and she forgot to breathe as shudder after shudder racked her body. Riding a feeling of euphoria that she had never imagined, Lauren shook uncontrollably. Elliott continued to stroke her as the spasms peaked a second time, holding her close and whispering soft words of endearment.

"Shh, it's okay. It's okay. Just enjoy it." She eased her caresses and gathered Lauren to her. Lauren's hands were still in her hair, and as they loosened their hold, Elliott lifted her head and looked at the woman she had just made love to. Lauren's eyes were closed and sheer pleasure was imprinted on her face; she was the most beautiful woman Elliott had ever seen. A sheen of sweat covered her neck and drew Elliott's lips once again. As she kissed and licked the sensitive skin, she began stroking her again. Lauren immediately lifted her hips in response.

Elliott quickly shifted her position and replaced her hand with the first tentative touch of her lips. Lauren was breathless, and her head began to swim as Elliott slowly used her tongue to explore every inch of her.

"Oh God, Elliott."

Elliott cupped the firm ass of the woman she was fully enjoying. She lifted Lauren slightly to allow greater access and opened her eyes; this time, she wanted to watch as Lauren climaxed. The clitoris beneath her tongue became hard and Lauren gripped the sheets with both hands, writhing on the bed. She came with a greater intensity than before, and Elliott almost climaxed herself watching this beautiful woman shudder with desire.

As Lauren came down from her orgasm, Elliott slowed her tongue, tasting the juices that flowed freely. Breathing heavily, Lauren gasped each time Elliott's tongue lightly slipped over her clitoris. Eventually Elliott left the warm, fragrant place and rolled over onto her back, taking Lauren in her arms and cradling her as the aftershocks of her orgasm left her body. Lauren settled in as if she had always been there. Elliott reached down and pulled the sheet up to cover them both. She gently stroked Lauren's back and moved strands of wet hair from her face.

"Are you okay?" she asked quietly.

It took Lauren several minutes to catch her breath and think clearly again. She had never imagined the exquisite pleasure that she'd just experienced. In fact, she had never had multiple orgasms. "I'm not sure," she said with a weak smile. "I feel like I just died and went to heaven." She moved her arm to encircle Elliott's waist and rested her leg over Elliott's hard thighs.

"I can honestly say that you are very much alive." Elliott chuckled and kissed the top of Lauren's head.

"God, am I ever. That was incredible."

The women lay quietly for several minutes, and Elliott was content to simply hold Lauren and feel her warm body against her. Even though her own body was on fire with desire, she would let Lauren set the pace for this side of their union.

Lauren had not drifted to sleep, and her mind was reeling with thoughts of the woman who held her close. *She was so gentle.* Suddenly she experienced an overwhelming desire to touch the woman who had given her such pleasure. She tentatively moved her hand over Elliott's stomach in a gentle caress. The muscles under her fingers quivered and Elliott held her tighter. *So this is what it's like to feel a woman respond to your touch. It's wonderful.* Feeling empowered by Elliott's response to her caress, Lauren moved her hand over the taut stomach, approaching the breast where her head lay. She noticed that Elliott's breathing was shallow and her body flushed.

"Elliott?" she asked tentatively.

"Hmm..." Lauren's roving hand was beginning to make her crazy. When she didn't continue after several moments, Elliott pulled her on top. *God, it feels good to have you there.* "What is it, Lauren?" she asked, brushing hair from her face.

Lauren hesitated, unable to get the words out. Elliott softly looked into her eyes, which gave her the strength to say, "I don't know what to do." Her eyes dropped from Elliott's. She supposed what had just happened was a lesson, but how could she be sure that Elliott would enjoy the same things? "I feel so inadequate. I feel like I'm a sixteen-year-old virgin again."

Elliott lifted Lauren's chin with her fingers, drawing their eyes to each other again. "Listen with your senses. Listen with *all* of your senses." Elliott's hands moved over Lauren's back as she continued. "Listen with your eyes and your ears. Listen with your sense of touch and smell to hear what your lover is telling you." She kissed her gently. "Lauren, anything you do will please me." *Just do it now!*

Lauren was overwhelmed with desire once again. She lowered her head and kissed the lips that had so recently given her pleasure. As their tongues met, she was driven by a desire to touch and taste every inch of Elliott and dragged her mouth away, kissing Elliott's neck as her hands grew bold in their wanderings. Elliott responded with a moan and began to move with her.

I heard that.

Lauren captured Elliott's nipple with her mouth, and Elliott's hands went into her hair and pulled her closer. Lauren felt the heat and wetness of Elliott's desire as she pushed against Lauren's thigh.

I felt that.

She reveled in the taste and feel of Elliott's other breast, and slid her hand down the tight stomach to settle between Elliott's thighs. She moved her fingers ever so slightly and Elliott arched her back as she groaned. "Oh my."

I heard that.

"You are so warm." Lauren was in awe as her fingers moved freely across the surface of this woman, then delicately traced her clitoris. Feeling bold, Lauren asked between kisses on her breast, "Do you like that?"

"Oh, I definitely like that," Elliott growled, regaining her breath. Seconds later Lauren touched her again and Elliott's voice was thick with desire, "If you keep doing that you'll know exactly how much I like it."

Lauren smiled and her heart surged with the knowledge that she was pleasing Elliott, whose breathing was now coming in quick gasps and body was moving in time to Lauren's exploring fingers. Wanting to give as much pleasure as she had received, Lauren slowed her hand and settled her body between Elliott's legs. She marveled at the woman exposed in front of her. A delicious scent propelled her forward, and she gently touched her tongue to the bright red surface.

Elliott gasped again. Lauren explored her fully, sensing Elliott's impending climax.

I heard you. I won't stop.

Suddenly Elliott arched upward as she rode the crest of desire. "Oh God, Lauren!"

Lauren climaxed again simply at the sound of her pleasure. She slowly returned to earth and rested her head on Elliott's thigh, drinking in the sights, sounds, and smells of her lover. *My lover.* Just the thought of that phrase caused her blood to surge again.

"Come here," Elliott urged shakily.

"I don't want to leave this beautiful place," Lauren protested, softly touching the glistening flesh once again.

With a sharp gasp, Elliott stilled her hand. "Don't worry. You can definitely go there again. Come here. I want to hold you." She patted her chest to indicate where she wanted Lauren to be.

Lauren moved up the warm body and settled into Elliott's arms once again.

"That was wonderful."

"I'm glad you liked it." Lauren was filled with awe at her ability to please the woman holding her.

"Oh yeah, I liked it. I liked it a lot." Elliott gathered Lauren closer, loving the feel of their bodies melded together. It took several minutes for her heart to return to its normal beat and her head to clear. "Are you okay?" she asked. Instinctively she knew the answer, but she needed to hear it. She felt Lauren smile as her warm breath caressed her breast.

"Yes. Actually, I am more than okay. I'm so okay I want to do it again." Lauren could hear Elliott's heart immediately race in response.

Elliott rolled over on top of her, a mischievous gleam in her eyes. "That's the best thing about being with a woman. You can do this all night." She lowered her head, tasting her own passion on the lips she began kissing again.

Suddenly Elliott was everywhere. Lauren felt hands on her body in places that she didn't know could feel such exquisite pleasure. Elliott tried to control her desire, but her senses reeled as Lauren responded once again, this time without inhibition. Elliott burned a trail with her lips across her face and the smooth creamy skin of her throat.

"Oh God, Elliott, that feels wonderful," Lauren moaned as Elliott's mouth moved to claim her erect nipple. Lauren moved her legs to press against Elliott's thigh. Whatever control Elliott had left vanished as Lauren roughly said, "Touch me."

Elliott shifted to bring her hand to the desired place, and Lauren responded with a moan of pleasure that again drove all reason from her mind. Elliott moved from the breast she was devouring to the mouth she could not get enough of. At the touch of their lips she slipped one finger into Lauren's warm channel and Lauren immediately responded, opening her legs to grant greater access. Elliott slowly pulled out her finger and gently circled the tender flesh of her lover's clitoris. She returned inside with two fingers and Lauren crushed her lips to her.

Lauren rocked in time with Elliott's thrusts. She had never felt her mind and body so in tune, and yet so out of control. The woman caressing her seemed to know exactly what her body needed even if she herself did not. Elliott's fingers continued their thrusts, her thumb moving to circle her clitoris. At the renewed pressure, Lauren exploded with huge spasms, tearing her lips from Elliott's and burrowing her face in the neck of the woman climaxing along with her.

They lay spent then, their breathing becoming more even as the minutes passed. Elliott moved off Lauren, causing a whimper. "Shh," she said gently and drew Lauren to her heart. As her body settled, warm and sated, Elliott realized that the woman in her arms had fallen asleep. She reached over, turned off the light, and pulled the covers over them both.

CHAPTER FIFTEEN

When Lauren woke, it was still dark and she felt heat on her back and breathing in her ear. Momentarily surprised, she tensed and then settled back into the warmth of Elliott's embrace. Elliott pulled her closer, nuzzling her neck and cupping her breast, and Lauren lay awake thinking that life would never be the same again. For that she was grateful; an entire new being had emerged in the arms of this powerful, giving woman. She started to move when the urge to take care of some personal business was greater than her desire to remain in Elliott's arms.

"I'll be right back," she whispered. She finished in the bathroom, made a quick detour to the kitchen, and quietly climbed back into bed, snuggling next to Elliott and falling instantly asleep in the warm cocoon.

Lauren woke later to the feel of Elliott's hands moving over her body in soft, gentle caresses while warm lips nibbled on her neck. Still half asleep, she felt herself falling when Elliott turned her over and moved over her. She came fully awake as Elliott's tongue touched her and was quick to orgasm with the sun just peeking out over the horizon.

"Good morning." Elliott placed a light kiss on her lips as Lauren caught her breath.

"Mmm, yes, it is," Lauren agreed, inviting her lover closer. Before their kiss became passionate again, she pulled away and said, "I'm not normally a morning person."

Elliott looked into eyes that were filled with the afterglow of lovemaking. "You could have fooled me."

"Must be the company I've been keeping lately." Lauren tickled Elliott's stomach.

A neighborhood dog was barking, signaling the beginning of another day. Elliott offered, "Coffee?"

"Later," Lauren said as she pushed Elliott onto her back and straddled her thighs.

More bold and confident than she was the night before, she explored Elliott's body, basking in her beauty in the early daylight hours. She saw how Elliott's flesh reacted to her touch and how her chest rose and fell with every shallow breath. She was mesmerized as she watched Elliott's eyes glaze over when her fingers entered and she stroked her clitoris. Elliott was right when she had talked about how her senses would tell the story of her lover's passion. The sights and sounds of Elliott climaxing under her caresses were overwhelming.

Lauren was happier than she had ever been as she got out of bed after yet another climax. Muscles she never knew she had spoke to her. She went into the bathroom, washed her face, and looked into the mirror. Her reflection showed the same woman with clear eyes and hair that definitely needed a visit to the beauty salon, but it did not reflect the change she now felt inside. She saw Elliott approach from behind as she put her arms around her, peering over her shoulder.

"What do you see?"

"A changed woman," Lauren replied calmly.

Elliott frowned. "I kinda liked her just the way she was."

Lauren looked deep into the brown eyes in the mirror. "I think you'll like this one better." She turned in Elliott's arms and kissed her.

After a moment Elliott pulled away and asked, "Promise?"

"I'll do my best."

"Well, you know the only way to get good at something is to practice, practice, practice." As she said each of the last three words, she bent her head and kissed Lauren softly.

Their kisses flamed into desire once again and Lauren felt

herself being lifted. The next thing she knew, she was seconds away from orgasm as Elliott's tongue worked its magic. "Oh my God, Elliott," she exclaimed as rockets went off behind her closed eyelids.

It took several moments for her to comprehend what had happened, and as Elliott gently moved her off the bathroom counter, Lauren flowed into her arms. She moved her hands down Elliott's back and cupped her firm butt. As she squeezed it, she growled, "I'm definitely awake now," and pushed Elliott back into the bedroom.

An hour later, lying comfortably in Elliott's arms, Lauren said, "Now I need coffee."

Elliott moaned in mock disappointment and looked down at the smooth tan flesh of the woman in her arms. Reluctantly, she got out of bed. "As much as I hate to hide this beautiful body, I don't trust myself." She handed Lauren a robe from the closet and she pulled on a pair of boxer shorts and an old T-shirt. Kissing her one more time, she took her hand and led her to the kitchen.

Lauren smiled shyly when Elliott leaned forward across the counter as they sipped coffee a few minutes later and said, "At the risk of repeating myself, you are so beautiful."

Lauren blushed. "I'm suddenly shy and I have no idea why." She paused. "It's kind of silly after what we did all night."

Elliott reached across the table and took her hand. "It's not silly at all. As a matter of fact, I think it's quite charming. It's refreshing to see someone in awe of something. You so seldom see that anymore."

"Yeah, well, it can go away anytime now," she said, unnerved. She had been in the same morning-after position before with men and had never felt as awkward as she did right now.

Elliott put her cup down and pulled Lauren out of her chair and into her lap. "I hope it never goes away." She gently kissed her parted lips. Instantly the kiss sparked passion, and Elliott untied the knot on the blue robe. She slipped her hands inside and captured Lauren's breasts, causing her to arch into the caressing hands. Elliott dragged her mouth away and took an erect nipple in her mouth.

"Oh God, Elliott." Lauren moaned. "It makes me crazy when you do that."

Elliott moved her mouth a fraction of an inch away from the enticing breast. "And it makes me crazy when you do that," she replied when Lauren tangled her fingers in her hair and pulled her tighter to her breast. As the desire pounded between her legs, she stood up and pulled Lauren back into the bedroom. There were no complaints from Lauren as Elliott took her fast and hard. While Lauren rode her thigh, Elliott said, "Touch me," and Lauren immediately did as asked. The instant her fingers touched Elliott's warm, wet center, they both shuddered in orgasm.

Their breathing slowly returned to normal as the two women lay spent in each other's arms. Elliott sighed. "I can't believe I'm saying this, but I have to get to the office."

"You what?" Lauren sat up, incredulous.

"I have a board meeting today that I absolutely can't miss. If I had any idea I'd be waking up with you in my arms this morning, I would have cancelled it."

"Well. I have absolutely nothing on my calendar this morning, so you hurry along and I'll be right here dozing in this soft, warm bed that smells like sex." Lauren lay back down and moaned softly as she stretched out on the luxurious bedding.

Elliott realized that Lauren was teasing her. "How did you manage that?" She knew just how difficult it was to get a complete morning without appointments.

"I called Michelle and told her that something had come up and to reschedule anything I had this morning," she said, proud of herself.

"When did you do that?" *Well, well, well.*

"Earlier this morning when I got up to use the bathroom."

"You dog!" Elliott exclaimed, sitting up and tickling her. "Not fair!"

"A good attorney always knows her next move," Lauren said between giggles.

Elliott leaned down and kissed her. "I certainly know what my next move is," she said as she moved on top of her once again. When Lauren was fully aroused, Elliott jumped out of bed. "Oops, I'd better start getting ready." As she moved toward the bathroom, she glanced over her shoulder to see the shocked expression on Lauren's face.

Elliott was still laughing as she stepped into the shower. She was rinsing her hair when she felt a draft and then Lauren's hands were on her. She could feel tight curls pushing against her buttocks as Lauren reached around her and long, slim fingers entered her. She was still wet from the teasing encounter in the bed a few moments ago, and her knees buckled when Lauren said, "Payback is hell."

Lauren intended to leave Elliott as aroused as she had been, but when Elliott got to that point she was totally overcome with desire and couldn't have stopped even if she wanted to.

Elliott gasped and placed both hands on the wall of the shower, the water cascading over her back. Through her haze, she knew that Lauren was touching herself with the same rhythm that she was touching her. That knowledge increased her arousal and she said, "That's it, right there," encouraging Lauren to continue. As she came, she cried out and her voice was drowned by Lauren's simultaneous cry.

After they settled, Lauren took the soap and washed Elliott. She inspected every square inch of the body that excited her, her passion rising again. She had showered with other lovers but none with the intimacy that she now felt with Elliott. Before she got to the point of no return, she rinsed her new lover and turned off the water.

"What are you doing?" Elliott dropped her briefcase on her desk and sat down with her cell phone cradled to her ear.

Lauren's heart raced at the husky sound of the voice on the other end of the line. "Lying here in your bed thinking about you." She had watched Elliott dress for her day at the office and thoroughly enjoyed witnessing the transformation from passionate lover to respected businesswoman. Actually, the more she thought about it, the more aroused she became.

"Really?" Elliott sat back in her chair, holding the phone as if it were Lauren.

"Yes, really. What are you doing?"

Elliott shook her head and smiled. "Thinking of you." A warmth spread through her body at the thought.

Lauren lay back on the pillow that Elliott had used for the few hours that she did sleep. "You probably know this, but you are an incredible lover."

Oh God. The warmth had settled in the spot directly between her legs that was already overheated. "You shouldn't say things like that."

"Why not?" Lauren inquired.

"Let me rephrase that. You shouldn't say things like that when I have to spend the rest of the day in a board meeting." *I'm sure not looking forward to trying to concentrate on financials and long-term strategy.*

"And why is that?" Lauren already knew the answer, but she wanted to hear Elliott say it.

"Several reasons."

"Tell me." Lauren loved hearing the caress of Elliott's voice.

Elliott knew that Lauren was enjoying their conversation as much as she was. "Well, first, I'm only as good as the woman I'm making love to, so it's all your fault. Second, I'd rather be there with you, and third, my panties are already soaked through and it's not even ten thirty in the morning." Lauren was quiet for so long that Elliott wasn't certain she was still on the line. "Lauren?"

"Yes, I'm here. I was just trying to think of something to say."

The uncertainty in her voice caused Elliott to draw a quick breath. "What would you like to say?"

Lauren took a deep breath and took the plunge. "That I want to see you tonight."

"I'd like that." *Actually, I want to make love to you right now.* "How about if I come by your place? I should be free about eight thirty."

Lauren tried to keep the relief out of her voice. "I'll be waiting."

"Okay, if I don't hang up right now, I'm going to be worthless for the rest of the day." *As if I'm not already.*

As she hung up she could hear Lauren's laughter.

❖

Elliott was a successful executive for the rest of the day but could not concentrate completely until she rang Lauren's doorbell that evening.

Lauren was standing in the doorway in a cashmere sweater over a pair of jeans. Her hair was down and her feet were bare. *God, she looks beautiful.*

"Hi. Come in." *So I can take you right here on the living-room floor.*

"Hi yourself." Elliott stepped across the threshold and turned to face Lauren as she closed the door. What she had intended to be a simple hello kiss quickly exploded into the fire of desire as Lauren answered with several of her own.

"I think you're overdressed," Lauren said, tweaking the business suit that fit Elliott so well.

"Then maybe you should do something about it."

Given free rein, Lauren slid her hands under the jacket lapels, lightly brushing Elliott's hardening nipples as she pushed the coat off her shoulders and let it fall to the floor. Lauren pulled the silk blouse from the waistband of Elliott's tailored trousers. Searching hands met skin simultaneously, and their passion exploded.

Elliott stepped away for an instant to pull the sweater over Lauren's head so she would have unimpeded access to the breasts that had filled her mind all day. She shivered when Lauren ran her fingernails up and down her back, then quickly moved to unbuckle her belt. At the sound of her zipper being pulled down, Elliott slipped her hand under the waistband of Lauren's pants and was met with warm wetness. She couldn't stop herself as her fingers slid over the engorged flesh, and she felt Lauren's legs begin to buckle.

"Oh God, Elliott, don't stop."

Lauren was breathless with desire, and Elliott wasn't sure she could stop if she had to. She expertly moved her fingers, and Lauren released her grip on Elliott's zipper to put both arms around her neck, drawing her closer. Elliott could feel Lauren's ragged breathing in her ear as she came closer to the ultimate release. Their passion was driving Elliott to the point of climaxing herself, but she pushed thoughts of her own fulfillment out of her mind, fully committing to the pleasure of the beautiful woman she held.

Lauren would have collapsed in a heap on the floor if Elliott had not pinned her to the door. Her legs quivered and her arms felt like lead weights across Elliott's shoulders. She wasn't sure she could move any part of her body and wasn't certain if she even wanted to.

Feeling the spasms subside, Elliott slowly withdrew her hand and gathered Lauren into her arms. She whispered, "I have thought of nothing but this all day."

"What…having sex at the front door?" Lauren smiled.

Elliott touched Lauren's check with fingers still wet with evidence of her desire. "No. You, coming in my arms."

The look of tenderness in Elliott's eyes made Lauren weak with desire all over again. "Come with me," she murmured, taking Elliott's hand.

They moved down the hall and Lauren finished what she started in the foyer, and none too soon she was pushing Elliott back onto the bed. She covered Elliott's body with her own and let out a long sigh. "You feel so good."

Elliott could feel the wetness from Lauren's desire on her thigh, and her own level of arousal increased. "So do you," she replied, lifting her leg just enough to make her point.

Lauren shifted slightly. "None of that right now, or I'll lose my train of thought."

"And just what are you thinking about?" Elliott knew the answer was the one her body needed.

"All the things I spent the entire day thinking about doing to you," Lauren said between kisses on Elliott's neck.

"Such as?" Elliott's hands were searching and exploring the soft skin under her fingers.

Lauren's eyes met hers, and the yearning reflected there made Elliott gush with anticipation. "Lie back and I'll show you."

The promise in Lauren's voice made Elliott murmur, "God give me strength."

God did give Elliott strength, and it was several hours before she was able to catch her breath. "Are you sure you haven't done this before?"

Lauren slowly snaked her fingertips across Elliott's chest and down her stomach before circling around her navel. "What ever do you mean?" she asked in an exaggerated Southern drawl.

Elliott laughed and reached down to stop the hand that was tormenting her once again. "You know what I mean."

Good wasn't a strong enough word to describe how they made love, and as if to prove it, they moved together again. Lauren was everywhere. Her hands continually explored and her mouth never stopped nibbling and sucking on the places that drove Elliott crazy with desire. The more Elliott responded, the more aroused Lauren became. Finally, after what seemed like an eternity, Lauren settled into the spot where Elliott needed her the most. It was not long before she knew just how desperate Elliott was for her tongue, and she held on tight while Elliott's body soared to climax.

"I think you said it earlier, Elliott." Lauren smiled at the thought. "I'm only as good as the woman I'm with, so it must be all your fault." She withdrew her hand from Elliott's and slid it into the warm, wet curls between Elliott's legs.

Elliott jumped at the unexpected contact. "Whoa, I've got to rest a minute." She eased the hand away from her sensitive clitoris. "You're like a kid in a candy store."

The teasing made Lauren chuckle and snuggle closer. "And I think I've developed a serious sweet tooth."

Fighting the lassitude of good sex, Elliott reached down and pulled the sheet up to cover them both. "Lucky me," was the last thing she said before she drifted off to sleep.

Lauren woke to chirping of the birds outside her bedroom window and the sound of a lawn mower across the street. They were lying on their sides facing each other, and she used the opportunity to study the woman who was still sleeping soundly beside her. Elliott looked at peace. The lines of stress had softened and her tousled hair made her look many years younger. *You are so wonderful. What's*

happening here? Her gaze moved to the hands that had given her such pleasure throughout the night, and her body began to tingle in remembrance. She reflected on the time they had spent together in the throes of passion and couldn't have ever imagined that she could feel this much pleasure over a basic bodily function. She now knew what the phrase meant: that women make love with their brains more than their bodies. Her connection with Elliott was unmistakable, and the desire to kiss her was overwhelming.

"You've had enough rest," Lauren whispered as Elliott began to respond to her kisses.

"Mmm. What time is it?"

"Time to do it again." Lauren took a rosy nipple into her mouth.

"Oh, God," Elliott cried out as Lauren gently bit down on the hard peak. She had woken fully aroused and she knew it would not be long before she was incapable of coherent thought. Quickly seizing the offensive, she rolled Lauren over onto her back. "Oh no, you don't," she said, straddling her thighs, holding Lauren's hands over her head. "It's my turn."

The possessive look in Elliott's eyes made Lauren's mouth go dry. *My God, I want you so bad.* "Is it always like this?" she inquired.

"Like what?" Elliott asked, already lowering her head to kiss her.

"Not being able to get enough of each other." Lauren tried to move her hands but Elliott held them firm.

She leaned down and whispered in Lauren's ear, "Turn over."

Lauren's blood raced through her body in a nanosecond, and apprehension began to creep up her spine. "Why?"

"Do you trust me?"

"Yes."

"Then turn over. I won't hurt you."

With Elliott's assistance, Lauren turned over onto her stomach. Her arousal skyrocketed as she felt Elliott's weight settle on her. The soft curls tickled her butt and the nipples pressed against her back were rock hard. Elliott started to move slowly up and down her body, making Lauren squirm on the bed. Elliott moved her hand under Lauren and instantly found the spot she was looking for.

Lauren moaned her pleasure as Elliott began the rhythmic stroking that she needed. Her body arched with each bold stroke, and the feeling of Elliott's fingers on her clitoris and her body pressed against her back quickly drove her to orgasm. As she descended she could feel Elliott moving against her more urgently than before. Lauren arched her back so that her butt was in direct contact with Elliott's thrusting pelvis, and after several moments, Elliott came and collapsed on her back. Listening to her ragged breathing, Lauren reveled in the knowledge that she could give Elliott equal pleasure.

Through gasps of air Elliott answered Lauren's original question. "With the right person, yes. It's always like this."

And am I the right person for you, Elliott?

COME AND GET ME

CHAPTER SIXTEEN

Lauren was reaching for the phone, planning to call Elliott, when it rang. "Lauren Collier," she answered briskly, planning to end the call as soon as she could.

"Is this *the* Lauren Collier?" The voice was soft and sexy, and her pulse began to race.

"Which Lauren Collier are you referring to?"

The voice became huskier as it continued, "The one who takes my breath away with just one look at her. The one who causes my heart to pound in my chest with just one look. The one whose fingers are like fire when they touch my skin and whose skin is as soft as a rose petal. The one who drives me crazy with desire, and the one who drives me even crazier with *her* desire." The voice was almost panting into the phone.

"I'm sorry," Lauren replied coolly. "You must have the wrong Lauren Collier. This one is just a plain old corporate attorney with a very reserved style."

"That may be the daytime Lauren Collier. I'm describing the nighttime one."

"Why didn't you say so in the first place!" Lauren couldn't hold on to the charade any longer. "Elliott, what are you doing?"

"I'm calling you."

"I know that."

"Actually, I wanted you to know that I've been thinking about you. I missed you."

Lauren laughed softly. "We talked every day." She'd been

out of town, dealing with the SEC, and Elliott had called her each evening.

"I would have sent you flowers but I was afraid it would generate more questions than you'd like to answer." It was Elliott's habit to send flowers to the women she spent the night with as a way of thanking them for the experience. Now it just seemed cheap.

"You're right, but I appreciate the thought and the thoughtfulness." Lauren tried to avoid receiving anything of a personal nature at work. The umbrella bouquet Elliott had sent just after they met was still being talked about. "How was your day?"

Elliott regarded the piles of paper on her desk and sighed. "It seems to never stop. How about you?"

"Not bad, but I have more fun with you."

"Wanna have some more fun, little girl?" Elliott's imitation of Groucho Marx was laughable.

Lauren was about to answer when she caught a movement in her doorway and looked up to find Charles Comstock standing on her threshold. *Oh shit! How much did he hear?* "Yes, I'd definitely be interested in that suggestion. I'll follow up with you later and we can firm up the arrangements."

Elliott was puzzled at Lauren's sudden shift in her tone and the conversation. "Did somebody just walk in?"

"Yes, that's right," Lauren replied, looking at her boss for any indication that he had heard too much.

"Well, tell them to go away. You're busy talking dirty to your lover," Elliott teased.

"Actually, I'd love to, but that really isn't possible." Lauren signaled Charles that she understood his hand gestures and would be in his office shortly.

"Okay, I'll cut you some slack, *this time*," Elliott said. "But next time you'll have to remember to close and lock the door."

Lock the door? Jesus, she's making me crazy. "You're absolutely right. I'll speak with you later." Without giving Elliott the opportunity to respond, she said good-bye and got to her feet. The last thing she felt like was a meeting with her boss and, from the taut expression on his face, it was not going to be pleasant.

❖

Lauren was furious. She'd just successfully argued to dismiss the SEC charges against Bradley & Taylor. While both men should have been ecstatic at the turn of events, they had been strangely subdued on the flight back, and now they were treating her like the enemy.

Charles was seated behind his desk and Thomas Merison was in the chair to the left. Charles's desk was clear except for a manila file folder. He preferred to have meetings and conversations at his conference table or the small seating area by the window. The fact that he was on the other side of the massive desk signaled this was serious and it involved her.

"Lauren, please come in and sit down." There was no informality in his voice.

Merison almost gloated as she sat in the adjacent chair.

"Lauren, something has come to my attention and I'm very disturbed by it."

Lauren's stomach tightened but she didn't say anything.

"I received some photographs that are, shall we say, not appropriate to the image we uphold here at Bradley & Taylor. I'm disappointed in you, Lauren. The company had high expectations of you, but it seems our trust was misplaced."

"Photographs? May I see them, Charles?" Lauren had no idea what she would see when she opened the folder, but she was not about to back away from whatever it was. She was relieved that her hands were steady when she picked up the folder Comstock slid across the desk. He had as little physical contact with the file as possible, giving her the impression that he was afraid he might catch whatever was inside. She felt rather than saw both men's eyes on her as she opened it.

Staring back at her was a photograph of Elliott. Her experience as an attorney enabled her to show no reaction as she studied first one photo then the next. She was locked in a passionate embrace in Elliott's arms. She recognized her back patio as the setting. Instantly she knew what this was about. *Oh my God, Elliott.* She was sick to her stomach and wanted nothing more than to vomit all over Merison's Italian leather loafers and Comstock's Persian rug, but she wouldn't give them the satisfaction. There were several similar photos in the stack. She flipped though them in an uninterested manner, then tossed the folder back on Comstock's desk without saying anything. She made cool, defiant eye contact with both men but remained silent. *Let them cast the first volley.*

"You can see why we're upset, Lauren," Comstock said.

"Over two consenting adults sharing their attraction to each other?" Her voice was strong and firm.

"It's disgusting!" Merison spat from his chair.

"Tom…"

"No, Charles. She's a pervert, and what she is doing in those pictures—and God knows what else they did after that—is disgusting. We can't have this kind of degenerate as a member of this company." He was seething. All the cards were now out on the table.

"Lauren?" her boss asked. "Do you have anything to say about this?"

Lauren knew what they wanted from her. They expected her to deny it or make excuses for kissing Elliott. They wanted her to resign in humiliation, and if she didn't they would hold it over her and make her life miserable. They might keep her on the payroll, but they would strip her of her duties, rendering her impotent to do what she loved, to practice law. How she handled these next few minutes would define her, personally and professionally, for the rest of her life.

"Lauren?" Comstock was waiting for her answer.

She looked back and forth at both men and made the most significant decision of her life. "No, Charles, I have nothing to say about this because it's none of your business. I'm a good attorney… no, I'm a *great* attorney, and you know it. My personal life is none of this company's damn business and I will not be threatened because of it."

She turned her attention to Merison, who sat smugly in his chair. "Tell me, Thomas, how is Summer doing? Is she back at school?

It's been what, two or three months? Wait, isn't that the same as a trimester?" The look of shock on Merison's face told her she had hit her mark perfectly.

Both men sat speechless. They had worked hard to make sure that the incident with Merison's daughter was handled discreetly and never hit the papers. To have the sordid details come out now would make Merison crazy.

Lauren stood on solid legs. "I'm not sure if I can ever come to terms with the moral degeneracy of a pregnant teen attempting to trade sex for favors from a police officer, and being supported in her illegal conduct by a father who should know better." She sighed. "The tragedy is, mistakes like Summer's are sometimes judged most harshly by people who have their own secrets to hide. Hypocrites need to deflect attention from themselves, I suppose." She turned her gaze on Merison. "You would know all about that, Thomas."

"I don't think the two situations can be compared." Comstock's indignation sounded hollow.

"No, they can't," Lauren agreed. "One involves a crime, and the other doesn't. Who sent the photos, Charles?"

"They arrived anonymously."

Lauren's mind raced. Had Merison engineered this? It was possible, since he was a homophobe and seemed to have a personal vendetta against her. But he had to know that Lauren would not guard his dirty little secret if she were hung out to dry over her personal life.

"I'm very disappointed that this company isn't the company I believed it to be." She held up her hand as Comstock opened his mouth. "Don't, Charles, I really don't want to hear anything else you have to say to me." She changed her tone from anger to pity. "You are my biggest disappointment in all of this. I respected you. I would have done anything for you and for this company, and this is what I get because I might want to bring my *girlfriend* to the Christmas party? Losing me makes you the biggest loser here, Charles." Lauren pointed her finger at the stunned man to emphasize her point. "You and this company, and I feel sorry for both of you."

She started to leave, then hesitated and turned back to the men.

"Oh, one other thing. If I ever hear that John Briggs has left the company for any reason other than because he's fed up with this bullshit, everyone will know Summer is more than just a season." She left the door open as she walked out.

❖

"Are you absolutely sure about this?" Elliott asked Teresa.

"I found them by accident. I was looking for the Colchester file. Mark tends to be a slob, so I was checking his desk, and…there they were, stuffed under some papers in the bottom drawer."

"In a folder with the business card of a private investigator?"

"I would have taken the folder, but he could just deny it then and act like he is being set up."

"Good thinking." Elliott gave a couple of different scenarios room in her mind. She could call Ryan and go about this formally, or she could just march in there and confront him herself. "I'll deal with this. Is he in now?"

"All two hundred pounds of irresistible manhood," Teresa replied with dour humor.

Elliott headed along the hallway and took the stairs down a level. As usual, she spared a thought for Stephanie, but her younger sister no longer factored into the equation; Stephanie had made her choice and would have to live with it. No doubt she would come up with a good excuse to explain why her husband had hired a PI to snap photos of Elliott kissing a woman.

Elliott did not knock. She pushed open his door and crossed the room to slap her hand down on his desk. One look at his guilty face and she knew he'd done everything Teresa said, and possibly more.

"El." He gulped down the mouthful of pizza he was chewing. "What brings you to my humble abode?"

"Don't waste my time." She put her hands on her hips. "You know why I'm here."

Her brother-in-law's gaze darted past her to the door as if he was actually thinking about making a run for it. Then, with a swagger he could not quite sustain, he said, "Chill. I don't know what you've been hearing, but the Gallien Company has absolutely no connection with the Syrians. There's no foundation to those rumors. I personally checked the principals' bona fides."

"What!" Elliott exploded, unable to believe her ears. Distracted from her intended course of action, she demanded, "Are you telling me you're still chasing that deal behind my back?"

Suddenly, some of the strange questions she had answered in the meeting with the FBI started making sense. Had she ever been to Syria? Could she provide a list of all business contacts in the Middle East? Did her company have business relationships with any French weapons providers? The final nail on Mark's coffin fell into place.

"I'm simply assembling the right information so that you can be in possession of the full facts," Mark said. "I know why you had concerns, but those rumors were circulated by a competitor. The deal is—"

"The deal is dead! I have all the facts I need, and that's not why I'm here." Elliott's mind was working overtime. Was the FBI interested in her because of Gallien? If so, she could clear that up in five minutes.

This time Mark had nothing to say. He scowled at her with a mixture of fear and puzzlement.

Elliott tapped his desk sharply. "Put it here."

"What?"

"The folder and photographs."

Mark's face turned bright red and he made a wheezing sound and clutched at his chest. *Please, not a heart attack.* Elliott was in no mood to administer life-saving CPR to this bloodsucker.

"Do it!" she yelled.

"I didn't know he was going to take pictures, I swear," Mark began blathering as he stooped to pull the folder from his bottom drawer. "All I asked him to do was watch you and report back, but those guys, they act like someone has cut their nuts off if they can't take photos."

Give me strength. "You hired an investigator to *watch* me?"

"It's not what you think. It wasn't my idea. That woman... Rebecca. She came up here one day—"

"You fucked her."

Even up to his neck in shit, he couldn't contain himself. "She knew I hated you. Hell, everybody knows I hate you. She seemed to be pretty happy having a real man for a change."

His gloating expression vanished when Elliott said, "You're fired, Mark."

"You can't fire me."

"I just did." Elliott picked up the phone and called security. "You have five minutes. Don't take anything from your desk or filing cabinets. I'll have your personal effects sent to the house."

For once, he seemed lost for words. The color leached from his face. "She said she just needed some insurance."

"Mark, a word of advice—think with your brain." Elliott leafed through the photographs. "Who else has seen these?"

He blinked. Elliott could see him constructing a lie. "No one."

Wearily, she said, "I can make things a whole lot tougher for you. Tell me everything and this stays here. I'll advise the board that you have resigned to spend more time with your family."

Mark's face sagged. "I sent them to *her* company."

"To Lauren's company?" Elliott was stunned. She forced herself to stay calm so she wouldn't strangle him with her bare hands. "Why?"

"She's a bitch."

Elliott regarded him through narrowed eyes, letting him know with a single cold look that he was on dangerous ground.

"Okay, she turned me down. Fuck, all I did was touch her ass, and I didn't even know it was her until I saw the pictures. It's not like I planned all this."

"But when you saw her you decided to take advantage and pay her back?"

He tried to show remorse. "What the fuck does it matter. She's just another one of your wh—"

Say it and I'll break your jaw. Elliott clenched her fists. "You're talking about the woman I love, asshole. And if you ever lay a hand on her again, so help me, I'll kill you."

She wasn't sure who was more flabbergasted; Mark stared with his jaw hanging, and she distracted herself by taking the keys from his desktop and locking his cabinets. Security arrived while she was making sure nothing could be removed from the building.

Mark's parting words were predictably craven. "Please, El... for Stephanie's sake...please, don't tell her."

Elliott didn't respond. Her mind had room for only one thought. *The woman I love.*

CHAPTER SEVENTEEN

I need to see you," Elliott said when she finally managed to get past Lauren's guard-dog assistant.

"This is not a good time." Lauren spoke carefully. She didn't want to sound discouraging, but she did not want her call to be overheard, either.

"It's urgent," Elliott said. "And we can't do this over the phone."

"Okay, but I might not be very good company. My CEO just dropped a bombshell on me."

Elliott fell silent, suddenly afraid. The situation she had hoped to preempt was clearly in play, and she could not predict how Lauren would react when she found out why her career was now under threat. "Lauren, just answer me one question. Does the bombshell involve photographs?"

Lauren gasped. "How do you know?"

"As I said, we can't talk about this over the phone. Please, can I come by tonight?"

An hour later, when they were settled in Lauren's living room, Lauren kicked off the conversation. "The photos?"

"My fault," Elliott admitted.

"How is it your fault?" Lauren felt queasy.

"Remember my brother-in-law?"

Lauren grimaced. "The man with a hundred hands?"

"I wish you had told me he groped you." Elliott looked pained.

"He's family. I didn't want to cause a problem."

"You're not the problem, he is." With a groan, she said, "Lauren, he sent the photos. He hired a private investigator to watch me. The guy took the pics. Mark recognized you and thought he could get some revenge."

"Because I gave him the brush-off?" Lauren was incredulous. "He tried to destroy my career over *that*?"

"What can I tell you? The man is a jerk." Elliott paused. "There's more."

"I'm afraid to ask."

The slight humor in her tone soothed Elliott. Her worst fear had been that Lauren would just lose it and blame her and that would be the end of *them*. Elliott's mind jumped back to her exchange with Mark, and she tried to place her comment in context. In the heat of the moment, she'd blurted out *the woman I love*. She studied Lauren, testing the words against her feelings. Nothing jarred, except that the notion was so foreign to her she wondered if she really knew what it meant.

There were people she loved. She knew what love was. Yet her feelings for Lauren were different. For a start, she could be apart from people she loved and not feel hollow and bereft. She could contemplate having a fight with someone like Victoria without the excruciating fear of losing her.

"Elliott?" Lauren was regarding her quizzically. "What else were you going to say?"

Elliott combed her fingers over her forehead and through her hair as she collected her thoughts. "Rebecca instigated this. She slept with Mark and...persuaded him to hire the PI. This was her idea of insurance, something she could use against me...us...later on, I guess."

Lauren was silent briefly, wondering if she should tell Elliott now what she had done. She could see that Elliott was incensed and barely controlling her emotions. Gently, she said, "First of all, I don't blame you for this. Rebecca and Mark are responsible. Secondly, I resigned today."

"Oh, God. No. I'm so sorry. I'll speak to your boss. This doesn't have to—"

"Wait. Listen to me Elliott, it was coming." She'd been struggling with the decision ever since the discussion about John Briggs. "I was starting to see exactly what kind of company Bradley & Taylor is and I didn't like it."

What are you going to do?" Elliott asked.

"I don't know."

"What do you want to do?"

"I'm a first-class attorney. I won't starve. There are three firms I could call tomorrow and I'd have a job."

"If there's anything I can do…I know a lot of people."

"I don't need any favors," Lauren said firmly.

Elliott smiled inwardly at the note of pride in her lover's voice. She should have known better than to offer. Lauren was not the kind of woman to climb the ladder through the auspices of powerful friends. She was too ethical, and too classy. She sighed as an unwanted thought entered her mind. This was always going to be a problem for Lauren.

Holding her breath, she said, "I think we should stop seeing each other."

Lauren shot up off the couch. "What?"

"Lauren, we are both in very public positions in very public places, and if we continue to be seen together, and photographed together, people will talk." Elliott thought about a photograph she had seen in *San Diego* magazine recently of two women attending a fund-raiser for battered women. The camera never lied and that was certainly proven by the look the women were exchanging when the shutter clicked. Perhaps they thought they were being discreet, but their connection was obvious.

"I don't want you to continue to be hurt by our relationship." *It will kill me if we end it. But I will for you.*

"You can't be serious?" Lauren asked in disbelief. Panic flooded her body.

"I am."

"Well, I think you're fucked up if you think I'm going to stop seeing you because of this!" Lauren began pacing the room. "I love you, Elliott Foster, and, God damn it, no one is going to stand between us, especially some twit like Charles Comstock." Lauren stopped when she realized what she had said.

Elliott drew the first full breath in several minutes. "What did you say?"

Lauren came over and knelt in front of her. "I said you're fucked up."

"That's pretty apparent, but I was referring to the other part."

"The part about the twit Comstock or the fact that I love you?" Lauren said with all the love she felt bursting from her.

Elliott's heart began to sing. She tried to speak but her throat was so unbearably tight all she could do was make a small groaning sound.

"I do love you, Elliott. I don't want to stop seeing you. I want to spend the rest of my life with you." She took Elliott's face between her hands and stared into her eyes with such passion and yearning, Elliott could not breathe. Her expression became grave. "Please... don't use this as an excuse to run away from me."

The words hit home with a force far greater than the soft delivery Lauren had chosen. Shaken to the core, recognizing that Lauren had cut straight to the truth, Elliott said, "I can't run away from you. I love you too, Lauren. You are everything to me, and it is killing me to see this happen to you. I can't stand that because of me, you've been treated this way."

Lauren sat on Elliott's lap. "Elliott, without you I'm nothing. You're my heart and my soul and my reason for getting up every day." Lauren's eyes shone with love. "I'm not afraid of anything if I know you are with me. So what if I resigned. Those people don't deserve me. I have too much self-respect to stay there now. That's nothing to do with you. It's *my* decision."

"God, Lauren, I love you so much," Elliott gasped as she kissed her.

They made love on the living room floor like they had never made love before. Words of devotion were spoken in whispers and moans as they shared in the culmination of their love. When they finally lay curled against one another, exhausted, Lauren said, "Take me to bed."

Elliott did just that. She carried Lauren into the bedroom and laid her on the bed, then gazed openly at the woman who set her body on fire like no one else. *You make me feel like a different person. Someone I've never been. And it feels good.*

Lauren looked up into sparkling brown eyes. "What?"

"Excuse me?"

"Why are you looking at me like that?"

"Like what?" Elliott was afraid of what Lauren might have seen in her eyes.

"I don't know, kind of..." Lauren thought for a minute before continuing. "Perplexed, I guess, is how I'd describe it."

"I guess I'm thinking about how it would be if we lived together...to come home to you. To share my life with you." *I have a feeling I would be perfectly content.*

A welling tide of happiness swept Lauren into bliss. She had dared to imagine such a scenario, but had thought it would be a long while before Elliott would give the idea any room. *You're full of surprises tonight.* Out of curiosity, she asked, "What would you normally be doing at home, if you were by yourself?"

Elliott thought for a moment. "Well, if I were at home, I'd probably be working." That statement was truer than she wanted it to be. She typically worked well into the evening either in her office or at home.

"And if we lived together?"

Elliott smile turned warm. "If I were with a woman as beautiful as you, I certainly wouldn't be analyzing financial statements."

"What would you be doing?" Lauren knew the answer to the question, and the way that Elliott was looking at her, her body was beginning to tell her as well.

"I'd be making love to her, soft and slow, until she begged me to take her fast and hard." Elliott saw a flame jump in Lauren's eyes that mirrored the one she felt in the pit of her stomach.

Lauren trailed a hand down Elliott's throat and placed it between her breasts. "Well, I don't want to ruin your track record."

"I think you already have."

Lauren smiled enticingly. "Can we skip the soft and slow part and go straight to the fast and hard?"

Elliott's heart skipped a beat and she suddenly felt dizzy from the desire that surged through her body. Lauren telling her what she wanted, and how she wanted it, was almost enough to set Elliott off. She kissed her hard and passionately.

Elliott's hands and mouth quickly had Lauren hanging on to her for support. She felt like she was on a freight train that couldn't stop, and she was powerless to control it. Her passion was fueled by Lauren's murmurs of pleasure as she slid one finger into her. Another finger joined the first and Lauren bit her hard on the neck, which fueled Elliott even more.

"Oh God, Elliott, faster," Lauren cried. Stars began to burst in her head as Elliott did as she was asked. "Yes!" Lauren cried as wave upon wave wracked her body. She was hyperventilating, her breathing was so ragged. Slowly she became aware of movement as Elliott moved her up the bed a little more and immediately replaced her fingers with her mouth, pushing Lauren to soar again with pleasure.

Elliott soaked up the remnants of Lauren's release and softly kissed the still-throbbing flesh. *You are the most beautiful, passionate woman I've ever known.* Finally, she lay still, her heart pounding with emotion, her head resting on Lauren's belly. Their lovemaking was more intense each time, to the point it took her breath away. *I want to please you so much.*

"Come here," Lauren whispered. She was physically spent, and it was all she could do to wrap Elliott in her lethargic arms. "You're wonderful." *That doesn't even begin to describe how I feel.*

Elliott lazily ran her fingers across the bare skin next to her. "It was my pleasure." *God, was it ever.* Elliott heard Lauren laugh deep in her chest.

"Actually, I think it was mine." Lauren kissed the top of her head.

Elliott lifted up on her elbows to look directly into Lauren's eyes. "Giving you pleasure gives me pleasure. The way you respond fuels me and makes me want to give you even more."

The lethargy that threatened to overtake Lauren suddenly disappeared, and in its place came the desire to give Elliott all she had just received. "I know exactly what you mean," she said, and rolled Elliott onto her back. With all the passion she felt, she said, "I love you."

Elliott could not believe how utterly happy it made her to answer, "I love you too, Lauren. I love you with all that I am."

CHAPTER EIGHTEEN

Lauren, what are you doing here?" Elliott inquired three weeks later when her lover showed up at Foster McKenzie.

"Is that any way to greet the woman you love?" Lauren felt as light as a butterfly with the joy of knowing that this woman loved her.

"I guess I'm just surprised to see you." Elliott noticed the recent lines of strain were gone from Lauren's face and she was absolutely glowing. "So, what's up?"

"Can you get away for the rest of the afternoon?"

Elliott recalled the last time she had left early with Lauren, and her stomach did a flip-flop. They had spent that afternoon in bed. "For you, anything."

Lauren took her hand. "My car's out front."

"Okay, where are we going?"

"You'll see. Be patient, my love."

Elliott's pulse jumped at the endearment. "You know I have no patience when it comes to you. Especially when you have your hands on me."

Lauren slid her hand up Elliott's thigh. "Patience. I promise I'll make it worth your while."

"You know that makes me crazy." Elliott wanted to make love to Lauren right here, right now, on her desk. But that would be unseemly during working hours. She reined in her hormones, gathered her things and told a smiling Teresa that she was leaving for the rest of the day, and dutifully escorted her lover to the elevators.

Ten minutes later they pulled into a small office complex. Cars were parked in front of the various businesses, which were grouped around a small courtyard.

"What are we doing here?" Elliott asked, mystified.

"Come with me."

The women got out of the car and Lauren took Elliott's hand and pulled her toward the rear of the courtyard. Lauren's pace quickened as they approached a vacant office, and she asked, "Remember Marcie Webster?"

"The Southern steamroller—how could I forget?"

Lauren laughed. "Well, that opportunity she told me about…"

"Lauren?" Elliott read the stencil on the front door.

"I turned down the offer from Powell and Powell." She had been offered the position of partner in one of the most prestigious law firms in the area. Lauren tightened her grip on her lover's hand. "I want to help people. I want to help women and children who can't help themselves. I can't do that from behind a big desk fifty-three floors above the ground. I want to work for people who don't care who I sleep with but only how I can help them. I want to make a difference in people's lives."

The look of excitement and conviction in Lauren's eyes was exactly the expression Elliott thought belonged there, and she was overcome with love for this strong, passionate woman. She gathered her into her arms and whispered, "I love you, Lauren," just before she kissed her. "And I'm proud to be your partner. Now show me around."

Before she opened the door to her future, the future she would share with the woman she loved, Lauren moved her hand lightly over the lettering:

LAUREN COLLIER, ATTORNEY AT LAW
SPECIALIZING IN THE PRACTICE OF LAW FOR WOMEN AND CHILDREN

About the Author

Julie Cannon is a native sun goddess born and raised in Phoenix, Arizona. After a five-year stint in "snow up to my #$&" and temperatures that hovered in the 30s, she returned to the Valley of the Sun vowing never to leave again. Julie's day job is in Corporate America and her nights are spent bringing to life the stories that bounce around in her head throughout the day. She can often be found making notes of story lines or character development while in the car on the way to work, going to the store, or sitting at a stoplight. Julie and her partner of fifteen years, Laura, live in Phoenix with their seven-year-old son and six-year-old daughter, two dogs, and Spencer the cat.

Julie has selections in *Erotic Interludes 4: Extreme Passions* and the upcoming *Erotic Interludes 5: Road Games*, and her next novel, *Heart 2 Heart*, is due in December 2007 from Bold Strokes Books.

For more information visit www.Julie-Cannon.com.

Books Available From Bold Strokes Books

Lady Knight by L-J Baker. Loyalty and honor clash with love and ambition in a medieval world of magic when female knight Riannon meets Lady Eleanor. (978-1-933110-75-2)

Dark Dreamer by Jennifer Fulton. Best-selling horror author Rowe Devlin falls under the spell of psychic Phoebe Temple. A Dark Vista romance. (978-1-933110-74-5)

Come and Get Me by Julie Cannon. Elliott Foster isn't used to pursuing women, but alluring attorney Lauren Collier makes her change her mind. (978-1-933110-73-8)

Blind Curves by Diane and Jacob Anderson-Minshall. Private eye Yoshi Yakamota comes to the aid of her ex-lover Velvet Erickson in the first Blind Eye mystery. (978-1-933110-72-1)

Dynasty of Rogues by Jane Fletcher. It's hate at first sight for Ranger Riki Sadiq and her new patrol corporal, Tanya Coppelli—except for their undeniable attraction. (978-1-933110-71-4)

Running With the Wind by Nell Stark. Sailing instructor Corrie Marsten has signed off on love until she meets Quinn Davies—one woman she can't ignore. (978-1-933110-70-7)

More Than Paradise by Jennifer Fulton. Two women battle danger, risk all, and find in each other an unexpected ally and an unforgettable love. (978-1-933110-69-1)

Flight Risk by Kim Baldwin. For Blayne Keller, being in the wrong place at the wrong time just might turn out to be the best thing that ever happened to her. (978-1-933110-68-4)

Rebel's Quest: Supreme Constellations Book Two by Gun Brooke. On a world torn by war, two women discover a love that defies all boundaries. (978-1-933110-67-7)

Punk and Zen by JD Glass. Angst, sex, love, rock. Trace, Candace, Francesca...Samantha. Losing control—and finding the truth within. BSB Victory Editions. (1-933110-66-X)

When Dreams Tremble by Radclyffe. Two women whose lives turned out far differently than they'd once imagined discover that sometimes the shape of the future can only be found in the past. (1-933110-64-3)

Stellium in Scorpio by Andrews & Austin. The passionate reuniting of two powerful women on the glitzy Las Vegas Strip, where everything is an illusion and love is a gamble. (1-933110-65-1)

The Devil Unleashed by Ali Vali. As the heat of violence rises, so does the passion. A Casey Clan crime saga. (1-933110-61-9)

Burning Dreams by Susan Smith. The chronicle of the challenges faced by a young drag king and an older woman who share a love "outside the bounds." (1-933110-62-7)

Fresh Tracks by Georgia Beers. Seven women, seven days. A lot can happen when old friends, lovers, and a new girl in town get together in the mountains. (1-933110-63-5)

The Empress and the Acolyte by Jane Fletcher. Jemeryl and Tevi fight to protect the very fabric of their world…time. Lyremouth Chronicles Book Three. (1-933110-60-0)

First Instinct by JLee Meyer. When high-stakes security fraud leads to murder, one woman flees for her life while another risks her heart to protect her. (1-933110-59-7)

Erotic Interludes 4: Extreme Passions, ed. by Radclyffe and Stacia Seaman. Thirty of today's hottest erotica writers set the pages aflame with love, lust, and steamy liaisons. (1-933110-58-9)

Unexpected Ties by Gina L. Dartt. With death before dessert, Kate Shannon and Nikki Harris are swept up in another tale of danger and romance. (1-933110-56-2)

Broken Wings by L-J Baker. When Rye Woods, a fairy, meets the beautiful dryad Flora Withe, her libido, as squashed and hidden as her wings, reawakens along with her heart. (1-933110-55-4)

Combust the Sun by Andrews & Austin. A Richfield and Rivers mystery set in L.A. Murder among the stars. (1-933110-52-X)

Sleep of Reason by Rose Beecham. Nothing is as it seems when Detective Jude Devine finds herself caught up in a small-town soap opera. And her rocky relationship with forensic pathologist Dr. Mercy Westmoreland just got a lot harder. (1-933110-53-8)

Grave Silence by Rose Beecham. Detective Jude Devine's investigation of a series of ritual murders is complicated by her torrid affair with the golden girl of Southwestern forensic pathology, Dr. Mercy Westmoreland. (1-933110-25-2)

Passion's Bright Fury by Radclyffe. When a trauma surgeon and a filmmaker become reluctant allies on the battleground between life and death, passion strikes without warning. (1-933110-54-6)

Of Drag Kings and the Wheel of Fate by Susan Smith. A blind date in a drag club leads to an unlikely romance. (1-933110-51-1)

Tristaine Rises by Cate Culpepper. Brenna, Jesstin, and the Amazons of Tristaine face their greatest challenge for survival. (1-933110-50-3)

Storms of Change by Radclyffe. In the continuing saga of the Provincetown Tales, duty and love are at odds as Reese and Tory face their greatest challenge. (1-933110-57-0)

Distant Shores, Silent Thunder by Radclyffe. Dr. Tory King—along with the women who love her—is forced to examine the boundaries of love, friendship, and the ties that transcend time. (1-933110-08-2)

Beyond the Breakwater by Radclyffe. One Provincetown summer, three women learn the true meaning of love, friendship, and family. (1-933110-06-6)

Safe Harbor by Radclyffe. A mysterious newcomer, a reclusive doctor, and a troubled gay teenager learn about love, friendship, and trust during one tumultuous summer in Provincetown. (1-933110-13-9)

Turn Back Time by Radclyffe. Pearce Rifkin and Wynter Thompson have nothing in common but a shared passion for surgery. They clash at every opportunity, especially when matters of the heart are suddenly at stake. (1-933110-34-1)

Promising Hearts by Radclyffe. Dr. Vance Phelps lost everything in the War Between the States and arrives in New Hope, Montana, with no hope of happiness and no desire for anything except forgetting—until she meets Mae, a frontier madam. (1-933110-44-9)

Innocent Hearts by Radclyffe. In a wild and unforgiving land, two women learn about love, passion, and the wonders of the heart. (1-933110-21-X)

Justice Served by Radclyffe. Lieutenant Rebecca Frye and her lover, Dr. Catherine Rawlings, embark on a deadly game of hide-and-seek with an underworld kingpin who traffics in human souls. (1-933110-15-5)

Justice in the Shadows by Radclyffe. In a shadow world of secrets and lies, Detective Sergeant Rebecca Frye and her lover, Dr. Catherine Rawlings, join forces in the elusive search for justice. (1-933110-03-1)

A Matter of Trust by Radclyffe. JT Sloan is a cybersleuth who doesn't like attachments. Michael Lassiter is leaving her husband, and she needs Sloan's expertise to safeguard her company. It should just be business—but it turns into much more. (1-933110-33-3)

Fated Love by Radclyffe. Amidst the chaos and drama of a busy emergency room, two women must contend not only with the fragile nature of life, but also with the irresistible forces of fate. (1-933110-05-8)

shadowland by Radclyffe. In a world on the far edge of desire, two women are drawn together by power, passion, and dark pleasures. An erotic romance. (1-933110-11-2)

Love's Masquerade by Radclyffe. Plunged into the indistinguishable realms of fiction, fantasy, and hidden desires, Auden Frost is forced to question all she believes about the nature of love. (1-933110-14-7)

Honor Reclaimed by Radclyffe. In the aftermath of 9/11, Secret Service Agent Cameron Roberts and Blair Powell close ranks with a trusted few to find the would-be assassins who nearly claimed Blair's life. (1-933110-18-X)

Honor Guards by Radclyffe. In a wild flight for their lives, the president's daughter and those who are sworn to protect her wage a desperate struggle for survival. (1-933110-01-5)

Love & Honor by Radclyffe. The president's daughter and her lover are faced with difficult choices as they battle a tangled web of Washington intrigue for...love and honor. (1-933110-10-4)

Honor Bound by Radclyffe. Secret Service Agent Cameron Roberts and Blair Powell face political intrigue, a clandestine threat to Blair's safety, and the seemingly irreconcilable personal differences that force them ever farther apart. (1-933110-20-1)

Above All, Honor by Radclyffe. Secret Service Agent Cameron Roberts fights her desire for the one woman she can't have—Blair Powell, the daughter of the president of the United States. (1-933110-04-X)